HATE HOUSE

JOHN C. FOSTER

Encyclopocalypse Publications
www.encyclopocalypse.com

HATE
HOUSE

Chapter One

"I want you to investigate Hate House."

Low beams clawed through the murk to pick out the gate and she feathered the brakes until the big Chevy Suburban halted on the muddy road. The gate was rusted iron, taller than head height. A fence in the same state of disrepair disappeared into the mist on either side.

It was interesting to be outside again, talking to people in person instead of over the internet. Unnerving as well.

She had expected it would be like riding a bike, you don't forget how to be out in public, right? But she missed her apartment. The well-worn path between desk and kitchen for snacks. Weather was something that happened to other people beyond the window glass, as fake as images on her TV screen.

Two heavy chains secured the gate, each with its own padlock. She had received the key to one in her briefing packet. Her counterpart would bring the other, trust was nowhere in the equation.

Hate House indeed.

Shifting into park she left the engine running and dry swallowed her Lexapro. Being out in the world gnawed at her like a plague of invisible mites. She brushed a strand of red hair from the steering wheel, wondering again how she hadn't shed herself bald. The doctor said it was anxiety.

No shit.

Ready or not. She climbed out, boots splashing onto the unpaved road. She checked her phone. Her counterpart was late. The cell signal was tenuous and she decided not to call him. Let the first point be hers.

The air was heavy enough to muffle sound and she was glad for the headlights, though dusk had yet to descend. A breeze might bring her the clean scent of the sea, but here she wallowed in the smell of brackish marsh. Generations of dead clams gave off the sulfurous stink of hard-boiled eggs, amplified by billions of dead crabs and whatever else once lived in the swampy rivers that wound from land towards the Atlantic.

"I want you to investigate Hate House," her employer had said in their first and only meeting.

"Why is it called Hate House?"

"It's the Versailles of Hate houses. The Empire State Building."

He was so old she wondered if he knew the Empire had lost the world record. Not that it mattered. His name was Abbott and he was wealthy and was paying her.

"She wanted to drive me mad," Abbott had alleged. "Ten years she kept me prisoner on that island. Her only purpose for the house was hate."

Hate houses. What a concept. That people had so much money to expend on bitterness—

The chains whacked dully against metal when she shook them, the noise quickly smothered. *Shhh*, mustn't wake the house.

A cigarette found her mouth, a lighter found the cigarette and her ass found the Suburban's front bumper—in that order. She rubbed the deep scar that cut across the bridge of her nose. She didn't wear sunglasses because of it. They tended to settle into the cut and made it impossible to forget. When she realized what she was doing she forced herself to stop.

It occurred to her that she should shut off the engine. Save the ozone layer and all that. Decided peevishly to let it continue burning gas.

Hate: intense or passionate dislike.

She studiously avoided thinking about the days and nights ahead. About accommodation. About spending so much time within proximity of a man she didn't know. She had been reclusive since Josh, avoiding people in general, but men in particular. Rebuilding the fortress walls around her life.

She amused herself by imagining The Righteous staring up at her empty apartment. Abbott's money was enough to lure her from the safety of her apartment but now, in the damp fog with the locked gate—a real and solid thing, doubts began to tunnel beneath her defenses.

An unfelt breeze snatched the ash from the tip of the cigarette and she glanced up.

"Megan French?"

"Shit!" She slipped from the bumper, landing hard in the mud.

A pale face was staring through the gate.

* * *

There were three outside the apartment but only one carried a sign.

YOU WILL NEVER KNOW PEACE.

French had become accustomed to them on days without rain, a handful gathered on the sidewalk across from her Locust Street apartment building. Some days a member of Josh's family stood with The Righteous. But the family showed up less often with so much time passed since the Dateline Special.

Not so The Righteous.

That was her name for them, of course. On social media they

called themselves *Friends of Josh Hargrave* and she developed the habit of checking their page to see who and what would be attending the daily vigil and whether anyone mentioned bombs or hanging ropes.

She ordered food and more importantly, alcohol. Twice one of The Righteous had tried to trick themselves inside this way, but were easily detected in their glassy eyed excitement.

French worked cases online, enough to keep the rent paid with heavy support from her credit cards. Though she was taking on fewer clients, of late her work had focused on domestic cases, scouring the internet and social media for infidelity. She knew she needed to generate more work before her credit card bills crushed her, but motivation was a scarce commodity.

She had one cat, few friends and no color to her skin, the milky pale of a cave thing. She stopped shaving her legs and unless it was too cold, her uniform was a t-shirt and underwear. Told herself that her hair was *shaggy chic*.

Once she mooned the group below, pressing her bare ass to the window in defiance.

She wasn't agoraphobic and she wasn't an alcoholic.

She just didn't like to go outside.

She insisted silently that a glass of wine for breakfast was French, not addiction.

She told herself it wasn't just fear of confrontation that trapped her in the apartment. She stood vigil over something she could no longer remember. In the dim reaches of her disassociating mind she hoped for a trigger. A bright flare in the distance. Something to lure her out, a rope to climb. A fucking fire in the building.

She considered setting the fire. If not for worry about her cat, Buster, she might.

When it finally happened it wasn't a flare and it wasn't a rope.

It was a letter.

* * *

Abbott was a mystery, a complete cipher online. Correspondence found her in the form of a handwritten letter and he insisted on a response via the same atavistic technology.

When she saw her name scratched in spidery ink on an envelope, she was surprised to discover an elevated heart rate.

A date, time and address inside.

It offered sufficient motivation to leave her home, and Doctor Acosta suggested during a tele-session that she seize the opportunity. She called Mrs. Pappas downstairs to ask if her son Mike would feed Buster while she was gone.

Google Maps helped her find the address in Rhode Island, a few hours north of her Philadelphia apartment. She liberated her Acura from the long-term garage and headed north on the date indicated.

High hedges surrounded the Abbott property and vines made the gate near invisible. There was a speaker of vintage make and she pressed a button, stating her name.

The gate rasped open, last oiled in the year the speaker system was new.

She wound down a long drive into a space too wide to be called a ravine but too small to be described as a valley. The house at the bottom was tall and narrow, reminding her of a fussy schoolteacher with his shoulders hunched around his ears. It had the sense of having collapsed inward on itself to grow thinner and taller, so much so it pulled the surrounding land closer and the whole sank below street level.

She pulled up to the front door and left her car, passing unkempt topiary on foot before ascending a high, thin staircase towards the front door, which opened at her arrival.

"I'm Hill." Her greeter was as narrow as the house, white hair pulled tightly back over a dark, angular face. A spinster who neither smiled nor offered to take her coat. "I'll show you to the study."

Abbott waited for her like a frog in the center of a puddle that he never left.

"I want you to investigate Hate House."

The library was tight but tall like everything else, two stories with a ladder on wheels, and she felt as if she were at the bottom of a well. It smelled of old smoke and old man and the origin of both waited in a Victorian wheelchair, moth eaten suit coat visible above the blanket thrown across his lap.

"Read this before we speak," he'd said as she entered and she went with the flow, taking the large manila envelope from his palsied fingers and sitting in a settee across from him without asking. There were printouts, a map, and handwritten pages. The family name Laurent was prominent.

"Your reputation is one of discretion."

She looked up from reading about a property on the Maine coast. "Discretion is critical in my profession, Mr. Abbott."

He fluttered a liver spotted hand.

She resumed reading and when finished, neatened the pages and slid them back into the envelope. "The property is yours."

"Hate House *is* mine." Fey light danced in his eyes and he jabbed with his smoldering pipe. "I earned it."

She nodded.

"*Her* estate wants it," Abbott continued. "I'm rich. They're richer. We've fought in court for decades and no one has been inside since."

"*Her* estate," she said. "The Laurent estate?"

"Simone Laurent, my late ex-wife." His lips twisted as if the words carried a foul taste. "We both, the estate and I, employ security patrols to keep the other out."

His froggish tongue slid wetly across his lower lip. "Now we're going in."

"We?"

He nodded, ignoring the pipe ash that scattered onto the blanket over his legs.

"You as my agent. They will dispatch a counterpart.

Together you will enter Hate House and together you will investigate. *You* will prove that it is mine."

"Why is it called Hate House?"

"It's the Versailles of Hate houses. The Empire State Building."

"I don't understand."

"You will."

At the door to the study she paused when he said her name. His voice was loaded and she braced for the question that everyone asked.

Abbott's purple lips were wet with expectation.

"Did you kill him?"

* * *

"Are you okay?"

French barely had time to register the words issuing from the pale face beyond the gate before he sprang up to grasp the top. The man was all knees and elbows in an alpine sweater and baggy cargo pants. He planted a boot on the locking chains and she was expecting him to vault clear over like New England's answer to Tarzan. Instead, the boot slipped off the damp metal and shot forward through the bars, somehow tangled in the chains.

"Fuck!"

She was up and running in an instant. "Stop pushing!" She planted her shoulder against the treads of his boot and pushed hard with her legs as he wiggled the boot free.

He chinned himself to the top of the gate and slid over to plop down with a *splat*, knees flexing to take the weight.

"Sorry." He looked at the muddy boot print on her windbreaker. He smiled awkwardly and offered his hand. "I'm Grady."

She was pissed so she asked, "Who wears sunglasses in the fog?"

He plucked his glasses free. "UV protection?".

After wiping the damp seat of her jeans she pulled out a pack of Salems, offering it without speaking. Alarm crossed his guileless face and she shrugged, shaking one out and plucking it free with her lips. She took her time with the lighter, enjoying the petty pleasure of ignoring social norms.

"Neither one of us is supposed to go into the house without the other present." Smoke leaked from her mouth. "That's the deal."

His smile was awkward and she wondered if he had trouble closing his lips over such blocky teeth. "I got here early and decided to explore, but I didn't get to the house."

"Didn't get to it?"

He fished in a front pocket and pulled out a key. "If you have yours, we can open up the gate and you can see for yourself."

She pulled out her key and he gestured, so she checked the two locks. The second said SCHLAGE, so she worked the key in against the grit and wiggled it until it turned. She unfastened the lock and removed it, the chain dangling. The Schlage went in a pocket and dragged her windbreaker down on that side.

Grady attempted the Masterlock installed by the estate and had it free in a moment.

"I parked back there off the road," he pointed back the way she'd come. "I'll get my truck and follow you in."

"Alright."

* * *

The rented Suburban bounced and jostled past a small, untended graveyard behind a falling down iron fence that did nothing to lift her spirits. The road on the inside of the gate barely deserved the name and her teeth were clacking together with every pothole.

"You're kidding me."

The bridge was out, reduced by years of battering Atlantic weather to a jumble of pilings furry with white barnacles where they rose above choppy water.

French shifted into park and shut off the engine before climbing out, the sea smell cleaner and clearer here. Grady parked his Dodge pickup beside the Suburban and he cut the engine before hopping down.

"So that sucks," he opined.

"How the hell are we going to get the gear across?"

They had exchanged logistical details over email earlier, including a division of equipment. She had a small generator and fuel as well as personal gear. He had food, camp stove, lights and more fuel.

She shook her head and stepped closer to stare down past the wet rocks to the water separating them from the small island a mere thirty yards away.

"It's almost like we're not welcome, eh?" He said.

French flicked an irritated glance his way but he ignored it and she followed the direction of his gaze, finally taking in the reason they were there.

Hate House.

It was three stories of stone and brick with a tower-like structure rising to a fourth story on the southernmost side. The windows were boarded over as if the house had closed its dozen eyes against the world. A low fence of rusty iron ran along the rooftop and she imagined some kind of platform. The kind of thing a Captain's wife would leap from upon news that her husband's ship was lost at sea.

The abandoned dwelling gave the appearance of a beast atop the small, rocky island on which it was built. Too tall for the tiny bit of land, it dwarfed the island, as if sucking its materials in through pyroducts like roots, the island shrinking as the house itself grew another story. The whole of it was bleached by sun and salt, here the color of bone, there the shade of decaying teeth.

Pale orange and pink strokes were gently brushing across the house as the sun set behind her, there and gone. It occurred to French that this was likely the best the house would look. To look past the house was to see a sky already dark with October night.

"I don't love the look of that current." Grady picked his way carefully down to stand beside her. The current came in from the north and swept by them going south. Beyond the small island was open ocean.

He pulled out his phone. "Lousy signal." The phone went back in a pocket. "It's a little past high tide. At low tide we might be able to wade across."

"Carrying the generator?" She watched a predatory mess of seaweed swirl like Medusa's hair along the surface.

He smiled and pointed. "That, on the lee side? I think it's a boat house." He wiggled his finger. "See there? Stone stairs down into the water."

She saw them now, steep and treacherous. "When is low tide?"

"Three, four hours."

"You want to wade over to the island in the dark?"

"No." The word exploded in a laugh. "But I don't know what else to do, unless you want to head back inland and find a boat rental."

French planted her hands on her hips and a sudden gust tugged at her windbreaker. A rusty weathervane spun atop the house, the squeak carrying to them over the water. She wondered about the dark interior, untouched by light in how many years?

"It's ugly," she said.

"I don't know what the fuss is about," Grady said.

Rich people, she thought.

"Rich people," he said. "Bet five bucks it's haunted."

French looked over her shoulder into the dark. "You see that graveyard we passed?"

"Yeah," he nodded. "Lot of those in New England from early settlements and stuff."

A metal screech drew their attention back to the weather-vane and French pursed her lips.

"It's totally haunted."

A seagull screamed overhead.

Chapter Two

The breeze picked up when the sun went down and French's windbreaker fluttered in defiance. She retreated to the Suburban for solitude, unconcerned with how Grady might spend the time. Being out in the world was exhausting.

She lit up a Salem, keeping the windows closed in an act of defiance. She wanted the familiar stink of cigarette smoke in her hair. In her clothes.

Hasty research prior to leaving Philadelphia had shown the Laurent estate was nearly as much of a cipher as Abbott himself. No social media presence. No newspaper articles announcing charity functions or donations.

It took money, but the internet could be scrubbed. She'd done it for clients on a smaller scale.

She had been gliding over the web like a spider on dancing feet when she stumbled across a connection of incredible importance.

Claude Laurent was the founder of Court Pharmaceuticals, one of the largest big pharma players in the United States. His obituary listed him as survived by a wife, Josephine, and single child. Simone Laurent.

Was her adversary employed discretely by the estate, or was

he the point man for Court Pharmaceuticals? Whether the former or the latter, it was clear at the moment that they wanted discretion, as did her own employer.

She dozed.

* * *

Dateline nearly destroyed her.

She couldn't prove Josh's family was behind the show's dogged interest in the case, but they were wealthy and connected and unwilling to accept the results of the police investigation. Josh's passing was a terrible tragedy. He leapt to his death after a psychological breakdown.

It was not a murder.

Dateline didn't care and the episode they ran nearly destroyed her.

* * *

She woke with a snort, opening her eyes to darkness. Emerging from the vehicle, she brushed ash from her jacket and shook feeling back into her legs before opening the back hatch to assemble some gear.

Her lips and mouth were working to clear away the taste of ashes and she privately admitted the recent petty rebellion had backfired.

"Oh for fuck's sake."

She could barely make out the figure of Grady standing at the edge of the slope that dropped towards the water. If it were a portrait it would be titled *Loneliness*. In the dark he could have been a stone road marker or a branchless tree for all that he moved. Her earlier grumpiness brought a trickle of guilt and she felt like she'd bullied Richie Cunningham. Worse, a young Beaver Cleaver before he got older and his voice broke and he wasn't cute.

She told herself she was leaving the vehicle to move around and get blood circulating, the notion of being social because it was *expected* something she wasn't ready to acknowledge. A moment later she was standing beside him looking at the black hump of Hate House, a deeper darkness against the night ocean beyond.

Grady seemed lost in himself—probably meditating or some yoga bullshit—and she stuck a Salem between her teeth before sparking her lighter to life. Cupping her hands like a convict afraid the wind would steal her flame, she lit her cigarette and drew deeply, relishing the thorny heat in her lungs.

Grady stirred when she blew out an industrial cloud of smoke. He started to say something but decided to shift himself until he was standing upwind of Megan the Environment Killing Smoke Stack.

"You ever hear of Hate Houses before this gig?"

His question surprised an honest response. "Nope."

"So I started reading—"

"Yeah," she interjected, nodding.

"—and didn't find much about Hate Houses but tons about Spite Houses. This stuff has been going on for centuries. Not just here. Europe too."

She tapped ash and smoked, content to listen.

"There was this place called the Marino Crescent in Dublin, I think it was Dublin." He rubbed his hands together for warmth. "Anyway, so this rich guy named Ffoliet—with two F's up front for some reason—he designs this project along Dublin Bay just to antagonize this earl named Caulfield who had a huge palace facing the bay. We're talking like the 1700's here. Anyway, Two F'ed Ffoliet designs this crescent shaped sprawl of houses along the bay to block Caulfield's view. Caulfield is pissed but he also owns the road that leads to the work site, so he starts charging crazy rates to use it. Ffoliet says *screw you* and has supplies shipped in by boat and makes sure to build each of the houses high enough to block

Caulfield's view. He even made sure the back side of the development, the one facing Caulfield, was built all crazy and ugly just to make it worse." He shook his head. "Imagine having so much money you could build something like that just to be an asshole."

She grinned around her cigarette, the expression hidden in the dark.

"Most of these Spite things seem to be from rich jerks, but I read about one called Redneck Stone Henge that was pretty funny."

He chuckled and nodded at her to continue.

"So this farmer named Rhett Cooper out in Utah had a neighbor." The glowing tip of her cigarette bobbed as she spoke with the butt held in her teeth. "Neighbor was a pain in the ass from the suburbs who thought Cooper's farm smelled awful. Cooper says, 'Okay, let split the cost of a fence between our properties' and the neighbor is all 'fuck you no.'"

"Big mistake," Grady said.

"Not sure if it was a big mistake but it was a funny mistake, because old Cooper had a sense of humor. He rounded up a bunch of car wrecks, took them to the border between their two properties and buried them nose down in the dirt. Started calling it the Redneck Stonehenge."

Grady laughed.

"Cooper promised to take it down but first he collected donations for a charity from people who wanted to come out and gawk. Needless to say, the neighbor stopped his whining and that was that."

"Redneck Stonehenge, I love it." His grin faded. "If people will put that much time and effort into a place just for spite, how much would they put into a place for hate?"

"It's a Spite House on steroids." She flicked her cigarette in a meteoric arc into the channel. "Of course the Laurent family didn't build this place. Catholic Church built it in 1850 to store some monks or something."

Grady tilted his head. "But it was in disuse when the Laurent family bought it and the surround."

"And still in disuse when Abbott made it his home."

Grady grinned at her riposte and said, "If we're gonna do this, we should do it."

She nodded and made for her SUV.

She wasn't sure if they'd find a boat in the dark or want to risk wading back across to shore, so she grabbed her sleeping bag, spare socks and Penn State sweatpants. She ate an energy bar and stuffed a couple more in a green and white Eagles duffle bag along with bottled water. Damn bag was so stuffed it weighed a thousand pounds.

A small pepper spray canister went into a front pocket on her jeans and a folding knife went into a rear pocket. It was a Spyderco, a gift from a friend who called it a *gravity knife*. Press the button and the blade appeared with the flick of a wrist, short, curved and thick, it was sharp enough to slice through a soda can.

Grady was making his own preparations, though of course he had an elaborate mountaineer's pack with straps and zippered pouches. He lifted a fishing pole in one hand and she shook her head.

"What are you doing?"

"You'll see," he grinned, teeth white in the dark.

The moonlight provided a silvery, deceptive illumination, enough to see the wavelets near shore, but the island itself was already lost in gloom. Grady snapped a small plastic tube and shook it until a green glow grew in strength.

"If we somehow get turned around." He stuck it in the grill of his truck, wiggling it to make sure it was fast. "We can key in on this. Better than leaving headlights on and draining a battery."

It was smart but she didn't want to give him a big head, so she said, "Let's go."

The beam of her flashlight picked out a path down the rocky

slope to the water. The scent grew stronger as she descended, the Atlantic smell filling her nostrils with warning. Her beam didn't stretch the thirty yards to the island and the water in between had a sly look that unnerved her. She imagined the grasping undulation of seaweed and shivered from more than the cold.

"Dawn and dusk," Grady said as he descended carefully without a light. "Sharks hunt at dawn and dusk."

"I'm not worried about sharks," she lied.

"They scare the shit out of me." He leaned forward and dipped the fishing rod into the water, grinning. "Not too deep here. I'll use this to check ahead while we cross."

"You a boy scout?"

A shake of his shaggy blonde head. "Nope. Grew up in Maine and came back after college. Spent some time teaching city kids in a program called Nature's Classroom doing mud walks and stuff."

"Mud walks." She shook her head. "You go first."

He eased himself into the water, feeling with his feet, arms out for balance. She was struck by how foolish this was but bit her lip, unwilling to show her unease to Luke Mudwalker.

"Oh mama," he muttered as water closed over the top of his boots and he stepped forward, wavelets splashing his knees. "So far so good but it's really cold."

She followed his path, her boots slipping on unseen rocks beneath the water. Her thighs burned as she lowered her center of gravity for balance, but she'd rather look awkward than lose her footing.

When she was beside him, teeth clenched against the cold, she blurted out, "This is so incredibly stupid."

"Right? I dropped out of law school for this?" He shook his head and probed with the fishing rod before stepping deeper. "I can feel the current pulling but it's not too bad."

"Why did you drop out of law school?" She asked to distract herself from the reality of wading into the dark ocean. Her boots kicked through debris that felt like shells and sand and she was happy to be off the rocks, though less happy as the water rose above her knees and gripped her thighs, tugging her south with the current.

"I was miserable," he said over his shoulder. "Didn't want to get a fat ass sitting at a desk while I went cross eyed looking at contracts."

Her heel skidded and she windmilled her arms before regaining her balance. "Desk sounds pretty good right now."

"Yeah—*motherfucker!*"

"You alright?" She started to rush forward and her boot crushed shells.

"Water reached my balls."

She laughed in spite of herself and realized she could see the island ahead. A new sound intruded over her labored breathing and splashing progress. The slap of waves against rock.

"I think we're almost there," she said, breathing hard from the effort. The water crested the top of her jeans and sliced an icy line of pain along her belly. "This is so stupid, this is so stupid." It became a mantra as she splashed ahead and then it was before them. The island. Grady jabbed it with his fishing rod as if making sure it was real.

"Go on," he said and she brushed past him, probing forward with her right foot until she kicked something hard and squared off.

"Stairs go all the way down."

She put one foot on an unseen stair and carefully lifted the other beside it. The stairs were slippery with seaweed and she shared the news.

Seconds later she was out of the water and released a long breath. The duffle bag on her back shifted up as she eased forward to brace her hands on the damp stairs ahead and she wiggled to keep it in place. While she wasn't thrilled about shoving her ass at Grady, falling had even less appeal and she began a cautious ascent.

She heard the splash and slap of Grady emerging behind her —cut off by a sudden yelp. Whirling, she caught a glimpse of his mouth open to scream before the weight of his pack dragged him shoulders first back into the water.

"Grady!"

She slid down on her ass, teeth clacking as she bounced down the unforgiving steps and then she was jumping into the water feet first, heedless of safety.

She doubled over, hands reaching through the water to no avail. Where was he? She thrashed deeper into the channel. "Grady!"

An explosion of water made her heart leap into her throat, but it was Grady flailing up, several body lengths to the south. The damned current.

He doubled over coughing and spitting and nearly overbalanced because of his pack, but she bulled towards him with reckless abandon and got a shoulder under his arm before he could fall.

"Let's go," she hissed as she dragged him towards the stairs. He was still coughing, shaking water out of his hair as she pushed him ahead, planting her hands on his ass to force him up the stairs. A moment later she followed using hands and feet like the world's most awkward ape.

He coughed and spat, head hanging between his knees.

"You alright?" She asked. Stupid, but it came out unbidden.

"Don't breathe the water," Grady responded with a weak smile. He coughed again before wrapping his arms around his torso. "Holy moly, the water is cold."

She shivered and nodded. "Let's get inside."

He resumed his ascent.

As she reached the top, French stepped into the moon shadow cast by Hate House and shivered again, the feeling in her fingers and toes swallowed by chill. She hiked a wet path to the nearest door and cursed at the sight of the chain and padlock.

"Our keys better work," she said, turning when she heard the crash of his backpack.

Grady crouched over it, trembling fingers ripping at ties to open a top flap. A moment later he pulled out a steel crowbar.

"This should work." He stabbed the metal tool through the chain and threw his weight against it until the hasps holding the lock to the door pulled free, screws pattering against the stony ground. Jamming the sharp end in between the door and frame, he shoved and pulled until the door popped open with a wooden crack, sharp in the night air.

A rank odor flooded out from inside like gas from a decaying corpse and French felt as if this forced entry was a violation of the house. The reality of cold interrupted the thought, however, and Grady picked up his backpack to follow her into the pitch-black interior. Seconds later her flashlight beam stabbed out.

"Kitchen." French stated the obvious. Counters, sinks and an oven. Pans hung from a rack on the wall and a wooden table and chairs occupied a corner.

"Look," Grady said. "We need to dry off and warm up before we explore. See if that table and chairs are dry enough to burn?"

Teeth chattering, French nodded her head and dropped her duffle bag.

"This isn't too bad," she said, sliding out a chair. He knocked it over and began stomping on the legs, breaking them free. She grabbed another chair and did the same.

"Let's use the oven so we don't burn the house down." Even his voice was shivering. "Should focus the heat at us."

They opened the oven and shoved sticks inside. French tossed several over her shoulder to clatter against the wall. "Rotten," she said in explanation.

Grady produced a short, thick stick from his pack and twisted one end. A bright red fire flared to life. "In you go."

He slid the flare beneath the pile of sticks in the oven. The wood began to burn reluctantly. The two of them knelt side by side, holding out their hands to the fire like primitives at prayer.

"Oh god." Grady peeled off his wet sweater and tossed it aside. A moment later his sopping t-shirt followed. "I'm gonna see how wet my clothes got inside the pack."

French nodded and crawled back to her duffle bag. A hard shove sent it sliding across the floor towards the oven. Hurrying back into the small circle of warmth, she started digging through her things. Her first handful of damp cloth filled her with dismay but the second wasn't as bad. Soon after she dragged her mostly dry sweatpants free. Socks and a long sleeved t-shirt followed. The hoodie she packed was, unfortunately, soaked through.

"I've got some stuff," she said.

"I'm mostly screwed but this will help." He shook out a shiny metallic square that unfolded into a thermal blanket. He stood and undid his belt. "Sorry, but I gotta get these off."

French looked away as his trousers fell, wincing as his belt buckle struck the warped linoleum floor. When she looked back he was squatting near the fire with the blanket around him. Dancing orange glimmered off his glasses.

"I'm going to see if I can find another piece of furniture to burn," he said. "You can change while I'm—" He jerked his head towards the dark arch of a hallway.

"Don't be an idiot, your teeth are still chattering," French said. "Stay by the fire."

"We need more wood."

He retrieved an electric Coleman camp lantern from the pack, shivering in his space age blanket. "Listen, the finish that kept that wood dry is toxic."

"I can smell it."

"Yeah."

"What should we do about it?"

He shrugged. "Just be aware, I guess."

His bare feet scraped across the floor and he disappeared

into the darkness, leaving her alone with the creaks and groans of the old building.

French fought the wet laces on her boots and scraped them off, one foot against the other. The wet socks came next. It wasn't until she stood that her situation sunk in and she turned to face the cavelike expanse of the kitchen, keeping her back to the fire while irrational fears capered through her imagination. The fire threw her shadow against the far wall where it danced drunkenly and she closed her eyes to banish the image. Rustling through her bag produced another electric camp lantern, this one from Cabela's. It cast a bright, actinic light over the scene and she blinked spots from her vision.

Alone, she felt the swamp like stink of the place return, sweet decay and age. The wind whispered secrets just outside the kitchen door and the slap of wavelets against the island sounded like a hand against flesh. Her skin crawled as the house settled around her, the old wooden frame recoiling inside the rock and brick as if offended by their intrusion.

She touched the scarred bridge of her nose as she often did when her nerves stretched taut. Strain as she might, she couldn't hear Grady's movements and—

"Enough." She said it out loud, her voice shocking in the quiet. Moving with haste, she unbuttoned her jeans and peeled them down her legs. The wet underwear followed and she stepped into the sweat pants as quickly as possible, hopping on a single leg for one brief moment of absurd semi-nakedness. Soon enough her wet shirt and bra joined the pile and she felt an immediate improvement in pulling on a dry shirt.

She dropped into a crossed legged seat on the floor, knees cracking, and felt the warmth pressing against her back. The creaky voice of the house spoke of age but not of Grady. She fought the urge to call his name and the night gained weight.

A stick popped behind her and she bit back a startled sound. Goosebumps danced along her skin and she forced herself to breathe. To remember the therapy. In through the nose and out through the mouth, the exhalation longer than the inhalation.

The house does not want to share its story.

Nonsense. An empty house could not harm her.

* * *

The burning fire sounded like a dozen people cracking their knuckles. Once the thought struck French she couldn't banish it. Between that and the dead smell it was impossible to relax and finally she stood.

"Grady?" Conversational volume. She held the Cabela's electric lantern in front of her like a B movie actress.

Details of the archway sprang to life, ornate molding and sickly patches of lichen, the top of the arch several feet over her head.

She decided to leave the lantern as a shining beacon on the kitchen floor and equipped herself with the flashlight before passing through the archway.

The corridor beyond yielded its details reluctantly. Wainscoting to the height of her shoulders and soiled, peeling wallpaper above that might have once been orange.

She noticed that the wallpaper had bubbled a bit. Slipped out of true. French assumed houses in Maine didn't sweat, but the wallpaper made a lie of that.

Secure behind the shifting cone of light, French walked down the winding hall leading into the belly of the house, traveling beyond the border of the known. She felt guilty and excited to see this without Grady and she smiled without realizing it. Where was he? Playing hide and seek?

Did she really want to share these odd, exhilarating moments with him?

The passageway was dark, the end lost in shadows, and though she was sure she was traveling in a straight line, the corridor seemed to bend and turn with no discernable pattern as if the house intended to confuse her. A pathway in a corn maze, not a proper hall at all. She began to wonder if the entire mansion was filled with a coiling twist of intestine-like hallways. She wondered what was wrong with the Laurent family that they would buy such a place and what it would do to her mind if she spent any amount of time trapped on this little island.

She ignored the doors on either side, following her light beam as if it were a will-o-the-wisp luring her forward.

Did some part of her notice the lessening brightness of her light?

One moment she was trapped within the tight confines of the corridor walls and then around her was only the void, her weakening illumination quickly fading into the surrounding black.

A sharp smack reinvigorated her flashlight beam.

What the Hell is this, a ballroom?

She was several yards into the nothingness when she thought to begin counting her steps, but continued forward despite growing unease. She was untethered in this space. Worried that somehow she would emerge from the seaside of the house and tumble straight into the ocean.

There was the brief sensation of a wall before her when her light glinted off a giant's eyes high above, and she covered her mouth with her free hand to hold back a shriek.

Her light clawed upward to reveal an enormous portrait occupying the high expanse of wall over the front door, it's colors muddied and darkened by time. The woman depicted was life sized in a short, early 20th century dress, streamers of grue dangling from her fingertips.

The woman's bone white face was melting with age and hunger, her expression the sly mien of a starving coyote slinking into town to attack new, inappropriate prey.

Simone Laurent?

"Fuck this." French backpedaled and pivoted with all the

grace of a drunken ballerina. Her retreat across the warped floorboards took her into a blank, white wall and she would have groaned in fear if her light hadn't revealed an opening mere feet away.

Hoping it was the same hallway so recently traversed, she stepped inside, her earlier confidence gone.

Where the fuck was Grady? If she shouted would she upset the house even more now that it was so clearly awake?

A strange thought. Strange but she knew in her marrow it was right.

"Grady?"

Floorboards creaked beneath her bare feet, cold against her skin and she ducked into an opening on her left. The room was long and narrow like a train car, lined with glass-fronted cabinets framed in black metal, presenting an outdated view of a future that never was. While most of the cabinets were intact, some of the glass was broken and she stepped carefully, lowering the flashlight beam to avoid the shiny shards.

The dining table was long, with four chairs along each side and another at the foot. It was lacquered wood with a vaguely Asian aesthetic. *Cocaine chic* decades out of date. Again she was reminded of an outdated view of future style, as anachronistic as The Jetsons and bizarrely out of place in the old stone and brick house—

Movement caught her eye and her head turned slowly towards it, tendons in her neck as stiff as wood, crackling like sticks.

A hooded figure sat at the head of the table.

"Holy—"

French backpedaled rapidly but missed the opening and banged off the hard wood of the archway. Her heart leapt to her throat as the hooded figure moved and her weak light flickered off silver.

"Grady?"

He struggled to stand and the thermal blanket slid off his

naked body. Ghostly white, he planted his hands on the table and the glass creaked beneath his weight.

"What are you doing?" French whispered.

"C-c-c-old…"

French edged towards him with her torch held before her like a talisman, as if he would suddenly spring into predatory action. But she could see his entire body shaking as she drew closer and her fear vanished. The shine of the blanket made it easy to find and she wrapped him in it. "Let's get back to the fire."

Did he nod?

"I…" Grady trailed off.

French wrapped her free arm around his waist and guided him back towards the hall. "Be careful of glass on the floor."

Chattering teeth bared themselves in a grin and she realized he was limping. "F-f-ound it," he stammered.

Close against his body, he smelled like a fish market. The dead sea stink of the house was in his pores. Soon enough she had him sitting in front of the diminishing fire in the kitchen and she forced him to open the blanket to allow the warmth to reach his blue white skin.

"I'll be right back."

Her feet were numb with cold, but she forced herself to return to the dining room and grabbed two chairs, trapping her flashlight beneath her right biceps and ribs.

Back in the kitchen she tipped a chair onto the linoleum floor and began breaking it apart.

Chapter Three

French awoke with a start, confused by her surroundings. It took her a moment to orient herself at the sight of the sleeping bag draped over a table tipped on its side, making a wall that trapped some heat.

Or had trapped heat when the fire burned. Nothing but ash and blackened sticks remained in the oven.

Her mouth tasted terrible and her eyes were gummy with grit, and she wondered if the headache was the result of toxic fumes or gratuitous misery inflicted by the world.

When she sat up from where she was slumped against the cabinet beside the oven, Grady stirred beneath his metallic blanket and his head emerged from the cocoon. His hair looked like a haystack that had been dynamited.

She was surprised at her lack of anxiety. The events of the previous night had brought out something competent in her. A solver of problems. The lack of worry worried her.

"Hey." Grady's voice was hoarse.

"I have to pee," she said by way of greeting and rose, stepping out of the nest. She crouched by her duffle and rooted inside until she found the damp roll of toilet paper and made for the door, passing the clothes, hers and his, she'd hung around the kitchen to dry. If Grady had a problem with bras and panties, he'd have to suck it up.

She gritted her teeth when the soles of her feet touched the ground outside and froze when the ground seemed to undulate away from her with a sudden rattle as of a million pebbles striking the rock. The earth swirled and scuttled until she realized she was watching a tide of pale crabs flowing away from the house towards the water. An army of them.

They had been creeping towards the house on ten thousand sharp feet when she startled them into retreat. She wondered what they ate, these crabs. Imagined two sleeping people would be a feast for the horde. The grim image of a skeleton picked clean settled in her imagination and she shook her head to dispel it, breathing in the frigid sea air to clean out her sinuses.

She moved in shadow, scuttling along the length of the house for privacy until she reached the corner and the bright glare of morning sunlight, the sun itself a metal disk hovering over the eastern horizon and making the sea molten with its light. The rock beneath her feet was slick with lichen and great swathes of white she imagined was seagull crap. Whatever the outcome, she was already earning Abbott's money.

Looking around as if it mattered, French slid her sweats down and lowered herself to pee, careful it didn't run down the rock onto her feet. *The glamorous life of an investigator!* She wiped with a bit of toilet paper and stood, yanking up her pants one handed, wondering what to do with the soiled wad in her hand.

"Okay, I'm the asshole." She tossed it and let the wind push it along the island towards the edge. Her gaze wandered out to sea and stopped on a small fishing boat bobbing on the waves.

It was off white with peeling paint and sported a small pilothouse near the bow, no bigger than a phonebooth. The open aft section carried a stack of empty lobster traps, but that's not what drew her attention.

It was the lobsterman, dressed in waterproof overalls and a

heavy sweater, a long, black beard dangling to his chest, binoculars held to his eyes.

"Are you fucking kidding me?" French cursed. She mouthed the words, *fucking pervert* and lifted her middle finger in his direction.

He kept the binoculars focused on her.

"Creep." She high stepped it back to the kitchen door, running on the balls of her feet. As soon as she was inside she closed the door and leaned against it, desperate for the meager warmth of the kitchen and an escape from prying eyes.

Unfortunately, Grady was awake and zipping up his baggy cargo pants. "The good news is they're still damp, and also soggy.

Defensive. "I did the best I could—"

He held out a hand. "I was joking. Thanks for hanging up my things. It's way better than they were last night." He smiled. "And that was smart, making a fort to trap heat."

She crossed her arms over her chest for warmth. "I make nests at home to watch movies."

"You're in Philly, right?" He picked up his shirt and shook it.

"How did you know?"

He pulled the shirt over his head, muffling some of his response. "I followed you on Twitter."

"Oh." French re-crossed her arms. She decided to follow him right back.

"You're on Toonz as well. I didn't figure you for blues."

She grabbed her hoodie and decided the damp garment was better than nothing as she shimmied into it. "What did you figure me for?"

This is where he says Melissa Etheridge because he thinks I'm a lesbian.

"Punk," he shrugged. "Ska. Something too cool for Maine."

"Oh." Cool was not part of her biography.

"I dig acoustic singer songwriter stuff," he offered. "Older stuff like Jim Croce."

French didn't care and pulled a bottle of water from her bag, asking, "Do you need water?" He shook his head and lifted a thermos.

"Tea."

Of course.

She wished she had caffeine but was too lazy to dig out the jar of instant coffee from her bag. Produced an energy bar and tore off the wrapper with her teeth as he hopped up to sit on the counter and drink his cold tea.

"Thanks again for last night," he said after a bit.

She shrugged, chewed and swallowed. "I think we should look for a boat before we check out the house."

He nodded. "And we should stick together when we do check it out, not just because we're supposed to monitor each other." Her face flushed with guilt but his grin reappeared. "Who knows how solid the stairs are and stuff."

* * *

French already felt the chafing from damp jeans and her feet were mealy in the moist socks, but followed Grady on a tour around the house, his first time viewing it from the front.

Morning light danced on wavelets and white buoys bobbed as a reminder of lobster traps below. French thought of the voyeuristic lobsterman but decided against mentioning him out of an instinctive need to keep her cards close to the vest.

The front of the island had been hacked into rough tiers descending towards the water. Steps made for giants.

"They're to welcome Old Man Atlantic." Grady nodded towards the tier-like steps.

"Who?"

"Old wives' tale."

The front of Hate House was washed clean of mystery by the morning light, more than one upstairs window gaping stupidly where tattered boards had fallen free. An enormous panel of wood covered a space on the second story nearly the size of a room and drew her curiosity. She was about to point it out when Grady interrupted.

"Look at that," Grady said.

Carved into the stone lintel over the door was the name SIMONE. Above that was the ghostly shape of a large cross, legacy of the onetime Catholic residents.

When a cloud passing over the sun draped them in momentary shadow, French felt as if Simone had passed a giant hand over the face of the house.

I don't like this place, she thought. The idea of reaching into the guts of this fetid manse became repulsive, as if it meant digging her hands into the belly of a maggoty corpse. Abbott's money held less sway in Simone's shadow and French indulged a momentary question. *Was the name itself not proof that the home belonged to Simone Laurent and not Abbott?*

The moment gave form to her thoughts of the night before, the sense of having violated the house. Breaking in and setting up camp was as crass and unwanted as if they had lifted the skirts of Simone herself and crawled beneath.

"Let's look for a boat," she said to force her mind to business. Grady nodded and followed her to the lee side of the island, trailing her down the shallow slope to the free standing structure they hoped was a boat house.

"There's a lot of birdshit on this island." Grady looked back. "It's all over Hate House."

"Shit House," she replied.

He grinned.

At the boathouse they discovered a lock securing the double doors, though the wood was rotten and flaking. French thought she could kick it in if need be.

Grady made quick work of the lock with his crowbar and pulled the hasp out of the rotting wood frame.

"Help me," he said and she hesitated, reluctant to maneuver

beneath his arms to grip the edge of one door. "Please, I need your weight on it."

She gritted her teeth and slid beneath his arched body to set herself against the wood, as aware of his sweat and seawater stink and his body heat as she was the soggy, splintered wood. She was glad he couldn't see her expression, lips drawing back from her teeth in revulsion.

"On three," he said and counted.

Together they wrenched the door open.

French ducked inside, her flashlight beam stabbing into the dusty interior, motes hanging in the air like muddy water. Rusting gear and rotting lines hung from spikes on the walls but she ignored them and approached the bulk of a big wooden rowboat. A short kick made her grimace.

"The wood's soft."

"Shit." Grady looked inside, playing his own light around. "We may have to rent—"

"Wait." French circled the boat to a low shape covered by a tarp. She ducked away from a hanging strip of fly tape, coated by a platoon of desiccated insects. "This might be..."

She covered her nose and mouth with one hand and yanked aside the tarp with the other to reveal the dingy grey of metal. "This one looks okay."

Pulling the tarp all the way clear, French kicked it into a corner while they both played lights over the smaller row boat.

"We can get our stuff over with two, maybe three trips," Grady offered.

"If we find the oars."

* * *

The crossing back was easy enough once they got the boat down the stone steps and into the water without falling in themselves. French was content to let Grady play Daniel Boone and tackle the oars. A minute later she was scrambling from the bow onto the rocks with a wax-coated line in hand. Grady stowed the oars and joined her before they pulled the boat up out of the tide and looped the line around a thin, upright stone, "Just in case," as Grady put it.

The hours passed slowly as they transported their belongings across the narrow channel. It was after lunch when they set out from the mainland the second time. French pressed her key fob and the Suburban chirped goodbye.

They broke for lunch, sitting in the kitchen amidst their gear. Energy bars were the food of the moment and Grady promised to break out the camp stove for dinner to, "Get something hot in us."

The plastic fuel cans stayed outside in a nod towards safety, lined up near the door. They agreed to use the generator sparingly and stuck the big lights on their tripods in the rear of the kitchen to get them out of the way until needed.

"I want to try something." Grady leaned over the sink and twisted the cold water faucet. Nothing happened.

"It must—" French was cut off by a deep, groaning sound in the walls.

Grady stepped away from the sink and *BLAT*. A burst of brown gunk splattered the basin. The faucet trembled and a gout of foul liquid followed, spitting and gasping with air bubbles. The groaning pipes quieted and after a minute, the water went from foul to merely murky and ran steadily.

Grady stuck a finger into the flow and lifted it to his nose. He touched the wet finger with the tip of his tongue and grimaced.

"Salt water."

"The pipes are probably rusted through," French said, but Grady chuckled.

"Maybe not," he said. "This is a Hate house. For all we know, the pipes deliberately bring up salt water."

"Weird." She wadded up the wrapper and stuffed it in the bag Grady hung up for trash. When she shook a Lexapro tablet from the bottle onto her palm Grady asked, "Headache?"

She shook her head and washed the anti-anxiety medicine down, too aware of him watching as her throat worked. She wiped her mouth with the back of her hand. "Let's check the place out while there's still daylight."

Grady hopped off the counter with a thump. He plucked his crowbar from the counter and stuck his flashlight in a baggy pocket. "I'm game."

Gloom gathered as they left the illumination from the open kitchen doorway and she snapped on her flashlight. Without the urgency of the night before, she had a chance to notice how narrow the hall was, the ceiling so high. It gave her a cramped, claustrophobic feeling that struck her as very *New England*, though if pressed she wouldn't have been able to explain why.

The ugly smell was thicker in the hall and she wrinkled her nose. A carpet runner had once lined the floor but age and atmosphere had rendered it more holes than whole. Faded wallpaper was peeling like dead skin.

Back at the opening to the dining room French panned her light across the furniture. Glass shards flashed from the floor.

"You're lucky you didn't cut your feet up," she said.

"Yeah." He coughed again.

The intact cabinets still contained china and the drawers contained table settings. She found candles in one. Moldering cloth napkins in another.

"Silver," Grady said from across the room. He closed the drawer and the metalware clanked.

"Even with security patrols it's weird that no one…" French gestured vaguely.

"Yeah, it is," he agreed. "But we're out in the middle of nowhere and you have to get here by boat. I mean, drunk kids aren't gonna cross the water."

French passed several doorways and pushed open a few doors as she passed, propping them open on this second, slower sweep. A large sitting room was festooned with couches screaming 70's chic, but the mod glory had long since rotted and the wall-sized stereo and speaker set up was draped in ancient webbing.

The next door opened with a screech of hinges. "Library here," she called out.

The library was lined with leather bound books and the connecting study was fit for Washington Irving his own self. The stink of mold in the library struck her like a blow and she worried about the state of books and papers inside, but it would require attention. A file cabinet drew her gaze and she crossed the tattered remains of an oriental rug. It was a low thing with only three drawers and an unhealthy amount of rust. The drawers were locked, however, and she made a mental note to borrow Grady's crowbar.

"I found the head," Grady shouted, voice muffled.

"The what?" She peered out into the hallway.

He emerged from a doorway. "Bathroom."

The reek of dead things grew stronger as they moved away from the fresh atmosphere of the kitchen and French had to breathe through her mouth.

"Stinks," Grady said and shook his head. "This place is a trip. It's like if the Soviets went atomic in 1972 and everything was frozen in time."

He was right but not completely. She saw a mix of eras in different rooms. Mod decadence side by side with old money. A modern (for the seventies) stereo set up with enormous speakers and an eight-track player alongside an ancient gramophone with a giant brass horn mounted atop.

The hallway dumped them into a large octagonal foyer opposite the enormous front door of the house. The *ballroom* from last night. The musty foyer was meant to be lit by a battery of windows circling the high-ceilinged space, but the drab Autumn light barely tickled the murk.

For the first time she could see the massive front door, or at least the sheets of plywood nailed across it. The windows to either side of the portal were similarly covered.

Far overhead, French made out a chandelier and noted several six-foot candelabras made of brass standing around the strangely shaped space like palace guards. Archways led to shadowy rooms on either side of the foyer and the dust lay untroubled by any breeze. Through one open archway she could just make out disturbing glimpses of furniture covered in dusty sheets, chairs dressed as Halloween ghosts. Silly really, but unsettling.

"Over here," she said as she headed towards the ghosts.

The huge living room was laid out with moldering shag rugs and more mod furniture in faded seventies colors of orange and brown. The fireplace was ancient stone with a dusty lava lamp on the mantle. She took in the rusted andirons and pulled her gaze away to stop a sudden flood of memories.

"Holy shit, push these together and you get a Yin and Yang symbol." Grady pointed at two settees that would fit together like puzzle pieces.

Wall art was a mixture of paintings and posters under glass. Pollock and Monet. The Boston Pops and Broadway's GodSpell.

Handprints speckled the walls with no rhyme or reason and she saw what looked to be the smeared ochre outline of a human form, the paint long since peeling. French had no idea what to make of them.

"Light or warmth," Grady said and French chose, "Light." They wrenched open a window, coughing against paint chips, and Grady kicked out the rotting plywood affixed to the outside. The light and air streamed in with cleansing power and French felt her hackles lower.

"What the hell is that?" Grady aimed his light at smeared painted spheres pressed together two feet above the baseboard. "Is that a butt?"

French shrugged, eager to get upstairs but curious as Grady

dragged his light across the painted figure of a man she'd noticed earlier, a matte pressing in earth tones.

"Bet that was Abbott getting bored," he said.

"Hi Abbott," she said.

"Except for the study, this looks like the ultimate bachelor pad," French mused. "Playboy Mansion in Maine."

"Let's check upstairs. It's the riskiest and we'll have plenty of daylight if we need it."

It occurred to her that she was lucky last night, retreating in more or less a straight line. Ending up in one of the rooms off the foyer would have sent her into a panic.

"Wow." Grady stopped abruptly and she nearly walked into his back. He was looking at the life-sized portrait mounted over the front door.

"It must be Simone Laurent." French blinked when she realized she was staring.

"It's hard to tell." Grady tore his gaze away with an effort and shook himself. He stepped closer to the front door and ran fingers along the plywood. "Forget the Playboy Mansion, it's friggin' Manderlay."

French nodded and her light danced around the room. Age darkened paintings lined the walls and alcoves contained marble statues and busts covered in lichen.

"Whoa." She blushed after staring more closely at a confusing statue. She moved the light to another and had the same reaction.

"This place wasn't decorated by puritans." Grady approached another statue both carnal and mythic in nature. "I mean, Abbott took residence in the mid 70's…"

French gave him a look and he trailed off, tracing his finger along the heavy, dark wood framing the blocked doorway, more like beams than a frame. "This wood is so old it's petrified."

His light slid up and across the lintel, careful not to illuminate the portrait above. "Some words carved into the top. Not English."

French shrugged and pivoted away, boots scraping on the gritty hardwood floor. She strode towards the room opposite the living room and stopped in the doorway.

"That's not terrifying at all," French said.

"What is it?" Grady clomped over and joined her in the doorway. "Whoa."

Twin beams lanced out across the room full of huddled shapes. Dust danced in the thick air and light sparkled off the mirrored walls.

"What the Hell is this place?" Grady stepped inside and French played her light around his feet.

"Look at the floor."

What at first glance seemed to be a parquet floor quickly established itself as something different. The black and white squares were large and a bold line ran around the outside edges of the chamber as if to denote a game board.

But what caused the investigators to hesitate were the draped figures scattered about the giant board. They came up to French's chest, each covered by a moldering sheet stained with damp streaks and green with fungus.

Grady reached out towards one but hesitated, looking at French. She nodded and held her light on the object.

Face twisting at the unpleasant contact, Grady grabbed the sheet and dragged it off to fall on the floor.

It was the color of an unhealthy tooth, cylindrical with a wide base and spherical top.

"I think it's made out of bone." Grady's voice was hushed as if afraid to awaken it.

"No way." French advanced carefully, steps spring loaded with tension. This time she looked at Grady and he nodded, playing his light across another hunched shape.

She snatched the heavy sheet away and dropped it, wiping her hand on her hip.

This one was the color of charcoal but otherwise identical to the first. "Nah, this is wood."

"Pawns." Grady laughed. "They're pawns."

French grimaced. "I feel seen."

She dragged the flashlight beam around the room and panned along the walls, shaking her head at the filthy reflections of an endless army of small ghosts.

Grady stepped among them. "It looks like they were left in mid game." He dragged another sheet free.

"That a bishop?" French asked.

"Yep."

"Screw this room." French backed to the entrance, unwilling to turn away from the creepy mob. "Let's check out the rest."

"Sounds good to me."

She returned to the foyer and her flashlight stabbed through the gloom to pick out ascending stairs.

"Here," she said.

The staircase was wide and grand with a landing and a turn. The carpet runner fared little better than that in the hall and was more shreds than weave, striking French as a warning or at least a wish. Don't come upstairs, the house was saying. You are not welcome.

Thoughts she kept to herself.

Up above, railings protected the second story, the balusters bonelike and intact. Her light flashed off something red and blue and she imagined stained glass in second story windows, but otherwise the darkness upstairs swallowed her light like the house was slurping soup and preserved its secrets for closer inspection.

Irritated by a sudden onslaught of nerves, French ascended several steps before touching the banister, which wobbled beneath her fingers. "Watch that."

Identifying a real-world danger grounded her and she took another step, wood creaking beneath her boot.

"I think the stink is from up there," Grady said.

French took another step and felt the nerves dancing over the surface of her skin. She paused as the fine hairs on the back of her neck rose in warning. Something old was moving inside her. In her gut more than her mind. It told her a stick had snapped in the dark woods and danger approached.

"What is it?" Grady aimed his light up past her.

"Shhhh." She cocked her head to listen and gave him a glance. "I think…something's breathing."

His voice was taut. "What?"

She eased cautiously back down a step, eyes locked on the landing above. "Something is, uh…" She shook her head and tucked her arms close to her ribs, ascending the rest of the stairs in a rush, slowing at the top where she paused to brace both hands on the wobbly railing, only realizing she held her breath when pressure forced her to open her mouth in suck in oxygen.

She forced herself back into the moment when Grady's light stabbed past her. She took aim with her flashlight as if it could deliver more than illumination.

Leaning against the wall in front of her was an enormous portrait of another hoary old Laurent in an Edwardian dress, a rectangle of lighter tone on the wall above showing where it had once hung. It was a large portrait, larger than life size, and the subject of the painting stared at her with a puritan's judgmental glare, tightly bound hair bristling with animal intensity even under the gray scum coating the thing. Simone had brought in reinforcements to torment Abbott during his stay. This frightening crone could only be her mother, Josephine.

French glanced right and left down the upstairs hall disappearing into darkness on either side.

Below her the foyer stretched out, a dead place, the plywood torn from the door a pathetic intrusion into a space that had not seen life for decades.

Get a grip, French thought, worried she might be sucked into a tide of paranoia. Still the elder Laurent's eyes seemed to crawl over her body, digging through her baggy clothes to stroke the nakedness beneath with sharp fingernails, peeling back her past. She shivered at the thought of Mistress Laurent looking back through her memories as if she could stand in the room on that awful night with Josh, the most private moment in French's entire life.

"You okay?"

She flinched at Grady's question and randomly started down the right hand hall, feet crunching and snapping over—

The flashlight beam dragged over crab shells, some intact, some dismembered. Colorless. Dry. She aimed her light forward and saw a carpet of them stretching out in the hundreds, maybe thousands.

"It's crab genocide up here."

"What was that?" Grady asked.

"I said it's—"

"Listen."

She cocked her head and was straining to hear when he added. "I hear a car horn."

Grady disappeared back down the stairs and she followed at a run, ignoring the sense of relief.

They would explore the upper floors, but she was no longer excited at the prospect.

* * *

"You can't be here," the uniformed security guard said, his voice thick with coastal Maine inflections. "This is private property."

Wind whistled across the open space near the shoreline and puffy clouds scurried across a graying sky. Even the weather wanted them gone.

"We're authorized representatives of the two parties contending over the property," Grady repeated again.

They stood beside the security guard's white Jeep, a yellow and white light strobing atop it. After fruitless minutes of yelling back and forth across the water, French and Grady had been forced to cross the channel to explain their presence.

"No one informed—"

French cut him off. "We have the keys to the gate. We're supposed to be here and we're supposed to be working inside the house."

The guard was heavyset, with a sleeveless fleece over his blue uniform. His cap sported a militaristic insignia and the words CERTAIN SECURITY. Beads of sweat glistened on his cheeks and forehead despite the chill and he gave off a vibration of unhealth.

He crossed his arms over his thick chest. "Look, you can leave now or I'll call the police." His thin lips pulled back to reveal small teeth set in his broad, fleshy face.

"Call the fucking president," French snapped. "We have work to do."

She stomped back down the rocks to the boat and began untying the rope. Grady joined her a moment later.

"What's he gonna do?" She asked.

He shrugged. "I told him to call his office and have them check in with the estate or your employer…he's not even sure which one he's working for."

"Asshole."

"Ahh, he's just doing his—actually, he was kind of an asshole." Grady pushed the boat into the water and French stepped carefully inside.

She looked back as they pushed off. The guard remained with his arms crossed over his chest, the light on his Jeep strobing in warning.

* * *

They were each carrying a metal drawer full of moldering files, liberated from the file cabinet with the aid of the crowbar. French dropped hers on the kitchen counter with a bang.

"We've lost too much light to check out the upper stories," Grady said. "Let's set up the generator and improve our camp in the kitchen. Get some of the boards off windows to get a little clean air inside. Maybe check out the downstairs some more."

"About the camp," French said. "I'm going to set up in the living room." She lifted a hand to interrupt his protest. "I'm used to solitude and need space."

His expression was childishly transparent, even as he tried to straighten the insulted twist from his lips. "I'm not a bad guy, you know."

It was a small voice at odds with his six foot plus frame and she thought she heard the boy in him.

"I don't care."

Fuck the boy, she needed her space.

Her knees popped like logs in a fire and she gathered things into her duffle bag, eager to escape the awkward tension in the kitchen.

He slowly descended into a crouch to mirror hers and handed over her still damp socks.

"I know something happened." He paused when she froze in mid motion. "I saw the Dateline—"

She stood so quickly it was if there was no motion in between. One moment she was crouched and like a frame of film had been cut, in the next she was standing.

"I know what the TV said was bullshit," he continued and French let his words disappear into the ever present white noise of the restless ocean beyond the walls.

She looked out from the kitchen door as the orange sun slid down towards the western horizon.

"First thing in the morning we go upstairs."

She gathered up her file drawer, staggering a bit under all the weight.

She left.

Chapter Four

Fucking fireplaces were the bane of her existence and the living room of Hate House offered the granddaddy monster fireplace of them all.

Of course. Fucking house.

It was carved into the grey stone wall, an ugly, arched mouth that reminded her of a surgically repaired harelip. Blocks of stone formed the arch, presumably so it wouldn't collapse on someone as they tended a fire (the stone mouth slamming shut with a grinding snap) and it was easily four feet deep, blackened with ancient soot. If she were to go mad and walk inside it, French would barely have to stoop as the opening was easily five feet high. The length of it was longer than she was tall and she guessed seven or eight feet, big enough to burn the entire bole of a tree for warmth.

It was bigger than her studio apartment during grad school.

Fuck.

The big space was too creepy without companionship, a thought she barely allowed to surface before shoving it back below the water to drown, and her first step was to snap the blinding Cabela's camp lantern alight and set it on a wide, low platform too grotesquely hip to be called a coffee table.

The andirons drew her eye as she knew they would, filthy and blackened from disuse, one with a hooked bill like a miniature polearm had toppled from the stand and lay beside its more vertical cousins.

She instinctively swayed to the left away from them as if they radiated her own personal history and she was worried about stirring them to life.

The lever for the flue was on the side opposite those old iron sentries, however, and she set the flashlight on the floor to grab hold. If there was any chance of the smoke escaping through the chimney the flue had to be opened—

Do not think about it

--and she threw her weight against it

Do not think about that case

--and grabbed it with her free hand, baring her teeth in effort as the rusty metal resisted.

And gave way.

With a muffled screech the flue opened and debris rained down into the fireplace. She raised an arm to protect her eyes and stepped back in horror as the body of a boy smacked down onto the iron fire grate.

Adrenaline dumped into her system like a dam, releasing uncounted tons of water, and darkness crowded her vision, sight becoming narrowed like a sniper scope aimed at the fireplace and its horrible filthy—

She whooped for breath and flailed backward for one of the ridiculous couch sections, landing heavily atop Yang and lucky it didn't break beneath her. She remembered what she had been taught and planted her feet, spreading her knees wide so she could drop her head between them and consciously focus on sipping air instead of devouring it. Eventually her breathing slowed and the blackness receded from her vision as the warm rush in her temples calmed.

Therapy had taught her to manage panic attacks but the

bottle was her own technique and her right hand dove into the duffle bag without thought, a mongoose hunting a snake.

She lost the cap in her haste to free the whiskey inside but the wet burn down her throat momentarily blotted out all thought. Liquid dribbled from the corners of her mouth as she coughed before managing a smaller, more ladylike swig of booze.

It was a bird, not a boy. A bird so blackened and desiccated she had no idea of its species.

The boy was in another place and another time. Her free hand gently massaged the deep scar across the bridge of her nose as she remembered that moment, that case. It had been the single most horrible moment of her life until the night of her disfigurement.

This was in the *time before*, when she went outside to work a case. It was a divorce, an ugly one, and after the husband lost the house to his wife it became a custody case.

An ugly one.

When the five-year-old boy went missing the police descended on the father's apartment, a shitty second story affair in a white clapboard building behind a CVS drug store.

They dragged him out blinking and unshaven in a t-shirt and painter's pants without shoes on his feet. He denied everything but all French had to do was look at his small pig eyes, boar like bristles on his jowls. He had bad news written all over him and despite the lack of evidence anywhere in his apartment or his steadfast denials, all attention was aimed at him.

Two weeks after the boy's disappearance French found herself wandering aimlessly through what had once been the family home. The mother had been rendered near catatonic by events and was staying with her sister. French was looking for…what?

She imagined herself like a baleen whale, cruising through the neatly appointed rooms with her mouth open to inhale clues like brine shrimp. It was a home done in cream and beige, upscale suburban. The mother a fan of Martha Stewart with the father's touch utterly absent—as if even when living in the house, he wasn't really there.

The ever present scent of sandalwood incense had diminished and she was in the living room with its low, bone colored couches when her nose twitched and her lip wrinkled in disgust. She actually noticed the movement of her lip before consciously registering the smell.

It grew as she became more aware of it and she drifted across the floor to the source, the fireplace with its perfectly stacked pyramid of white birch logs.

Knees popping as she squatted, she braced her hand to form a three point stance like a football lineman and leaned forward, craning her neck around to look up inside the fireplace.

She saw a whole lot of nothing and scooted back to stand with a grunt. The flue lever was easy to find and she grabbed it before realizing it was open.

What the hell?

Back down in her three point stance then, French produced a blue Bic lighter and spun the wheel to spark a flame.

It was hard to understand what she was seeing so she dropped to her knees, accepting a dry cleaning bill in her future. Now freed, her left hand reached up and probed something familiar that eluded her understanding until she began to tug on it and a small Converse sneaker came free.

Her mind went white as a humming sound filled her ears. She eased back to her haunches to examine the child's shoe in her hand. It had been blue once.

The sliding sound took too long to register and she was still far too close to the fireplace as gravity took hold of the bloated thing and a stiffened leg swung down, the small foot wearing only a sock When the other Converse clad foot descended. French thought she really was going to see the boy land in a grinning crouch. King of hide and seek. *Look what I did ha ha!*

The tumbling mass of boy that finally free itself from the

stony hold of the chimney struck the birch logs with a wheezing explosion of bodily gases, a horrifying fart of eye watering dimensions that had her scuttling back on her ass until her back struck a couch.

The fireplace coughed forth a billow of dust and ash infused with dead child and she gagged while a rain of plastic action figures followed the corpse, tiny paratroopers bouncing off his distended body to scatter over the blonde hardwood floor.

She blew her nose into her hand to push the stink and particles away. She stuck out her tongue and scraped her blunt fingernails over the meat of it, the pain bringing tears to her eyes but she couldn't abide the thought that the shit she had breathed, that she had tasted, was a dead kid.

That was the first panic attack, whooping and gagging until her system slowed of its own accord. She pushed up from the floor, a long trail of spittle connecting her to the hard wood was wiped away with the back of her hand.

It took several tries to dial 9-1-1 on her cell phone and she had trouble articulating to the problem to the operator, finally just demanding *the police, the police now!*

They came with speed and aside from brief questioning, French found that her part of the terrible ordeal was done. They surmised his motive, the boy wanting to hide from his parent's incessant strife. Following logic that only a five-year-old could understand, he brought a small army of heroes for emotional support and managed to climb up inside the fireplace.

And got stuck.

And died.

And that was it for the police. That was it for the parents. That was it for French.

Except for the memory.

* * *

Using two moldering cushions like slices of bread, she scooped up the dead bird and held it away from her body as she marched to the open window and dumped the lot of it outside.

Calm and in control, she returned to the task at hand.

After years without the tickle of smoke, the stone throated chimney was clogged. Still, she managed to breathe life into a small fire in the massive living room fireplace, hoping that the spaciousness of the room would protect her from asphyxiation. Shoving broken pieces of furniture onto the rusted iron firedog inside the stone cave, she disturbed sedimentary layers of ash and wound up smeared grey like one of Dickens' urchins. Creating space for oxygen to flow beneath the rack of the firedog would have been simpler with the help of the dirty andirons only feet away, but andirons were something French had deleted from her existence after that last night with Josh. When she saw them she insisted she *did not* until her conscious mind surrendered beneath her desperate will.

Knees complaining, she sat cross legged before the growing flames and let their warmth caress the exposed skin of her cheeks. Indian style, that's what they called this position when she was a kid.

The smoke made her cough but wasn't terrible and she retrieved a new pack of cigarettes from the duffle. It was already opened, which depressed her because it meant running out more quickly, but she lit one in a gesture of defiance against the fireplace smoke and blew a grey stream at the small flames.

When French was tired she was prone to maudlin thinking…and she was very tired.

Concentrate on your surroundings, her therapist was wont to say.

The outside chill pushed in through a broken window after she went outside and pried off the plywood. She did the same to a window alongside the massive front door to create airflow. The work would have been easier with Grady's help but she couldn't go back now and say she needed help from a big strong man. The openings allowed a steady current of air to flow through the living room and the sea sounds were loud in the quiet.

A smirk twisted her lip in a sneer that others found cruel, but had become so common it might as well have been her resting expression. Of this she was unaware.

French rose and moved through thickening gloom away from the safety of her fire and into the eerie expanse of the foyer. It took an effort of will to avoid looking up the grand stairs to the ominous black of the second story. The lewd statues around her hid within their recesses, satyrs and maidens and harpies in their animal dens. If she stared her eyes played tricks and she saw movement in those caves, so she never let her gaze rest on them very long.

Enough. A quick march took her to the boarded over front door and the cleared window beside it.

It was near evening at that point and the east side of the house, her side, was in shadow, sharpening the lines of the rocky tiers leading down the water and the skeleton of a dock, long since collapsed. The tiers really were like shallow steps for giant feet, but the thought fragmented when she saw the lights.

"What the hell is that?"

Two red lights slid up and down out on the dark water, rhythmic and mesmerizing.

Probably another lobsterman. She inhaled the clean air but couldn't shake the uneasy feeling that someone was watching her from the boat.

Wind hissed and the house sighed in answer. A minute later Grady must have flushed the toilet because the walls vibrated and pipes groaned in pain.

French fought down a shiver and applied herself to another cigarette, studying the orange tip as she held the delicious smoke in her lungs. She was wearing several layers for warmth and was tucked snug as a bug inside her hoodie. She pushed the hood back to listen in case Grady approached. Static popped on her hair. When she held her hand before her face she saw several strands clinging to it.

Eventually she decided Grady was respecting her space and hurried down the hall, forgetting her flashlight. She pulled out her phone and found the bathroom. Salty sea smell filled the cramped room and she sat to relieve herself. Even a semi-working toilet made the job less awful.

She tried to wash her hands without thinking but cranked the faucet off as soon as the sink rattled. The mirror was dusty but she leaned closer because spots on the mirror created the illusion that her childhood freckles were returning. She remembered her worries about that, about being in the sun, while waiting on the rental lot for the Suburban. The salt smell from the toilet eased her anxiety. There was precious little vitamin D to be had in this moldy old mausoleum.

"Screw it," she muttered after trying to pat her shoulder length hair into some semblance of order. It's not like she wanted to catch Grady's eye.

She was too anxious to return to her nest and headed for the library, deciding that traveling through this mausoleum with only the tiny light from her phone was almost worse than fumbling blindly in the dark.

The library was windowless and cluttered, bookshelves built into the walls were filled with leather bound volumes, their spines marked with fading gold calligraphy. The rug had moldered into tarlike fragments on the floor and the desk struck her as odd, a confusing sensation until she realized there was no computer. Instead, she saw a mug holding pens, a pile of rotting notebooks and an old Panasonic cassette player.

She pressed a greasy button on the machine and a clear plastic window rose to reveal a tape nestled inside.

French ran her fingers along the spines of several books and screwed up her face at the moldy odor. She pulled one from the shelf at random and held it up to see a forest of pale mushrooms growing from the exposed edges of paper, fusing the book shut.

They look like ears.

"They're listening to us," she muttered aloud and shivered at her own observation.

Shoving the book back, she tugged out several more, all of them fungus gardens. Her phone's light glinted off glass and she circled a deep reading chair to a tall cabinet with a glass door.

The door opened easily enough and she touched the spine of a tall book, discovering some kind of vinyl instead of the expected leather.

The encyclopedia sized book seemed to welcome her touch and slid free with a rasp. Opening it at random, she lowered her light over pages filled with familiar spidery script.

Abbott's?

Careful not to rip the heavy paper, she turned the pages.

She gasped when a pen and ink drawing caught her eye. A creeping sensation made her shiver and she felt the sudden need to be back at her camp, near her fire.

* * *

The yawning blackness of the foyer beyond the archway freaked her out, so French dragged a loveseat across the floor to block it. The effort dislodged roughly a trillion spores of ancient and unfathomable mold and she managed to inhale every one of them. A runny nose and sneezing became her companions back at the fire.

Still better than Grady.

She sneezed and grimaced at wet drops on the old pages she was trying to read by the light of her electric camp lantern. She was leaning against the Yin couch (more spores) and after experimentation, discovered that putting the lantern over her right shoulder on the couch cast light down on the pages without throwing giant scarecrow shadows across the ceiling and walls.

No shadows, no Grady. Just me, the spores and our book.

She wasn't sure when during the ten year residency Abbott decided to write a cookbook, but it was deep enough into his sentence that diagrams and recipes for seagull—not just one but seven—were deemed good enough to write down.

She chewed Ritz crackers and sipped water from a plastic bottle as she read, nauseated and fascinated by the diagrams accompanying the more esoteric preparations for kidney and liver and heart. Gizzard had its turn alongside the more prosaic fried seagull. There was brief reference to a stew that had included clams stolen from a nearby beach by the light of the moon, but the combination had brought out that which was most awful in both meats and was abandoned.

He wasn't a bad artist, old Mad Abbott. Acid rose in her throat and she coughed into her fist when she turned to the chapter on rat, but she pushed forward, wondering if he began eating the island rats because Simone Laurent was starving him or because he was bored.

Why the fuck didn't you just leave?

She was getting oblique glimpses of Simone from what she read, a horrid crone lurking backstage, pressuring Abbott's thoughts. Still, she found it hard to sympathize with her employer, a warped wreck in his dotage who seemed to have been at best *odd* in his youth. Uncomfortably odd.

The cats were next and she wondered where they came from, if Abbott had hunted the fields beyond the bridge at night, setting traps and leaving out food for unwary felines.

That Abbott had eaten everything he described she was certain, and she continued reading with growing caution.

When she came to two heavy, yellowing pages stuck together, she dabbed her finger and thumb against her tongue before prying them apart and turning the next page with care.

"Nope!"

A knuckle of wood popped in the fireplace and she jerked where she sat, before slamming the book shut with a bang.

Holy shit.

She side armed the book, spinning it across the floor.

Closing her eyes, she tried to banish the ink drawing that had so shocked her, shrinking from the knowledge that there were pages and pages after the place at which she stopped.

Instead of vanishing, the drawing grew stronger in her mind. The fading ink gaining density and growing more sharply black, the recipe beside it unimaginable.

She thought about crawling after the book to look again, to be certain what she saw, but stayed in place. She knew what Abbott had drawn.

It was a human hand.

* * *

The idea that had first nibbled at her mind was that the house was Simone herself. The resistance to their entry was Simone telling them to get out. The oddities inside reflected Simone's very own eccentricities.

French was beginning to think she was mistaken. She was inside Abbott's mind. His deteriorating mind.

She glanced at the ochre shape depicting Abbott on the wall, now just a smear in the darkness.

His mind was not a safe place to be.

Chapter Five

French awoke to a world of red light streaming in through the open window. The light consumed the last images from her unsettling dreams so that she was left with a feeling of nameless unease.

Shivering, she groaned as she uncurled from a clenched position before the dead fireplace, stiff muscles protesting, aging her by a decade as she sat up. Glass ground inside her joints as she rotated her shoulders and pain shot through her neck when she tried to roll her head in a circle.

Muttering curses as she stood, she stomped feeling back into her feet, more sweatshirt than woman in her multiple layers.

The room in red, as if seen through bloodshot eyes. Through rage.

Disoriented, she wondered if this was still a dream, the awakening merely trickery performed by the inner Megan who tortured her over Josh.

Molten stuff, the crimson light, and she decided she wanted more. She wanted to gorge in its bloody effulgence.

The windows were the easiest choice and the sanest, but she was giddy in the sanguinary glow and hipped aside the loveseat from the doorway, dragging scratches in the abused wooden floor.

The statues in their tiny caves hid as she flowed barefoot across the octagon. Unphased by the repellent gaze of Simone Laurent, French set herself against the plywood concealing the front door.

Though the frame of great beams around the door was as hard as iron, she discovered the plywood was soft when she attacked it. Wood splintered and blood swelled from pricks in the pads of her fingers and needing a tool, she found herself standing before a recessed alcove, snatching the stone statue of a cormorant and returning to the plywood to use its beak.

So singular was her determination that soon she had one edge free enough to slide her fingers beneath. She heaved and pulled, her stiff muscles swelling with blood. She braced both feet against the doorframe and clung like a furious tick, throwing all of her strength against the wood until nails tore free with an old woman's scream and French landed hard on her back, the sheet of plywood slowly falling to cover her.

She caught her breath and kicked it aside, earning more splinters for her feet before rising, heedless of pain, to wrestle the rusted deadbolt of the front door open. Again the shriek of an old woman sounded in the houses as the metal gave up its hold and slid aside.

The knob ground like a knee joint without cartilage, bone on bone, but turned under her will and she pulled the door back to flood herself with the red dawn.

It was a sea of blood, shining red with the gore of a thousand shark attacks. The peeking edge of the sun was unabashedly red, not yet giving to orange and eons yet from yellow. She bounded down the steps in the mad dawn's light and skipped down the tiers until the next stride would put her in the ocean where Old Man Atlantic waited with open arms.

A lobster boat bobbed several dozen yards off shore and she threw both fists skyward, jabbing with her middle fingers.

"FUCK YOU!"

And the light grew less like carnage and more like morning and the cold came through the rocks to her feet. Chill spray leapt up from the sea and dampened her face as she panted, no longer in the grip of the waking dream, the morning madness of Abbott or Simone or both.

A throat cleared nearby and Grady said, "How'd you sleep?"

He was sitting twenty yards to her right with his fishing rod forgotten in his hand, face blank with shock at her pagan display.

"Fuck you too," French said, making a dignified retreat up the tiers to the gaping front door and a much needed date with Lexapro.

* * *

After a half assed toilet, which consisted of wiping her naked body down with a wet cloth, French dressed, pulled her hoodie over a Waffle House t-shirt and looked for the book she had tossed aside the night before.

She finally discovered it beneath an overstuffed chair with rotting cushions, as if it had tried to hide in shame.

She thudded down the long hall, straight and not at all winding in daylight, and called out as she approached the kitchen.

"Are you decent?"

Passing beneath the arch she caught Grady rising from beside a camp stove where he was boiling water.

"I'm dressed, at least."

He was tentative, spine curved to reduce his height and she realized she was coming off a little manic but didn't care.

"Sorry about this morning." She thrust the book out in both hands until he took it. "I think Abbott was a cannibal."

It was funny to see someone's jaw actually drop open in

shock and French laughed, unaware of how the sound matched her ever present sneer.

While he held the book, French reached out and opened it, flipping pages with none of her earlier care until she got to the drawing of a human hand.

Lifting her gaze from the page to his face, she watched his pale skin grow corpse white as he turned page after page and from his reaction, saw something he didn't think she could handle.

He closed the book and set it on a counter before turning away and bending to pick up another book, this one also large and leather bound.

"I feel a little less guilty about borrowing this from the library last night," he said. When her eyes narrowed he added, "It's Abbott's diary."

She hefted it in her hands.

"I've got a bad feeling about both of them, Abbott and Laurent—"

"It will get worse when you start reading," he interrupted. "I'll make us some instant coffee—"

Now she interrupted. "I'm getting a bad feeling about the house too," she waved her hand to indicate the space. "It doesn't want us digging deeper. It doesn't want us to go upstairs."

"That sounds—"

"Nuts, yeah," she stepped on his words again. "Hate house, mad house, I think it's both. Let's get upstairs now, before we waste any more of the day, before it can distract us with security guys or looking for boats or whatever."

She handed back the diary, nearly big enough to be a coffee table book. *The ego, eh?* "Get your light and tell me what you read so far while we go up, I'll read it later."

"Okay." He set the book down beside the cookbook. "Okay."

* * *

They aimed their flashlights upstairs like snipers and this time Grady noticed the colors. "The stained glass window. Think there are more?"

French shrugged. "Wait'll you see the portrait."

"Huh?"

"You'll see."

She planted a boot on the first step, fighting the urge to be furtive. It was broad daylight in an empty house and she had backup.

"Ugh," she said, pulling back from the ancient balustrade. A slick of mold had piled up as she slid her hand along it and she shook green flecks from her fingers. She didn't remember the mold from yesterday.

A glance to her right and she saw the ancient face of a harpy leering at her from a recessed alcove. Round, pupil-less eyes bulging over a hooked nose gave it a decidedly ugly visage and she wondered why anyone would own such a thing. *Who picked this, Abbott or Simone?*

Enough.

She climbed with resolute steps, eyes on the stairs before her. She knew what awaited her and had no need to see it before it was absolutely necessary.

She half expected the portrait to be gone, or the ancient Laurent woman to have changed her pose into something more openly leering and predatory. But it leaned drunkenly where it had leaned the day before and the beslimed crone maintained her posture of regal disdain.

Josephine. Monster. No wonder Simone turned out to be such a bitch.

Eager to break away from the staring contest with the long dead matriarch, French glanced in either direction to regard the expected darkness.

"You okay?"

Grady appeared at her side, boots crunching over shells. He

flinched away from the portrait and aimed his light down the left hand hall.

"You weren't kidding," he said. "World War Crab. What the hell happened?"

"I dunno," she said. "Weird."

"This whole fucking house is weird."

She stepped forward, glad for her heavy treads, crushing thoraxes and claws and spindly legs. She drove away thoughts of crabs scampering over her feet and counted the closed doorways as she passed, noting the rusted metal lock plates with wide apertures for skeleton keys.

She tried a few doorknobs at random.

"Locked," she said. "We'll have to look for keys."

"Or my crowbar," Grady responded.

French's beam flickered as she walked and the light swayed back and forth as if she were riding swells at sea. Shadows moved across the painted landscapes and portraits that seemed to cover every wall in the place, giving the illusion of faces turning to follow as she passed, that eyes fixed on antiquity were lowering their gaze to examine the newcomer. It was a funhouse effect and should have been no more worrisome than her own theatrics...

She shook her head. Took in a deep breath and released it.

Her steps crunched and crackled on the carpet of crustaceans. She heard Grady exclaim behind her but paid him no mind.

How many doors had she passed? *Hallway can't be this long,* an abrupt thought she dismissed immediately. Unease nibbled at her until she tried a door and it swung open.

"This one's unlocked."

Rays of dusty light slipped through the boards over the window to illuminate faint details. A tiled floor, dingy with mold. Broken mirrors over twin sinks. A toilet and a long, clawfoot tub from which some kind of crawling vine had sprung.

She left the door open and he took a look while she moved on, a faint noise drawing her forward.

Was this the breathing she had heard yesterday?

The scrape of wind born things came from behind a door and when Grady said, "Wait" she ignored him, turning the stiff doorknob with a sharp jerk of her wrist and bumping the portal open with her shoulder.

Crookedly placed plywood covered the far wall, the sea facing wall, and she stalked around moldering furniture towards it, not waiting for Grady as he entered behind her.

She placed a hand on a slimy wall for balance before rearing back to stomp her thick heel against the plywood. It popped free with a screech of nails and she held a hand out in a STOP gesture when Grady sought to intervene. Moving to brace herself against the opposite wall she kicked again, and more nails released their hold. The water logged weight of the wood was too much for the remaining nails and with a cry of protest the large piece of wood sagged and tumbled free.

Sunlight and clean sea air washed in with physical force and French smiled in relief.

"Holy shit!" Grady said, coming up to her side near the edge. "She really was messing with his head."

"What?"

Grady gestured around the room and she turned to see the moldering rot of bedroom furniture. A massive sleigh bed with carved wooden head and footboards slushy with rot. Desiccated cushions on toppled chairs, the smashed mirror on a vanity, a splintered wardrobe. Lumpy white paint covered the furniture, the floor and spattered the walls. Ancient, crumbling gull feathers were trapped like prehistoric beasts in a tar pit.

"Bird shit?"

"Yeah, in the Master Bedroom." He grinned at Simone Laurent's diabolical mind. "I don't think there was ever a wall in this room. It's just open, exposed. A public restroom for seagulls. Fucking with Abbott's head like the salt water from the faucet."

French shook her head, speechless at the pettiness of the long dead heiress. "Imagine how tired he must have been psychologically when he got here and the first thing he discovers is there'll be no easy sleep."

She fished out a Salem and lit up.

"Really?" Grady asked. It was the first time she'd seem him anything less than cheerful.

Of all the things she could have said in response she chose, "You're not as charming as you think you are."

"What?"

She looked out to sea and a stream of smoke jetted from her pursed lips.

"Why are you such an asshole?" Grady asked, forehead creasing in anger. "I haven't done a damn thing to deserve it."

"So you say."

"Yeah, so I say!"

She sucked in a greedy draught of smoke and pivoted to face him, letting the grey toxins dribble from between her lips as she spoke. "You work for an insane billionaire who kept my client prisoner for ten years."

"*I* didn't keep him prisoner," Grady said. "And it's an estate, not a person."

She laughed in his face.

"You know, it's not that fucking clean." He made for the doorway. "Abbott was no angel."

Then she was alone as his stomping retreat crushed an army of crustaceans beneath his hiking boots. The mud stomper become crab stomper.

Would she have been disappointed in herself to see the sneer settle back over her features, cigarette dangling from the corner of her mouth?

Fuck Grady and fuck Simone Laurent. Fuck Abbott too.

She dropped the remains of her Salem and ground out the butt amidst decades of dried birdshit.

"Grady!" She called down the hall, following the path of shattered shells. "Grady, don't be a fucking baby!"

Oh, that should help.

"Fuck—"

Grady stepped away from the wall and shot out his arm like a driver afraid his passenger would fly through the windshield.

She felt the urge to flinch back as the circle of her flashlight beam raked over him.

"Look here," he said, flicking his flashlight on.

She and Grady steadied their lights on the red ochre form of a man smeared against the wall, arms flung out in a Christ like pose. There was another next to it. She pushed past Grady and crunched forward far enough to see another. Beyond that another.

French shrugged, concealing her own unease.

Grady lowered his head and muttered but the hall was quiet enough to make out his singsong recitation.

"'But I don't want to go among mad people," Alice remarked. "Oh, you can't help that," said the Cat: "we're all mad here. I'm mad. You're mad." "How do you know I'm mad?" said Alice. "You must be," said the Cat, "or you wouldn't have come here."

"You think it's that bad?" French asked.

"Yeah," he said. "I don't know where it went off the rails, if it was straight up vengeance at first or if Simone Laurent was insane when it began. I think Abbott may have been sane when he first arrived here, but the place got to him."

"He told me she wanted to drive him mad."

"She succeeded."

Without thinking he held his flashlight beneath his chin and the clichéd eeriness made her smile.

"We could leave," he said with sudden urgency. "We jet and

forget about this place and these crazy rich fucks fighting over it."

She couldn't make the adjustment from his recent anger to the sudden earnestness. Cynical as she was, she believed him. He wanted *both* of them out for their safety.

She looked past him down the hall and aimed her light at the boards over a narrow window at the end. "Let's get some light in here."

His head drooped in defeat.

Why didn't she just tell him to go if he wanted to? Was she afraid to stay in Hate House alone?

She tromped to the end of the hall and bent to set her flashlight among the dead crabs. Grabbing a weathered board, she jerked at it until she got one free. She looked out through the gap before removing the next board and felt a chill in her veins as her stomach sank.

"Grady, we're not going anywhere."

"What do you mean?"

He kicked his way through the shells like a frustrated child and she stepped back so he could look through the gap. He twisted his head to look at her.

"Where the hell are our cars?"

Chapter Six

After shouting pointlessly at the empty swath of grass on the other side of the channel and trying their useless cell phones, French agreed to join Grady for lunch out front.

The sun was directly overhead and glared down through gathering clouds as the wind grew, whipping her nylon windbreaker with a steady *fwip-fwip-fwip* sound. She put on her shades, shifting them when they settled into the scar on the bridge of her nose.

Grady was gutting and cleaning two fish he had caught that morning, and her gorge threatened to rise at the thought of Abbott's hideous cookbook. When Grady heaved the guts away to splat on the rocks she looked away.

"For the gulls," he said and indeed they were already circling overhead like raucous sports fans. Drunk, angry and excited. They reminded her of Pittsburgh fans the one time Josh took her to a Steelers game...

She was distracting herself from the two things that upset her. Well, *two* more things.

The first was something she had already noted. Hate House did not want them digging into its guts (splat went the bird entrails). Even determined as she was to reach the top floor this morning, it thwarted her, distracted her, gave her reasons not to continue.

The will of the house was palpable in a way she didn't understand but could clearly feel. Though she loathed to admit it, she was considering Grady's idea of leaving the job unfinished. Even with their cars gone they could reach a main road with a few hours hiking and flag down a passing car.

The other thing smacked of paranoia—or would smack of paranoia if she hadn't been so certain they were filthy the night before.

The andirons beside the living room fireplace were polished clean and shining.

Why were they clean? How were they clean?

The smell of grilling flesh reached her and she heard the crackle of burning skin. Grady had a small fire going in a ring of stones and had pierced the fish with small sticks to cook over the flames. He had brought a salt and pepper shaker with him on the job and he wasn't shy about using them on the fish.

Grady wanted to talk about the diary but she needed to discuss something else first before it drove her mad ("we're all mad here").

Wind brushed her hair back from her forehead and she shook it to let breezy fingers comb through it. She decided to approach the conversation with the thoughtful honesty of a therapy session and crouched across the cookfire from Grady, who eyed her warily.

"You saw the Dateline special?" She asked bluntly. So much for the therapy approach.

He nodded and bent a stick in his hands until it snapped. He fed the ends into the fire. "When I was researching you I found it and watched it."

"And?"

"And it's lying trash."

A seagull landed not far away and casually wandered closer. French was surprised at how big it was up close, grey on its folded wings, the beak very long and egg yolk yellow. She was struck by the sudden image of a black ink sketch, a seagull split open. *Spatchcock* was what Abbott called it.

"Fuck off," she snarled, slapping the ground between them. It fucked off, retreating a dozen feet to eye her balefully.

When she looked back Grady was watching her and she sniffed hard. Considered spitting into the fire. "Do you think I killed Josh?"

"No," he said, staring into the opaque gaze of her sunglasses. "I think the show exploited a tragedy for ratings and it was disgusting."

She shrugged, almost unbalancing herself from her squat. She eased down into a cross legged position. A low sound reached them from across the water, a ship's horn far out to sea.

"His family thinks I did it." She brushed her hair from her face before it could blow into her mouth. "People stand on the sidewalk outside my apartment with signs. Sometimes the family is there too."

He forcibly jabbed another stick into the fire and sparks flew up. "They're hurt and they're being exploited. It's fucking gross."

"It is fucking gross." French removed her sunglasses and touched the scar on her nose. "He got drunk and had a breakdown. Like a psychotic break. I was stupid and argued and he just lost it. He hit me with an andiron and then…" Her throat grew too thick to allow words passage.

"And then he jumped."

She nodded.

"I'm sorry," he said, leaning towards her until heat and smoke made him pull back. "Really."

She shrugged and asked, "Did you clean up the andirons in the living room?"

"I—what?"

"They were dirty last night but they're all shiny this morning. I sniffed them. I can smell fresh polish."

He pressed his hands together as if he was finishing his yoga class. Instead of *namaste* he said, "I swear I did not touch your andirons."

"They're not mine."

"*The* andirons."

She shrugged again. "Fish smells good, what is it?"

"Mackerel," he said, carefully turning the skewers. "My dad used to take me deep sea fishing as a kid and we'd catch them and sometimes Cod or Bluefish, but Mackerel are my favorite."

She closed her eyes and inhaled the delicious aroma, the best thing she'd smelled since arriving at Hate House.

"I generally don't believe that a house can have a personality or a will, that's just stupid," she said. "But I think this place doesn't want us here. Look at today, we couldn't even get all the way upstairs before it fucked with us."

"You know that sounds crazy," he said.

Her eyes narrowed in anger and she jammed her sunglasses back in place but he raised a hand.

"But, as nuts as it sounds, I think the same thing." He stood with a grunt of effort and she was reminded again of his height. "Watch the fish, I'll be right back."

He trotted up the rock to the open front door and disappeared inside. French turned one of the skewers, nearly dropping the fish in the fire. She set the skewer back in place and decided to let chef Grady handle the cooking.

She heard his approaching footsteps behind her but didn't turn as his shadow passed over her. He sat down on the other side of the fire with the big diary in his hands.

"We need to talk about this, about Abbott's state of mind, about Simone Laurent and what this house means."

After a beat, she nodded. "Okay."

* * *

They ate by the fire with the rising tide crashing against the rocks while the seagulls and some kind of black seabird she couldn't identify fought over the scraps. Her knees protested sitting crossed legged and her ass wasn't thrilled about the hard stone, but there was something about the moment that relaxed her, sweeping away the cosmic funk with an invisible broom.

The stone of the island itself became their plate as she copied Grady, pulling the big Mackerel off the skewer and placing it on the rock, burning her thumbs when she slid them inside the slit in the belly and peeling it outward to open the fish like a book.

They plucked chunks of pale flesh with their fingers and ate. Soon they both wore greasy grins as the hot meat of the fish filled their bellies. When Grady turned his head to spit out a bone she stared and he arched an eyebrow. She mimicked him a moment later and allowed her expression to lighten if not into a smile, into something within shouting distance of a smile.

When they finished they scattered the bones, heads and tails for the mob of hungry birds and descended the tiers to rinse their hands where the waves slapped against the rock beneath their feet. French didn't mind the spray that dampened her face and clothes. The salt water that swirled around her boots.

Fresh air and fresh food were a powerful balm.

"Time to read," she said at last.

She returned to the fire and opened the book, not noticing when Grady left her alone.

* * *

My name is Marcus Aurelius Abbott.

French put the book down and her sneer shifted rapidly through the gears from first to fourth. *Oh, for fuck's sake, Marcus Aurelius? Really?*

She returned her attention to the book.

My name is Marcus Aurelius Abbott and I was twenty four years old when I married Simone Laurent, some thirty years my senior.

Talk about May December…

I am twenty-eight at the time of this writing, the first day of my imprisonment by my ex-wife, Simone Laurent. I have admitted in front of her attorney to infidelity with one Sophie Cohen, age twenty-seven, and to conspiring to bank fraud and an attempt to illegally transfer funds from Simone Laurent's estate. I have agreed to a sentence of ten years in Hate House, never to leave the island, and Simone Laurent has agreed not to press charges which I am assured would result in state prison. My allowance will be continued during my term of incarceration and it will be mine in ten years if I agree to annul our marriage.

I have agreed and am awaiting the paperwork.

French flipped forward, less gracious with the pages despite their age. She didn't much like Abbott, the current iteration or this much younger version.

Phrases leapt out at her as she fanned pages deeper into the book.

The cat haunts me.

I hid among the ochre men.

Funhouse.

"Shit." She resigned herself to reading if not entire thing, then much more than she wanted so she could understand the nature of Abbott's decline.

Chapter Seven

Simone has had six months to work mischief on the house and I am filled with dread on our approach.

We are on the barren coast of Maine. Barren only because the Laurent family purchased the land decades ago and kept all attempts of development at bay. The locals dislike the family and the fishing community of Paper Bay sees them as invaders, but haven't the financial resources to dislodge the Laurents.

I am in the back as the limousine bounces along an unpaved road towards the coastline and my prison. Her man is at the wheel, a tall, bony fellow with acne scarred cheeks who is more than capable of disabling me if I lose my resolve and resist.

My window is down and I've removed the headphones of my Walkman so that I may hear the native sounds of my new home.

Distant birds and wind. Beyond that there is only the sound of the engine and crunch of tires.

The smell is pungent and speaks of eons of dead things in the marsh. It smells of living sewage and my heart drops.

When we park Simone's man says, "We're here."

He comes around to open my door and I step out to lay my eyes on my prison. My heart sinks like a stone.

It is cold and terrifying, several stories of indigenous stone topped by a small tower at one end and several chimneys. The small island is lifeless, connected to land by a narrow footbridge over a thirty-yard span of black water. Simone has promised I can furnish it as I see fit, placing orders when her man arrives with my weekly delivery of food, but there is no way to make this horrible place warm and livable.

The wind is cold and slate colored clouds skid across the sky overhead. Wavelets in the channel are tipped with white and I feel the incoming storm.

"Go ahead, sir," Sophie's man waves a long arm in the direction of the footbridge. "I'll bring your things."

It will be a long ten years.

* * *

A faded photograph was inside. Color, though yellowed with age, depicting what French believed was a young Abbott in tight, white bell bottoms and a flowing, long sleeved shirt. His hair was long and parted in the middle and he was attractive enough to be called pretty. She could see how an older, wealthy lady might amuse herself with him as a toy and wondered how he managed to climb from there to the more exalted position of husband.

She didn't realize it was raining until she saw the ink running from a wet splotch on the page. Another fat drop struck, then another. She began to feel it on her neck and head and heard the *thock* of rain against the windbreaker.

Thunder rumbled, slow and distant like Old Man Atlantic clearing his throat after a long slumber.

In the next second the sky opened.

"Shit!"

It was pouring rain, the rock around her foaming with water. She slapped the book closed to protect it and stumbled upright, dashing for the open front door of Hate House.

Once inside she skidded on the wet floorboards and used her hip to start the front door swinging closed. She shoved her shoulder into it like the world's smallest football player and forced it shut.

Lightning flashed outside the open window beside the door. Seconds later the thunder boomed and she knew the storm was still distant.

"C'est la vie." She made for her camp in the living room, hanging the wet jacket over a long dead lamp and gathering up several pieces of wood to start a fire.

Wind whistled through the open windows and thunder was her constant companion as French settled down against the same couch she used the night before, shoving aside a stack of disintegrating folders from the library file cabinet. Boring stuff. Schemata for the house. Shipping information for various gewgaws, window glass, the front door, furniture.

The fire was catching at last and her electric lantern was still where she had left it. She lifted her head and looked around when the guts of the house gurgled, pipes rattling as Grady flushed the far off toilet.

It occurred to her on a distant level of consciousness that there had been no lobster boat voyeuristically lurking off shore while they ate lunch. She hoped the fisherman or men had grown bored with them and found other entertainment.

The book. In spite of herself, she was intrigued.

Abbott went better with a cigarette and she lipped one from the pack before bringing it to smoldering life.

Fuck it. She opened the book at the halfway point and started reading.

Chapter Eight

They've been in the house again, I'm certain of it now.

Are they yours, Simone? Or envious fishermen from the village?

The kitchen was plundered, the cheese and bread gone and the brandy drunk. The toilet seat in the downstairs bathroom was spattered yellow with urine.

A fire was built in the living room and a chewed cigar butt was on the floor beside it. Though the arm had retracted, a record still revolved on the turntable and static scratched from the speakers.

I heard the music but was too afraid to venture down to discover the source.

They are growing bolder, ranging about the lower level while I sleep above in one of the monk's cells. Soon they will gather courage and climb to the second story and then the third. Should I move my bedding to the tower? Is my prison to be reduced to a single cramped room?

Are they yours, Simone?

I wonder what your driver thought when, among my usual groceries and supplies, I asked for pieces of dark sandstone? Did he understand the old way of making red ochre?

Surely those that range about the first floor of Hate House do not and I will use their ignorance against them.

I sat in a kitchen chair to rub two pieces of the sandstone together, careful that the dust fell inside a bowl held between my feet.

I added water, stirring with a spoon until it was roughly the texture of water color paint. When I had enough I carried it to the living room where the brutes had enjoyed relaxing without invitation. I would introduce them to my idea here, so that when they roamed upstairs they would pay its brethren no mind.

Stripping naked in the blasted cold, I smeared myself from head to toe with the freshly made paint. When I was completely coated except for the eyes, I pressed myself against a bare stretch of wall with my arms thrown out to either side. It took practice, grinding my body against the hard wall, hurting my nose and my cock, but eventually I had created a red image of myself in the ochre paint.

I laughed at the sight and padded nakedly through the house to the kitchen, where I threw open the door and descended the slippery stone steps into the channel, safe at low tide. The salt water scoured me clean and I laughed again at the confusion I would sow.

I plan to cover the walls above with similar artwork and when the invaders grow bold enough to venture upstairs, I will cover myself again in paint and hide among the ochre men. I can imagine them walking right past, close enough to touch. The fools.

I am ready for them.

Are they yours, Simone?

* * *

French set the book down and crawled to her duffle, too relaxed to stand and walk over like an adult. She wormed her hand inside until her arm was buried to the shoulder as her fingers sought...glass.

Like the world's most boring prestidigitator, French produced a bottle of Red Breast Irish whiskey, brought along for medicinal purposes.

If she was going to read about an alcoholic sinking into madness, she needed shoring up. She lifted the bottle towards the Ochre Man painted on the wall and said, "Cheers, Marcus Aurelius."

The cap came off and tried to flee under the couch but she blocked it by slamming a heel down in its path. Bottle to lips. Whiskey to gullet.

She sighed involuntarily as gentle fire sent tendrils of warmth through her body like the spokes of a wagon wheel. Her eyes watered and she coughed, not bothering to cover her mouth. Another swallow and she set the bottle down without recapping it.

White light filled the room and threw black shadows against the wall. Two seconds later the thunder arrived and she knew the storm was much closer.

More whiskey found her mouth and throat and stomach.

The image of Grady grinding his naked, paint covered body against the walls was—*Grady*?

Abbott. Young Abbott was prettier but despite the obvious and weird sexuality of it, the image was not remotely stimulating.

French flipped back through the pages to look for a date and realized that Abbott began hiding among the ochre men only three years into his incarceration within Hate House. Did that speak to his weakness of character or Simone's deviousness? She suspected that the intruders, assuming they weren't phantoms from Abbott's sick imagination, were directed by Simone Laurent. Fucking with his head. Making sure he never felt safe even in his own house.

Simone's own house.

Their house of Hate.

* * *

I need a break from this nutcase.

In French's experience, so much of investigation was combing through the boring shit. She set aside the diary and dragged over the metal drawer liberated from Abbott's library to leaf through more of the files inside. She imagined herself less as a searcher or a hunter, but more of a giant net sweeping through the ocean to pick up tiny details as she passed.

There were purchase orders with dates appearing to be prior to Abbott's incarceration. There was furniture. Appliances. Cases of wine and liquor. She found orders for object d'art, some of them quite expensive.

Among the things bought were several oddities. There was wood purchased from a British museum, part of a gallows exhibit from Exeter where the very last witch in England was executed by hanging in 1684. The Latin caught her eye but was only a curiosity as she'd never studied the dead language. There was kitchenware from the USS Eldridge, which she knew from the Discovery Channel was a ship the Navy had made *disappear* in the 1940's. She got serious Roswell vibes around that one. There was a painting bought from the house where Sharon Tate was murdered by Charles Manson's cult.

There were other files in other languages. They had names like Tunguska and Baikal, Uruk and Baal.

Bad juju, all of it. But not of Abbott's doing. This was Simone's handiwork.

Did you believe in this stuff, Simone?

* * *

Boom! Thunder shook the house, rattling her teeth.

French returned to the diary and opened to the next place

Grady had marked but decided on more whiskey before encountering the haunted cat. She used the couch to push up to her feet and picked up the book and whiskey bottle, in that order.

"Grady!" She shouted ahead as she thudded down the hall towards the kitchen. "Did you pick the craziest shit in this diary for me to read?"

She had an idea that as clean and healthy Grady was, he might not mind a snort of the necessary. A quieter voice admitted that the storm and story had combined to make her uneasy and she wanted his company.

"Grady?"

She entered the shadowy kitchen and found his electric lantern on a gloomy counter. Cold light soon confirmed what she already knew.

Grady wasn't there.

The kitchen door was closed and she thought he might be outside communing with nature, but before she could open the door and interrupt his zen, she was distracted by the smell of recent cooking.

A small pot rested atop the unlit camp stove and yes, her nose guided her correctly. Inside were Swedish meatballs.

She borrowed one and stuffed it whole in her mouth where it bulged against one cheek while she chewed. She bent and plucked up a torn bit of cardboard from the neat pile of recycling he had built.

"Ikea?"

French had found her single visit to an Ikea store traumatizing and the idea of buying the meatballs displayed near checkout lines struck her as one of life's absurdities. Now she knew someone who *actually* bought them.

A different kind of madness.

The meatball kicked a little stomach acid into the elevator that rose to her mouth, so French scooped up Grady's ever present thermos of tea, sticking the flashlight under her arm to hold it while unscrewing the cap that was also a cup. The tea was as earthy and herbal as expected but washed her mouth clean of the acid taste and made her throat tingle pleasantly, so she slugged back some more and called it a win, screwing the cap back on, replacing the thermos in its original spot so Grady would be none the wiser.

The silliness of the action brought a curve to her lips that others rarely saw, even before her life of isolation.

"Grady!" She borrowed another meatball and sauntered back towards her camp.

Thunder banged like a truck crashing against the side of the house and she felt the stone vibrate.

Another bit of wood found its way to her diminishing fire and she coughed against smoke, though the open windows did a decent enough job of pushing it away with a cross breeze.

She found what she now considered her reading spot and picked up the diary.

Chapter Nine

The cat ate the rat. Who eats the cat?

"I do."

The windows were fogged with steam from pots boiling on the stove and the kitchen was an explosion of cooking odors, roasting meats and boiling stews and sizzling vegetables in a frying pan all going at once. I smelled rosemary and thyme, garlic and shallots. There was mint and lemon and baking cod and a live lobster scratched in the metal sink basin.

I flew from station to station like a whirling dervish, the table dusted with hillocks and fields of flour as I assembled the bread beside a mixing bowl filled with tuna salad.

My secret weapon.

"Aye said the Hatter, you'll make the cat madder."

I'd been waiting for the weekly food shipment for days by then, getting by on the small portion of supplies that had not been destroyed. When I heard welcome rumble of the limousine's approach I threw open the kitchen door and raced across the foot bridge, for once not terrified to encounter Simone's driver.

He emerged from the limousine, unfolding like a six foot jackknife, and stopped as still as a deer hearing the crack of a branch. Though his eyes were hidden behind dark sunglasses, I saw his black eyebrows arch into view and realized I had forgotten to put on a stitch of clothes.

No doubt he would report success back to his mistress, that I had gone stark raving mad, but I was without care because my goods were here. I would have food to eat and all the fixings for a great feast.

The troubles I would soon fix started six nights ago.

Six nights prior, I had struggled through a night of terrifying dreams. An anvil crushed the breath from me, held to my flesh by sharp steel screws.

Dawn dragged gentle fingers across my twitching eyelids and I awoke to find tiny black hairs on the breast of my white T-shirt, surrounded by tiny pin pricks red with blood.

Confused and hungover from the previous night's brandy, I stumbled downstairs to the kitchen for a pot of coffee. I caught the ugly stink in the hallway and froze in the archway when I saw the disaster of the kitchen.

The cabinets were opened and the dry goods inside scattered about the counters and floor, bags and boxes shredded by claws.

The acrid stench of cat piss burned the inside of my nostrils and I swore when I stepped in a fresh lump of catshit.

It didn't so much smell like a spraying tomcat, but like the cat's bladder had exploded. A urine-filled grenade.

Stepping more carefully now, I crossed the cold floor to open the kitchen door for air, jerking back with a grunt when a black shape hissed from the rocks outside and vanished like an oily streak around the corner.

"You shithead!"

I didn't realize then that the cat was Simone's agent.

Instead I was busy with the unpleasant task of cleaning the kitchen, scrubbing every surface with diminishing supplies of dish soap. When it was as done as I could do, I left the window and door open to speed drying and made myself a meal of Campbell's soup.

The cans, though scattered, had withstood the destruction.

I didn't see the cat again until that night, when it appeared once more as an anvil on my chest to crush the breath from me. My sleep was horrendous, my t-shirt again marked with black fur, when that bitch we call Morning herded me from bed and down towards coffee.

The refrigerator door was open and until I hit the wall switch, the interior refrigerator bulb cast a wedge of light across the floor to display the bits of meat and cheese scattered amidst more turds.

I opened the refrigerator door wider and it was only then I realized the cold had diminished the stink of the feline spray on the shelves inside. A cardboard container of lemonade had been slashed and the sticky liquid was everywhere. The meat and cheese drawer had been pulled free and dumped on the floor.

Only a few hardened targets remained intact, along with the condiments.

Slamming the door hard enough to rock the entire, aging refrigerator, I stormed to the kitchen door and threw it open with a shout.

This time the long, lean black cat took time to arch its back in defiance and hiss a warning, but I didn't hesitate as I charged out with the intention of kicking it all the way to the channel.

It fled before I could reach it, shooting around the corner of the house like a slice of obsidian lightning.

And so it went. It would not let me sleep and would not let me eat. At least not in peace. I hunted through the big house for the beast but had no chance of finding it. Thinking I might bash in its head during the night, I kept a rolling pin on my night-stand, but the anvil it became each night held me as paralyzed as I was breathless.

Rinse and repeat.

Again.

"Simone!!!" I grew convinced it was not simply the old witch's agent, but the wrinkled bitch herself. "Simone!!!"

I rationed my canned food, carrying it with me throughout the day in a pillowcase. The muffled clank and thump of cans made me more dispirited than before. How quickly she had she reduced me.

That damned cat.

So...I developed a plan. A madman's plan for sure, but I decided a party was in order. A hatter's party with one guest invited, me as host along with friends from the sea would fete the damned cat. All of the food would be there. Irresistible bait for the beast.

We would feast until we were fat and slow. When the last plate was licked clean and the last crumb chewed one of us would walk away.

The other would die.

* * *

I waved at the lobsterman as he pulled up traps near my island and though he ignored me at first, eventually he looked my way and I gestured him closer, descending the long stone steps until I stood inches from the water, the spray dampening my pants.

He nosed his boat cautiously towards me and tossed over a line while he dropped a stern anchor. The rope was wet in my hands and I wasn't sure I was much of an anchor if the sea decided to grab the boat, but it worked well enough.

His face was fishbelly white with a coal black beard, suggesting Spanish sailors in the family woodpile. On his head was a sun bleached Red Sox hat and his gnarled sweater was the color of seaweed and driftwood.

"What?" He finally said after looking me up and down and failing to be impressed.

"I want to buy a dozen lobsters."

He glanced behind him at three traps in the back of the boat. "Got fifteen."

"I only need twelve."

"Gonna send me back with three lobsters?"

Yankees don't bark and holler like some bargainers, but don't let it fool you, they are crafty.

"I'd like to buy fifteen lobsters," I amended my order.

"Alright." He removed his hat, scratched his bald spot while he did the math and quoted me a number.

"Wait right here." I dropped the rope and ran up the rocks to the open front door of Hate House, looking for something interesting. When I returned to the water's edge holding a long candle stick holder he said, "What's that?"

"Solid silver and worth a helluva lot more than your asking price."

I tossed it and he caught it with the deft hand of a professional fisherman. He weighed it in his palm and scratched a nail against its length.

"How do I know it's really silver?" Crafty as ever.

"If it's not you'll come back with friends and beat me silly or drown me in the ocean," I shrugged.

He set the silver down beside the boat's steering wheel. "Ya know, people talk about you."

"I've seen you and a few other lobsterman watching from your boats."

He turned and hawked a wad of spit over the side away from me. Fortunately, the wind was in our favor.

"We made kind of an unofficial pact to keep an eye, case any kids go missing or cows get cut up."

He said this while he was hauling up a big, dripping trap full of shiny dark lobsters and holding it out. I grunted from the weight and couldn't answer until I set it down on the stone without falling forward into the water.

"Your cattle are safe from me."

He put the hat back on his head and picked up another trap. "Fuck the cows. What about the kids?"

"Them too." This crate was even heavier and I overbalanced backwards, sitting down hard on the unforgiving stone with the wet trap landing against my lap and chest. The furious movement of the crustaceans inside was terrifying and I shoved it off to the side.

He cupped a cigarette to his lips and lit it to give me a chance for a dignified ascent to my feet. When I was upright he blew out a well rounded smoke ring.

"People in town figure you're a witch or a pervert."

I laughed. "Only a fool."

It was his turn to shrug. "Once you empty those traps, just leave 'em near the water, high enough so the tide won't take 'em. I'll swing by to pick them up tomorrow morning early."

I tossed back his line and he pulled up the stern anchor, reversing the engine to putter away from the island until he had enough clearance to make forward speed away. He left without a wave.

I looked down at my incarcerated party guests and said, "Let's get you ready for the big to do."

* * *

If I squinted I could imagine a long feasting table, but without the squint is was definitely several coffee tables of different sizes laid end to end with bed sheets for table cloths.

I fashioned low seats along both sides for the lobster guests, each with its own bit of cloth fitted as a scarf or waist coat. My crafting skills were limited, but they were lobsters and didn't care. Six armored guests on each side and three for the pot was the plan.

At the far end was an ottoman dragged from the living room and before it the dish of tuna salad laced with very special herbs.

A wind whistled across the water as the sun dipped, temperature chasing after it like an obedient dog.

I set out a motley collection of cups and glasses for the lobsters and splashed wine in each. The creatures themselves showed little interest, occasionally crawling away from their seats until I carried them back.

The long shadow of Hate House encased the feast and I lit the lanterns running down the center of the tables. Before the match burned my fingers, I lit my pipe and inhaled the sweet opium smoke.

As the last gulls cried and the waves slapped against the rocks, I smoked and drank and listened the music drifting from speakers inside the house. Edith Piaf, Simone's favorite.

Darkness was swift and a heavy wind pushed against my back. I shivered inside my wool pea coat and my hair danced ridiculously, which made me laugh.

Cracking lobster claws with my hands I stuffed my mouth with white meat while juices ran down from the corners of my mouth. I tossed bits of food to the sluggish lobsters and tried to engage them in conversation.

"Quick death. Slow death. What death? Your death?" I said to the green speckled guest nearest on my right, but it was unimpressed.

Opium is a glorious thing.

I stretched an arm out to pick up the nearest crustacean on my left and blew smoke into its face.

I said, "Have you ever enjoyed something so much?"

Antenna waving it replied, "It's impossible to smoke beneath the waves."

I clapped a hand to my forehead and set it on the table so we might continue. "I'm an idiot."

"What time is it?" Said a dying lobster further down the table.

Spying small bubbles around its mouth in the uneven lantern light I said, "It's very late, I'm afraid."

I was clever and continued this conversation while the cat ate tuna salad at the far end of the table. It skipped the ottoman entirely and crouched on the tablecloth beside the bowl, having appeared without fanfare.

Beyond the bowl was a platter full of mashed island crabs and a few chunks of cooked meat from a lobster that hadn't made my guest list.

The cat stepped daintily forward along the table and enjoyed the crab I had prepared.

For my part I discovered I had ceased speaking to the lobster guests and was staring into my bowl of soup, occasionally commenting on the shapes I understood within. The lobster to my right with its wrap of blue felt had gone still and I suspect was dead. The lobster to my left was also unmoving and the green in which I'd draped it was gone, perhaps stolen by the wind.

Being right handed I grabbed the lobster in blue and threw it pinwheeling at the cat.

The lobster struck the plate of crabs and the plate struck the cat. The opium drunk feline squawked and sprang away.

I was on my feet and hurled a ceramic bowl, struggling not to watch its slow arc and thistledown fall towards the earth as I charged down the length of the feasting table with the green clad lobster cocked like a quarterback in motion.

The bowl shattered in the cat's path and it darted away from the explosion, directly towards me.

I whipped the lobster at it and unbalanced, the bedsheet slipping from my feet so I flew headlong off the table.

I too floated like a thistle and barely felt the contact with the rock. The cat, drunk on poppies and confused, recoiled from the crashing lobster and crashing human in that order and I sprang upon it.

"Simone!" Someone shouted. Was it me?

I bashed the cat against the stony island and it clawed my hands and wrists in sudden fury. Unfeeling and unheeding of danger, I pressed it on its back and spread my hands apart as if flattening dough, pushing the forelegs up and hind legs down to expose its belly.

I used the only weapon at my disposal and my head darted down like a heron spearing fish. As my teeth met its fury belly the damned cat screamed like a woman. No feline ever made such a sound.

A man's teeth are not made for such efforts but I was determined and raised off my knees onto my toes so that all of my weight was behind my chewing mouth.

It wriggled and fought and bit. I felt wounds on my ears. My temples beneath the hair. But its flesh parted and my chomping teeth were soon into the pink secrets of the thing.

Did I swallow? Yes I did, though my plan had been destruction not consumption. Soon enough I had ravaged enough of its interior that it appeared a red and gleaming stew of indefinable organs and the damned cat went still.

I coughed and spat. Sat back on my haunches and panted while applause sounded from the remaining party guests.

The cat ate the rat. Who eats the cat?

"I do."

When I awoke the lanterns were very low, though not defunct like the cat. Edith Piaf had long since stopped her crooning and the only music was that of wind and waves. I was sprawled on my back beside the remains of my nemesis, my face crusted with blood and fur.

I sat up and realized, "I can see in the dark now."

I slept again.

Chapter Ten

French stood at the base of the big staircase leading up into the black void of the second story. Even the bright light of her electric camp lantern only crawled halfway up the risers.

She slugged whiskey from the bottle clutched in her free hand and when thunder cracked, white light screaming in through the high windows in the foyer, she shouted.

"YOU'RE A CLICHÉ!"

Adamantine light outlined every object in the foyer. The busts and statuary shivered in albino awakening and the Latin carved into the front doorframe door dripped fire.

"Don't read the Latin," she stage whispered.

The orange glow of her fire drifted from the living room entrance and she decided it would be enough to find her way back if she lost the lantern. Why would she lose the lantern?

She was atop the second floor landing, her bright light sparking colors from the stained glass windows but rendering her blind to the cavernous hallways stretching in either direction. She still had the bottle, which was good. It still sloshed with brown liquor, which was also good.

Her steps crunched over armies of dead crabs and door after

door swung resisted her ferocious charge. The stories of whoever slept in them long dead and beyond her reach.

Crunch. Crunch. When the first Ochre Man turned slyly to follow her passage she aimed her gaze at the tips of her boots.

She ignored the rustling as the rest of his tribe reacted to her intrusion. Their heads twisting. Lips baring over sharp, heathen teeth.

Another door, stuck. Her shoulder slammed into it hard enough to bruise but she was floating above the pain and nearly stumbled to her knees when the door gave way.

The room was cramped, little more than a walk-in closet. A drab, spiral staircase of dull iron rose towards the ceiling and punched through into the mystery above.

"Yes!" she crowed in victory. "I'm motherfucking Magellan! Found you first."

She heard the rustle of voices and dull applause from the hall, but saw nothing when she looked out. When her gaze fell on the Ochre Men they were sly and still.

She clomped back to the spiral staircase, feet booming hollowly over the uneven wooden planks of the floor in the small room. By the time the sound registered she was holding her lantern high.

Wait, what?

She stomped her heel and looked down as if she could see the hollow space beneath her. She hopped up and down and listened to the subterranean echo. Crouched, swinging her lantern around in a slow circled until…was that a deadbolt in the floor?

Knees lifting high, she mudstomped towards the deadbolt—

The crack was sudden. Gravity was immediate.

She plunged down into darkness.

* * *

The boat rocked on the waves and she rocked in its damp, metal bosom, nauseated by the smell of sea things.

Her hair was woven with dead crabs, her clothes wet and abrasive with salt. She was beyond cold. Jaw pained from chattering. She wore a bib of vomit on her chest.

When a light stabbed down her boat was abruptly shoved by something larger. A lobster boat bullying her aside.

"Hey! Hey!" A man's voice, harsh like a seagull's scream.

Wellington boots slammed down into her boat hard enough to nearly capsize it. She tried to move. To care. He was towering in the dawn's light, beard bristling and furious, eyes wild.

Was she too numb to feel the hand cradling her head or was his touch so gentle?

"Alright now," the lobsterman growled. "Gonna be okay."

Chapter Eleven

The doctor's office smelled like coffee brewed sometime the previous century. Back when coffee came in Styrofoam cups and blinking fluorescent lights drove people blind.

"Drugged?" French said.

"Have to do a blood test to be sure, but from what you told me and those pupils of yours." Doctor Booth shrugged his ancient shoulders. At least she hoped he was a doctor. He did have a stethoscope and an office behind his white clapboard house with an examination table and a poster on the wall diagramming the sinus. But he wore a red and black checked shirt, his hollow cheeks and loose neck were flecked with white stubble, and there was more hair sprouting from his ears than his skull.

She herself had been cleaned up and was wearing a borrowed hospital Johnny.

"I don't do drugs," she said and he shrugged again, lined face unmotivated towards expression. "But I was roofied once. I think that happened last night."

He *tsked*, whether at her libidinous lifestyle or at the idea a man would drug a woman for sex she wasn't sure. His hands wore knuckles like enormous coconuts but his touch was as gentle as a dove's kiss.

"I drew blood for a tox screen so we'll know what hit you." He paused, one bushy eyebrow rising. "You're out at that there house on Laurent property?"

She nodded and he clucked because he was feeling her glands.

"Sorry," she said. "There's a dispute over ownership and I represent one of the parties in contention."

"Tall fella represent the other?"

"You've seen Grady?"

Booth turned away and peeled off rubber gloves, stepping on a lever to open a trashcan lid so he could drop them inside.

"Nope," he said. "Some of the boys seen him and you scampering about." The metal trashcan lid clanged shut and he paused.

"What?"

He leaned his narrow flank against the sink and crossed his arms over his chest, sucking on an invisible toothpick. She suspected he used to smoke.

"Bad business when that house is occupied," he finally said.

A wave of cold prickled her skin. "What do you mean?"

"Town was here before that stone heap sprouted up on the island. Real secret like, the people who moved in. Priests who didn't have no congregation. Never came to town." He met her eyes. "Couple kids went missing."

She shook her head, remembering the conversation with a lobsterman that Abbott described in his diary. About how the local men agreed to keep watch.

"They weren't monks, were they?"

"No, they weren't."

"After they left," she said and he nodded. "When Abbott moved in—"

"Crazy as a shithouse rat, that one," the doctor interrupted.

"—did anyone from town go missing?"

He pushed off the sink to stand straight, cracking his swollen knuckles. "Who you say you representing again?"

"Abbott."

He nodded. "Let's get you some dry clothes over at the general store and I heard Bruce Flynn towed a vehicle to his yard. Bet it's yours?"

She nodded. "Bet you're right."

* * *

The town bore the uninspiring name of Paper Bay and there wasn't much to it. The bay and docking facilities not big enough to be much of a commercial enterprise, the houses hunched under the relentless scouring of sea and salt, fresh paint a luxury no one cared to indulge.

Her clothes were still damp as was her wallet. Her credit card strip had given up the ghost, but she was able to buy Boston Bruins sweat pants and a hoodie at the general store, the proprietor squinting at her through a sea of wrinkles but happy to take her money via PayPal, since she had her phone.

"We got the internet," the proprietor told French.

A bell tinkled over the door and French turned to see an old woman in a grey knit shawl. Her flyaway hair was barely held back by a length of yarn and her thick face was lined with wrinkles deep enough to evoke memories of dry riverbeds in the desert.

The old woman stumped inside, the eye unhidden beneath a faded black eye patch was fixed on French.

"I know you."

French shook her head. "I doubt it."

An ancient grin revealed crooked teeth. "You moved into Hate House."

French turned back to the counter but a hand gripped her arm, the fingers tipped with long, cracked nails. French jerked free and stepped away.

"Get your hands off me," she said, unnerved. "I didn't move into Hate House."

"You woke it up." The old woman nodded and looked at the proprietor. "Watch your kids."

The proprietor shook her head. "You gonna buy something, Rebecca Nurse?"

The old woman laughed wetly and produced a pipe from somewhere in her layers of clothing. She jabbed the chewed stem at French.

"It'll be your fault for waking it up."

The old woman, Rebecca, clumped her way to the door and left, bell ringing in her wake.

French took her things and looked outside after a moment of hesitation. Rebecca was nowhere to be seen.

As soon as she stepped into the street Rebecca Nurse emerged from behind the corner and blocked her path.

"I know all about that place, missy," Rebecca said. "These folks won't go nowhere near it but I been inside. I'm the only one knows what's going on."

French backed up, mouth working but at a loss for words. She swung wide around the old woman who turned to follow as she passed.

After a dozen steps she looked over her shoulder to make sure the hunched woman wasn't following, but Rebecca Nurse had vanished.

* * *

A few cars slowed as French trudged through town carrying her wet clothes in a plastic bag. The streets bore names like Mill and Saw, Boat and Net. Uninspired names taken from the uninspiring industry of the place.

On Captain's Way she passed a low roofed bar with broken neon beer signs in the windows and thought about a drink but didn't like the two men hunkered outside the door, smoking.

They had flinty eyes and regarded her with a mixture of invasive curiosity and hostility. She could feel their eyes on her chest as her meager tits shifted beneath the sweatshirt and wished she'd put on her bra, even if it was still damp.

At least the storm had passed and it was a clear, sunny day without too much chill. Important since she was taking the heel-toe express out to the tow yard.

The walk was uneventful.

After near a half hour of trudging she reached Flynn's Towing Service, just over a mile beyond what passed for the center of town. Her rented Suburban was shining in the yard beside several wrecks. The metal rowboat was tied securely to the roof.

"Yah, Steve brought your boat over already," Flynn said. He was missing a few teeth and his whiskers were white, but he was a friendly sort and she liked him immediately.

"Thanks." She glanced at the cigarettes poking out of Flynn's breast pocket. "Can I bum a smoke?"

He gave her the pack and she shook one free, leaning forward when he held out a flame.

She blew out smoke. "Is my friend's truck here?"

"I only towed your beast here," he nodded at the Suburban. "Don't know nothin' about a truck."

"Huh." French didn't know what to make of this intelligence. "Do you think that fat security guy will get me towed again? I mean, I'm supposed to be out there working."

The tow truck driver laughed his way into a cough. "Tell you what, if he calls me out I'll make sure you have a chance to give him a piece of your mind before anything gets moved." He winked. "'Tween you and me, I think you can take the chubby bastid." He coughed again.

She climbed behind the wheel of her Suburban while he was still spitting to clear his mouth.

"Thank you," she said out the window.

He nodded. "Yah."

She started to raise her window but hit the button to send it back down. "Hey, is there a bar around here that isn't the one in town?"

* * *

French drove easily with the window lowered, the cold air tossing her hair around into a fright show wig. The trees around her were mostly shed of their leaves, bony, unhealthy things in muted greys. The grass resembled uncut wheat but rustled peacefully in her passage and she thought it might be wisest to keep on driving straight past Hate House on down to Philadelphia.

That she had been drugged was obvious though she wasn't sure how. Her memory was full of black gaps but she remembered the glowing electric outline of objects in the foyer after the lightning struck.

"I was tripping balls," she muttered.

Sand crunched under her tires and she straightened her wheel to avoid the shoulder. The futility of her expedition was bright and apparent now that she was away from the cloistered confines of Hate House, a place that smothered her mind as much as her breathing.

The money was good. Really good. But Abbott had been insane, clinically so, during his incarceration at Hate House and she wasn't so sure of his sanity now. She felt almost as if she were more his cat's paw than investigator, sent to spar with Simone's agent in continuation of their decades long contest.

Still, suspicion shaded every thought and she pictured herself back in Flynn's tow yard, asking about Grady's truck. His vehicle went missing the same time as hers but what if security hadn't had him towed? Just her?

Was Grady working with the security service to mess with her? If so, why? And where the hell was his truck?

When a dirty brick blockhouse appeared ahead on the right,

she flicked on her turn signal despite the lack of traffic. An unlit sign proclaimed the establishment was FISHERCAT'S SALOON and below the name smaller letters said, KITCHEN CLOSED.

She nosed the Chevy Suburban in beside two dirt spattered pickups and a few Harleys, her vehicle standing out like a pearl among rocks but she didn't care.

She blew her nose and stuffed the tissue in her pocket before climbing out and slamming the door shut, the sound muted by the emptiness all around

A windowless door opened at her touch and she moseyed inside.

* * *

"You talk funny," said the old man a few barstools over.

"No I don't," she said.

"He means you don't sound like you're from around here." A giant in a biker jacket sitting just past the old man leaned forward to look at her. His face spoke of pot roasts and potatoes, and his eyes were friendly.

She sipped her bourbon rocks and hissed through her teeth. "Philly."

The old man slapped the plywood bar with a sound like a rifle shot.

"Hey!" The bartender shouted perfunctorily. She was a sturdily built woman in a stained t-shirt and looked capable of playing bouncer when the need arose.

"I been to Philly!" The old guy crowed, stringy hair bouncing off his shoulders in excitement. "I had one of them cheese steaks for breakfast, if you can believe that! One of the real famous places where there's two sandwich shops staring across the intersection at each other like gunfighters."

"Pat's and Gino's?" French asked.

"That it's! Pat's and Gino's!" He reached across the empty

space above the two stools separating them and she shook his hand. "I'm Mike." He cocked a thumb at his friend. "This big fucker is Percy."

Percy nodded and she nodded back.

"You guys work the boats?"

Percy smiled. "I'm a school teacher—"

"—and I'm on the disability," Mike interrupted. "What about you?"

She gave a mental shrug and said, "Private investigator."

"No shit!" Mike turned to Percy. "She's a detective."

"That your local camouflage?" Percy asked.

French glanced at her matching Bruins sweats. "Fell in the water and all my stuff got wet, this is all I could get in town."

Mike slapped the bar again. "Hey, Marie," he cawed. "Put another round for the lady on my tab."

"You gonna pay your tab?" Marie snapped her dishtowel in the old geezer's direction but fetched a bottle from the shelf.

"Soon as my check comes in," Mike grinned with the devil in his eyes.

French rolled her gaze around the place. A single, rectangular room with a few booths, a jukebox and a scarred dance floor. The cinderblock corners didn't quite seem to line up and she decided the place was both ugly *and* cheaply made. But the booze worked so screw it.

A heavyset lady all in denim was shoving quarters into the juke and the opening clang of AC/DC's *Hell's Bells* filled the air.

"What's a Fishercat?" French asked.

"Like a bobcat that hunts fish in the swamp."

"Ain't like a bobcat," Mike said.

"It works in this context," Percy shot back.

"It works in this context," Mike mimicked him and Marie laughed as she set fresh drinks down for the three of them. She leaned her elbows on the bar and her biceps popped impressively.

"What are you investigating?" Marie asked.

French decided that in for a penny was in for a pound and said, "Hate House."

"Huh?" Mike contributed.

"She means the old stone house on Laurent property," Percy said.

"You came to the right place," Marie said, straightening and wiping down the bar in front of French.

"That you staying out there the last couple days?" Mike asked.

"Me and another investigator," French answered.

Mike and Percy exchanged looks but Marie interjected.

"Yah, we heard all kind of things over the years." Her accent made *over* sound like *ovah*. "Like the reason there's so much land undeveloped around it is because they were up to things."

"*They* like the Catholic Church?" French asked. "I heard they built it to be a monastery."

Marie dropped her towel on the bar and leaned forward, voice dropping. "Masons."

"That land is undeveloped because this place is blighted with poverty," Percy said.

Mike cackled, "Poverty!" and Marie shot back, "You don't drink like you're living in poverty."

The way the conversation ricocheted back and forth on well-worn paths, French suspected she was seeing a daily ritual play out.

"Some bad shit happened out there," Mike said, smile draining from his face. "Stuff happened again when that crazy man took ownership."

"Masonic shit," Marie nodded.

"Folks are uncomfortable seeing lights in those windows again," Percy added.

French lifted her tumbler and sipped, ice cubes bouncing off her lip.

"You think Abbott was crazy?" French finally asked.

"That man needed a funny farm," Mike said.

French nodded. "I think you're right. I've been reading his diary."

"Holy shit!" This from Marie.

"What's it say?" This from Mike.

"Crazy shit." This from French.

Percy coughed into one ham sized fist. "Who hired you to investigate him?"

Before French could answer, Marie said, "Shit." She left to attend to a tall man all in black who was seating himself in a booth. His five o'clock shadow was so black as to be blue and he set a black Fedora on his table. Sunglasses with round lenses in the style of the late John Lennon hid the direction of his gaze, but French thought—

Mike cleared his throat dramatically and French smiled. She set her drink down, careful to place it exactly atop the moisture ring on the wood, milking the moment.

"I'm not investigating him," she said. "I'm investigating the house."

Mike nodded knowingly and French had a thought.

"You guys seem pretty okay about that."

Percy and Mike glanced at each other and shrugged.

"I mean," French continued. "People in town didn't seem too thrilled to meet me. There was one old lady with an eyepatch who said I was *waking it up*."

Percy grinned and shook his head but Mike slapped the bar again. "Hah! Rebecca Nurse says she can see the future in a pile of fish guts and use a willow stick to play water witch. Says she can make it rain when there's a drought."

"It's always raining here," Percy grinned.

French smiled. "So she really *is* a witch."

Mike laughed again and Percy leaned closer. "She's been nuttier than a fruitcake since I was in grade school. Kids throw rocks at her house on Halloween."

"Every town's got a nut and she's ours," Mike added.

In the pause that followed, a fisherman approached the

other end of the bar and Marie headed over, but as she passed she mouthed the word, "Masons."

"I gotta piss!" Mike pushed off his stool and took a weaving path towards what French presumed was the Men's Room.

Percy glanced to make sure Marie was busy with her customer and offered in a low voice, "I don't know anything about Masons and that crap, but that house out there has been bad news for a long time, since it was built."

"How so?"

Something ugly moved behind Percy's eyes. "It wasn't a monastery. It was a halfway house built by a group called Opus Bono Sacerdotii.

"I don't know that group."

"They're sole purpose is hiding pedophile priests."

* * *

In the parking lot outside Fishercat, French discovered she had a signal and called Abbott.

"Hello." A woman's voice on Abbott's phone, her tone steely.

"This is Megan French, I need to speak with Mr. Abbott."

"Mr. Abbott is not available."

"He'll want to hear this."

"He is unavailable."

"You tell him we've uncovered some very sensitive materials inside Hate House and that the Laurent's agent has become aggressive." French caught herself before she could add the word *bitch*. "I have no signal at the house. You tell him he'll want to get on the phone next time I call."

The woman on the other end hung up the phone.

* * *

French was prepared to ram the gates but the crack security patrol had failed to secure the padlocks. She clomped to the black iron barrier with an eerie sense of déjà vu, unwinding the chains and throwing them and both locks on the passenger seat of her SUV.

Was she a little drunk? Yeah, but it put her in the right frame of mind for the confrontation to come. She'd left Fishercat with an unopened bottle of Cutty Sark and planned to break it over Grady's skull if he didn't have a damned good explanation for what had happened to her.

After that, staying or leaving was a toss up. Hate House was seriously bad juju and she felt a crawling dread as she bounced down the dirt track toward it. Passing the old graveyard didn't help, with its tumbledown headstones and untended grass surrounded by a sagging black iron fence.

Her heart sank like a stone when she saw the ugly pile of rocks on its homely island. Hate House gleamed in the setting sun and still managed to look sly and untrustworthy. Had Abbott actually been involved in cannibalism in that horrid abode? Had predatory priests kidnapped children from town and dragged them back to its dark rooms where screams would be muffled and crimes hidden?

She wanted a drink, a cigarette and sleep. She wanted to give Grady a concussion. She wanted to be home in her apartment with Buster purring in her lap.

At the lip of the world she threw her SUV into *Park* and cut the engine. Unplugging her phone from the console she checked the signal in vain hope, but there was nothing. Hate House was a dead zone.

Breath steamed from her mouth as she clambered out and the frigid wind cut through her sweatshirt. "Shit." Cursing and snarling, she undid the knots Flynn had tied when he attached the metal rowboat to the Suburban's roof. One fingernail split and she sucked at the blood, swallowing it rather than spitting it on this blighted land.

The boat rang against the ground like an aging church bell and she dragged it down the slope to the water, her damp clothes and the Cutty Sark safely inside.

"GRADY, YOU MOTHERFUCKER!"

Nothing stirred behind the windows of Hate House and the kitchen door hung open as if the place waited gape-mouthed for her return.

Water slapped against the hull as she clambered in, the boat rocking precariously but failing to toss her into the channel. She rowed with alcohol fueled anger instead of technique and fire blazed through the muscles on her back.

Gonna feel that in the morning, she thought.

The bow scraped against the island rocks and she maneuvered until she could climb out onto the slick stairs with the bowrope in hand. She tied it off on the metal railroad spike pounded into the rock for that purpose and climbed on three limbs, cradling the whiskey and clothes to her belly with her left hand.

"GRADY!"

She stood atop the stairs and the western sun threw her shadow out ahead to make her a giant. The kitchen beyond the open door was dark and she thought he might be hiding.

That thought dissolved like a gossamer in a gale as soon as she clomped into the kitchen.

The empty kitchen.

Grady's camp was gone and no sign of him remained. Even the stove had been cleared of ash and debris from his fires.

"What?"

The as yet unused generator remained and she had passed the kerosene cans outside, but everything belonging to her counterpart had gone up in a puff of smoke, even the bag in which he collected his trash.

Had he found something definitive to prove the Laurent ownership and was at that very moment enroute to his masters?

It was difficult to see in the gloaming of the long hallway

but she knew its mysteries and made her way easily, glancing into rooms for signs of the other investigator as she passed.

Her own camp was hidden in shadow and she located her flashlight on the coffee table. Swept its beam around the animal den she'd made and felt something was out of place but couldn't put her finger on it. Panning her beam around the room beyond her camp she made out the ochre painting of Abbott on the wall and asked, "What the fuck is going on, Marcus?"

Where was her electric camp lantern?

She shivered, set down the Cutty Sark and plopped down on a love seat to rifle through her duffel for clothes.

Underwear and a bra, a t-shirt to go under the sweatshirt.

"Grady?" She cocked her head to listen but heard only the lonely wind hissing through the opened windows, so she stripped quickly and dressed herself, moaning with relief as she pulled thick socks over her cold feet.

Fortifying herself with a swig of the Cutty Sark—terrible but potent—she set about building a new fire in the cold fireplace. It was only when the fire began to lick the wood with an orange tongue that she realized what was different.

The andirons were gone. A trill of fear tried to slither up her spine but fatigue muted its cry. Made it one more strange detail in a sea of strange details.

Grady had left. Oh, she would look for him, but she could feel it in the whistling inhale and exhale of the house. Grady was gone.

A full but opened pack of Salem's was on the coffee table and she pulled one free, using the fire to light its tip. An odd sweetness rode her first inhalation and she wondered if cigarettes could rot.

Possibilities danced in the smoke but she couldn't understand them. *What the Hell is going on?*

Her stomach made unseemly noises and she was struck by

sudden hunger, but the memory of Ikea meatballs stirred her guts to nausea and she had to fight back the urge to puke.

"Whatever." It wouldn't be the first time she'd had cigarettes and booze for dinner.

She cradled the bottle to her chest and settled back against the love seat as the fire crackled and smoke ticked her nostrils. Fatigue was a warm blanket and she decided to sit for a moment before continuing her search for Grady, even though she knew in her gut he was long gone.

She was unaware of sleep taking her.

* * *

French awoke from a dream of crabs swarming over her naked body and jackknifed to a sitting position, brushing and swiping frantically at phantoms that failed to follow her into the waking world.

"Fucking hell."

Silver moonlight revealed a floor free of crawling horrors and she realized she was awake and desperately had to pee in rapid sequence.

Her limbs were less ready for action and she rolled to her hands and knees, breathing hoarsely against stinging bile in her throat and enjoying the cool breeze blowing in through the window. A silent count to three preceded her effort to rise and she climbed to her feet with more creaks and groans than a rusted Tin Man.

She grabbed at the Cabela's lantern and actually managed to snag the handle, shuffling towards the archway as her fingers searched blindly for the switch.

Blue white light flooded the foyer and her shriek was wordless as the lantern fell to the parquet floor.

The ghost was tall and billowy white, standing in her path.

The lantern bounced towards the apparition without breaking and French's mind filled with static as the big muscles in her arms and legs clenched, refusing to move her body to flight or fight.

A sudden gust caused the hem of the ghost to flap wildly and *It's a sheet!* was immediately scrawled across the tabula rasa of her tortured mind. Several heartbeats later, French realized the significance of this revelation and rushed forward before fear could freeze her again. She lunged at the hidden face of the thing and grabbed a fistful of dusty cloth before yanking it aside.

The bone white Queen was revealed, deadly and still.

French waited for it to move, to speak, before surrendering to emotion and shoving the giant chess piece over to crack hard against the floor. "You fucking thing!"

It would be a good hour before her mind cleared enough to wonder at the Queen's frightening appearance in the foyer. In the moment it was of a piece with the hideous portrait of Simone over the door and the toxic atmosphere of Hate House. Surging with adrenaline, French muscled the fallen chess piece to the front door, opened the portal and tumbled the Queen outside onto the rocky island. In so demeaning the Queen she felt a surge of anger from the chess room off the foyer and realized she could not leave the evil bitch's army at her back.

She would have been shocked to see her own face in the next frenzied minutes, spittle leaking from lips peeled back to revealed clenched teeth, eyes wide and bulging with manic intensity as she dragged piece after piece from the chess room and heaved them out the door into a pile with the White Queen at the bottom. Sometime during her trips back and forth she turned on the floodlights but had no memory of doing so, consumed with the greasy feel of Bishops and Rooks.

And then the pile was built, awaiting the splash of kerosene. The flame it conjured was huge and pagan, and she raised clenched fists.

"Fuck you, Simone," she hissed through her teeth before the crazed energy fled her body and she felt the crushing weight of fatigue. The humbling reality of her bladder motivated her to leave the bonfire and pick up the rugged, unbroken camp lantern before she made her way down the hall to the bathroom.

The fire outside Hate House's front door had weakened by the time she returned and though some vague Girl Scout notion of fire safety whispered that it shouldn't be left unattended, French didn't care.

She shuffled back into her camp and lowered herself into the nest she'd built, made secure by the scent of burning wood.

Still, she left the lights on in the foyer.

Just in case.

Chapter Twelve

There was a physical sensation to the emptiness and French relished the feeling upon her awakening.

The house was hers.

Unscrewing the cap to a water bottle, she rinsed out her dry mouth, pleasantly surprised by the absence of a hangover. She padded in her socks to the foyer, enjoying the golden beams of morning light blazing in through the unboarded window near the door.

"It's only us now, Simone," she said to the massive portrait over the doorway. "And since you're dead, that means it's only me."

She pulled open the door and inhaled the brisk morning air, a chill wind scouring her even as bright sunlight warmed her skin. The ground undulated as the pale crab army retreated but she felt strangely undaunted.

She surrendered to an urge to laugh, pulling off her sweatshirt as she strode outside, followed by her t-shirt. Her skin pebbled with goosebumps and her nipples tightened painfully when she shucked her bra, but this only made her laugh again, caught in a victorious giddiness.

A distant white boat bobbed on the water and she wondered

if the lobsterman was watching the show, waving before she slid her sweatpants down over her hips and hooked her thumbs in her underwear to send them down as well.

She advanced naked towards the ocean, descending the giant steps until the high tide splashed up over her feet and she released an unintended squeak of surprise.

The next step down brought the water to her knees and she knelt, teeth chattering until she could stretch out in a plank position with the seawater swirling in her face and the salt smell filling her nostrils.

She sucked in a breath and lowered herself in a push up until she was submerged, immediately rolling to the right along the smooth stone until she could stand the cold no more and jackknifed up with a sputtering shout.

Wind whipped against her wet skin as she dashed back up the giant steps, gathering clothes as she went. She felt like a selkie or a mermaid. She felt ridiculous in the most wonderful way.

The front door stayed open as she skidded inside on slick feet and hurried back to her camp to fetch new clothes. The Bruins sweat shirt and pants became her towels and she rubbed her flesh red before dressing.

Today she would climb to the third floor. Today she would reclaim the memories lost when Grady drugged her.

First, though, she needed caffeine.

* * *

The living room and foyer blazed with light as French ascended the wide staircase. In Grady's absence she decided to splurge, dragging the generator into the foyer where exhaust could be drawn out the window. She rigged several standing lamps in her camp and the foyer to drive away the gloom.

She was coming to know Hate House as it manifested the warped imagination of Simone Laurent. Abbott was correct in noting that the place was designed to drive a person mad. Tricky. Resistant to exploration.

Even dangerous.

At the second floor landing she felt the wind in her sails. The light behind her leaked in both directions and would be easily visible. The generator's growl a sound she could follow from anywhere in the big house.

She had gone to the left, she remembered. She had discovered stairs.

Deliberately kicking a path through the crab shells she trailed the fingers of her left hand along the Ochre Men as she passed. Her right hand held the flashlight and she followed its confident beam until she reached an open doorway.

She remembered this room. Small, dominated by the flimsy spiral staircase in its middle. She even saw her electric lantern on its side beside the staircase.

Memory failed when she turned her gaze to the black hole in the floor.

Had she fallen through?

It filled her with sudden fear, recent confidence blown out like a candle. Anger rode on the heels of the fear when she realized the house was once again thwarting her efforts to reach the top.

"What are you hiding?"

She aimed her flashlight down through the broken boards and saw the spiral stairs descending into the coal black dark.

She had been down there, she was certain.

And something down there had terrified her.

"No you don't," she said to the house. "Let there be light, bitches." Crouching swiftly, she righted the lantern and flicked it alight, brightening the room around her.

Thus fortified against the dark, she stepped carefully around the hole and placed a foot on the stairs.

It was rickety and old and she blinked against orange dust that drifted from the metal steps above her. Like the first story, the second had ceilings around eleven or twelve feet high so she ascended carefully, free hand firmly on the rough iron railing as her tread drew metallic moans from the shivering tower.

Even moving with caution, the ascent was swift. As her head broke the plane of the third story she swung her flashlight beam around the room to discover a cramped chamber similar to the one below.

The floor seemed solid beneath her feet and hasty examination showed the room to be unadorned and windowless, with a single wooden door.

A locked wooden door.

"What the hell?"

The hasp was rusted with age but the lock was new. A Masterlock padlock and French was prepared to bet it was the same damned lock Grady had removed from the front gate to the property.

She shoved the door and found it solid, though her hand detected what found like recent gouges. Her light revealed big awkward letters carved into the wood.

DANGER INSIDE

"This is bullshit." French kicked the door before banging down the steps to the floor below, unheeding of the shaking staircase. She was trying to remember what tools she'd seen in the boathouse when she reached the bottom and stood over the hole through which she was sure she had fallen.

That feeling of being a cat's paw returned. She was being coerced into action, denied access above, aimed like an arrow at the darkness below her feet.

In the silence she pondered, the thrumming of the distant generator restoring a sense of calm.

Moving too quickly for second thoughts, she slid the electric lantern closer, slipped her flashlight into the waistband of her jeans and sat, dangling her feet down into the hole.

It wasn't much of a drop and she caught the far edge of the broken boards with her hands, grimacing against splinters as she swung down in a motion like lowering herself from a chin up.

Her kicking boots clanged off unseen stairs and she released first one hand—flailing for a handhold on the central column in the spiral—and grabbing the lantern with her other hand to bring it through with her.

Despite the chill, sweat was beading on her upper lip and she licked the salty moisture free. She held the lantern out and saw stairs descending into impenetrable murk, going deeper than the first story into some kind of basement.

"Geronimo," she whispered and began her descent.

Chapter Thirteen

"No."

She stood in the stone chamber with the lantern held high over her head. The air was as still as a tomb and twice as quiet.

"No…no…no…"

The roof of her mouth was as dry as the Nevada desert and her mouth clicked as she muttered her denials like a chant.

I did not kill him.

"No…"

The floor was poured cement instead of natural stone, the rest of the huge, subterranean chamber carved out of the island rock itself. She stood in the bright circle of electric light, the walls beyond the reach of her lantern.

A blood stain was on the floor in front of her.

"I did not kill him."

The stain was black in the white light of the lantern, dried in an irregular shape on all but one side where it was cut off in a straight line.

A fireplace poker smeared with more blackish grue lay several feet away from the blood spill. The same poker that was missing from upstairs?

Of course it was.

"I did not kill you, Grady."

She crouched and reached out with her index finger to touch the stain, not sure what to expect. It was nearly dry, but not quite and her fingertip left a print.

Fingerprints at a murder scene.

Of course it's a murder scene.

"Oh, fuck me."

Head wound, she thought. Head wounds bleed savagely. She remembered the wild spray of blood when Josh slashed her across the bridge of her nose with a fireplace poker. The Sydney Pollock painting she made of the living room with her blood flung about.

She scuttled around the gruesome dried lake and lowered her face to study the straight edge on one side. There was a near invisible seam in the cement, revealed by the blood.

Standing with a grunt of effort, something in her hip popped painfully. She had a choice to make.

Should she go to the police?

Or should she clean up the mess and dump the evidence at sea?

She had no memory of being in this awful place and no memory of hurting Grady. She had no memory of cleaning up Grady's possessions from the kitchen...but someone had. Someone was already trying to hide his presence.

Had she done it herself?

If she went to the police would she sound innocent or would she sound insane?

Worse, would she sound like a killer?

Did the fireplace poker have her prints on it? What happened to Grady's belongings? If she had done it, if she had erased his presence from the house, where had she put everything? Without a car, the ocean would have beckoned. The lobsterman who found her in the rowboat...had she been out at sea dumping Grady's stuff? Oh God, his body? How functional had she been? What if she just dumped it all in the channel?

She was hyperventilating and closed her eyes, trying to remember her therapist's lessons on breathing, thinking she needed a Lexapro stat. She had worked with and sometimes against police departments throughout her years as a private investigator and experience told her that if they thought it looked like a duck and quacked like a duck, it was a duck. They weren't going to dig for some wild solution beyond the obvious.

This looked like a fucking duck.

It looked bad.

After all, she'd killed before.

* * *

Sitting on the metal steps in the spill of electric light, French accepted what she had decided upon first realizing she was looking at the sight of Grady's death.

She was going to clean it up. She smoked a Salem and thought about where to look upstairs for cleaning supplies. Thought about heading out to buy bleach. All thoughts of the third floor were smothered beneath her need to conceal the evidence.

Yes, Simone's maddening house had won another round and kept her from whatever secrets were kept on the top floor, but French had to be practical. Grady was missing and likely dead. It was quite possible she had killed him. His things were missing and either she or whomever killed Grady had removed his belongings. Unless Grady wasn't dead and had left under his own power.

Yes, there were too many questions, but one certainty was that the locals were already suspicious of Hate House and even a cursory investigation would reveal a possible murder scene.

Glancing around the walls, French walked the perimeter to discover shelves with tools and racks holding shovels and pick axes and similar heavy gear.

The pickaxe, then.

When she was done the tool would make short work of Grady's padlock upstairs—

She had to remain focused.

She thought about kerosene and decided to head upstairs to find whatever she could to begin removing all traces of Grady.

Hell, she couldn't even remember his first name.

Chapter Fourteen

In retrospect, fire may not have been the best plan.

Hair sticking to her sweaty forehead, French caught her breath and smoked a cigarette. Lugging basins of salt water from the kitchen tap downstairs had exhausted her. The only cleaning agents she discovered upstairs were dried and useless, so she went with plan B.

Setting the smoldering cigarette on a metal step, she carried a plastic water bottle full of kerosene to the blood stain and splashed the accelerant across the gory mess, careful not to get any on her boots.

Back to the steps then and her cigarette. She inhaled until the tip glowed angrily, then flicked it in a short arc.

The kerosene went up with a whoosh and the hot wind surprised French as a fireball rose, detaching itself like a flaming amoeba from the conflagration on the floor as it rose to smash against the ceiling. The heat baked her skin and she felt her eyebrows singing.

"Fuck!"

She immediately grabbed the nearest basin and forced herself to advance on the fire until she could dump the contents into the flames.

Salt water splashed and spread across the cement floor, burning kerosene riding the sudden wave.

"Fuck!"

Pockets of flame careened towards the walls and she dropped the empty basin to snatch up another one, ignoring the strain in her back. Four big steps took her to a burning patch and she buried it in a waterfall, scattering and splashing the flames into oblivion.

A quick glance told her the rest of the spreading fire was already burning itself out, finding no appetite for either cement or the stone walls.

She touched her cheeks, tight from the sudden heat as if she'd been out in the sun. The water pooled where the floor was uneven and she decided she'd now turned a localized mess into a giant, cellar wide mess.

Brilliant.

Fluid was also draining into that straight line gouged into the floor, now with an added extension at one end haring off at a right angle, making the cut a giant letter L.

A mystery for later, she thought, eager to erase the scorched bloodstain with a mop found in a hallway closet. Sweating more, feeling the trickle of liquid from her armpits weaving a path down her ribcage. The water around her feet was red, the charred meat stink thick in her nose, filling it with mucus. Realizing that she was going to have to leave Hate House and get bleach and proper cleaning supplies,

Discolorations in the cement tickling her ability to understand.

Old cement.

New cement.

Those lines where first blood and then salt water seeped into cracks definitely denoting new cement.

She suspected (knew) something awful but refused to acknowledge it, because this mystery was not her job. She has been hired by Abbott to find evidence that Hate House was his, incontrovertibly his.

Her boots were gonging on the stairs before she made a conscious decision, the mop leaning against a wall, the electric light relentless in her wake.

She didn't need her flashlight in the second floor hall, the glow and noise from the generator powered lights in the foyer a beacon drawing her.

Go towards the light.

What's in the cellar?

Head for the light!

What is buried in the cellar?

Down the stairs with a child's reckless speed, she skidded onto the black and white tiles of the foyer before angling to the right and making straight for the Cutty Sark on the coffee table. It wasn't until she shifted the fireplace poker from her right hand to her left that she realized she was holding a probable murder weapon.

I should leave now.

The urge was strong but she caught herself before thought became action.

If that blood in the cellar was Grady's—

If she *did* have something to do with it—

She had to clean up the evidence before she left.

"Oh, goddammit."

The booze roiled her stomach like she was a teen trying her first Schnapps. She released a wet belch and took another sip.

If anyone showed up at this stage while she was away from Hate House, it would look like she was cleaning up a murder scene in the cellar.

She was, of course, but her primary objective *had* to be eliminating any evidence of a crime.

Not digging for evidence of another crime.

She looked up, startled. Pipes were groaning in the walls as if the toilet had been flushed. Shifting her grip on the fireplace poker, French strode quickly to the hall, making no effort at stealth.

But the bathroom was empty, the toilet running quietly until she jiggled the handle and it stopped.

A sudden weight stifled her energy as she exited the bathroom. Found herself staring up at the enormous portrait of Simone Laurent, her pocked and aged face grinning hollowly in victory.

"I don't have a choice, do I?"

Simone didn't bother responding to the pawn below her.

French shuffled to the door and shoved it open, staring at the ocean stretching out to the horizon, a desperate sun striking white caps into flame.

There were no lobster boats in sight and without conscious thought she descended the giant's stone steps to the edge of the sea and hurled the deadly fireplace poker out as far as she could.

Was there a message in its inconsequential splash?

She didn't care.

* * *

The handle was slick with dust as French raised the pickaxe over head and brought it down on the crack in the cement floor.

She flinched at the sound, palms blazing with pain as a cruel vibration shivered up the metal haft. Before the pain could fully manifest she lifted the tool and swung again. Chips of cement flew and the clang of steel deafened her. She squinted to protect her eyes and brought down the pickaxe again. Again. Atrophied muscles complained as they awakened and she swung again with a grunt until a large chip of cement spun away and she paused, leaning on the tool, breath harsh in her lungs.

The hole was the diameter of a tea saucer, the cement only an inch thick.

The stink that erupted was immediate and awful, more so

than the ever present odor of Hate House. Her gorge rose and she buried her nose in the crook of her elbow. But it was the flash of milky movement that dialed her mind white with panic.

Grady? Had she buried him alive? Thrusting his mouth to the hole to suck in greedy gulps of air—

Unthinking, she retreated until her hand clutched the spiral rail that led up towards safety.

Stop.

She forced herself to breathe. To return to the world of fact and real possibility. It was not Grady. The cement was older than anything she could have poured.

The breathing helped as it always did. She gathered herself and held the lantern over the small hole, crouching. Her vision was baffled by the obsidian dark.

She was scaring herself. Nothing had moved down in the hole. Until she cracked the cement, there was no air to breathe.

There was nothing to fear.

She grabbed the pickaxe and renewed her attack. Chips flew and a painful blister rose on the palm of her right hand. Her shadow was a grim automaton on the wall, lifting and swinging, lifting and swinging.

A shard of cement struck her eye and she staggered back, rubbing furiously. The tears cleared her eye and she blinked painfully at the destruction she'd wrought.

The jagged hole was now more than a foot long and almost as wide with lightning bolt cracks fissuring outward in one direction.

She dropped the pickaxe with a dull clang and took a step towards—

The hole erupted.

French shrieked and found herself halfway up the stairs before her mind caught up with the moment.

Boiling like lava from the hole was a flood of pale crabs.

A bone covered army skittering in every direction, including the stairs.

She was overwhelmed with a sudden wave of humiliation, despite the lack of an audience. No one would know how she had squealed like a little girl and ran away. Embarrassment sparked into anger and within seconds she banged down the stairs and stomped a deadly path towards the hole, crabs squishing and cracking open beneath her heels, fleeing from the murderous giant.

She was the power in the cellar.

And then the space was clear as the crustaceans fled her and the blazing light, clacking and scuttling around the murky edges of the underground space in search of escape.

What was in the hole? Her flashlight beam picked out senseless shapes so she found the water bottle with its residue of kerosene inside and held it over the opening in the cement. She brought a lighter flame close to the bottle's mouth, burning her thumb until the fumes caught and for a split second she held lightning in a bottle.

She dropped the flaming meteor into the crevasse and crouched lower to see.

Even with recent horrors dancing through her imagination, French was able to steel herself and slip her hand down inside, reaching deeper, past the elbow now and feeling about blindly with her fingers until—

Something.

She shifted to give herself leverage and slid her fingers around what felt like a furry stick, gripping it tightly as her thumb found its place. When she pulled there was weight, resistance, a muted crackling noise.

She yanked and the branch snapped. Shuffling back on her belly, she was careful as she withdrew her prize. It became stuck until she angled it such that it emerged into the bright illumination.

Setting it down on the floor, she moved into a cross legged sitting position, studying it, recognizing it immediately but silently arguing against its size.

It was a humerus connected to ulna and radius, shreds of fabric still attached. There was only part of a hand but she expected further digging would produce the rest of a human skeleton.

A small human skeleton.

A child's skeleton.

* * *

Around the skeletal wrist was a plastic digital Swatch. Children didn't wear digital watches during the decades the Catholic monsters inhabited Hate House.

The child had died while Abbott was in residence.

She didn't fight it when her stomach rebelled again and a hot flood of acid and whiskey splashed from her mouth across the floor.

* * *

The sun was dropping through the western sky as she carefully descended the slimy steps towards the boat waiting in the channel.

She needed cleaning supplies and a resupply of food and drinking water.

And...

A dangerous idea had taken hold of her mind and she tingled with purpose.

Even more than she needed the cleaning supplies, she needed to make a phone call.

Chapter Fifteen

The parked SUV shuddered in the wake of a passing oil truck but French ignored it. As soon as her phone had shown a signal, she pulled over onto the shoulder of the two lane road leading to Paper Bay.

Her call was answered by a familiar cold, female voice.

"This is Megan French, I need to speak to Mr. Abbott."

"Mr. Abbott isn't available," the woman said.

French chuckled without humor. "He'll want to make himself available for this."

"He is unavailable," the woman said.

She caught a glimpse of her own hungry expression in the rearview mirror. "You tell him that I've been in the cellar," French thought about adding more but decided on ambiguity. "We need to discuss our arrangement."

She heard the clatter of a phone placed in the receiver on the other end, but her smile turned to a grimace as she rolled her aching shoulders. She mentally added ibuprofen to her shopping list.

She wondered if Abbott envied her ability to come and go from Hate House as she wished.

The big Suburban surged to life and she drove towards

town, eventually stopping at a gas station with a convenience store. She bought a cup of coffee and brought it back to the vehicle, taking advantage of the signal to search online for information about missing children in the area during the time of Abbott's residence in Hate House. To help narrow the years in question, she began with a simple query.

WHAT YEAR WAS THE SWATCH INTRODUCED?

* * *

Abbott didn't return French's call and she eventually drove back to Hate House. Sore muscles from her labors in the cellar transformed the short channel crossing into a period of pure agony.

Once inside, she washed down four Advil with bottled water from the case of Evian she bought at the store. She had picked up canned food and beer as well, soap and two bundles of cut firewood.

Before she could talk herself out of it, she carried bleach up the main stairs and then down the spiral staircase into the cellar, splashing the liquid about liberally until the fumes forced her to retreat.

What she needed was a hot tub in which to soak her aching muscles. Why were the muscles in her ass hurting? Her abdomen? Hand modeling wouldn't be in her immediate future either. Her palms were a mess of torn blisters.

Drifting behind her flashlight beam, she made her way along the second floor hall to the open door to the bathroom. Inside, her steps echoed in the way of gym locker rooms and reminded her of school. Of public pools.

The clawfoot tub was filthy and some kind of vine had taken hold, but she was bored, unable to finish her work down below until it ceased being a gas chamber and she did have all those cleaning supplies.

French lit a cigarette and went to work.

* * *

She met the ridiculous project with ridiculous determination, electric lights blazing in the foyer, fire blazing in the living room fireplace. The house moaned and chuckled around her as ancient pipes were whetted, dry throats grew moist and spat rust and then salt water into the tub, draining the bleach and Comet back down into the pipes to tickle the house into greater volume.

She gathered rocks and bricks and heated them with the simple expedient of shoving them into the fireplace. When she decided through no scientific method beyond guessing that she had enough and they were hot enough, she tumbled them into metal basins liberated from the kitchen and hauled them upstairs, more Advil chased by beer reducing the pained cry of her muscles to a lullaby.

What time was it when she finally piled her clothes beside the tub in that long unused bathroom? She didn't know and didn't care, still riding the thrill of her call to Abbott, despite his lack of response.

The tub was big enough for sex and she sank into the warm water up to her chin, using her feet to shove the rocks and bricks to the far end, taking perverse pleasure in the dark hair springing up along her shins.

It wasn't hot, not really. Barely warm if she were honest. But it scratched an itch that needed scratching, providing an almost meditative calm, a needed isolation that reminded her of home.

She smoked and drank as the water cooled and soothed. She ran through potential conversations that loomed in her future and let her imagination roam. In her mind's eye she saw herself walking from a tropical beachfront home down to the ocean's edge. She saw herself behind the wheel of a sleek coupe on the California coast. She saw her own portrait over the doorway of Hate House, replacing the hideous visage of Simone Laurent.

Eventually, ash speckling her breast, French's eyes closed

and her lips went slack. The Salem tumbled from her mouth and into the water with a kitten's hiss and she slept.

* * *

She awoke briefly from slumber with a thought clear in her mind. The Latin in the purchase order for the old English gallows might match the Latin etched in the ancient wood that made up the front door frame. She promised herself to check it in the morning and sunk back into her dreams.

Chapter Sixteen

The pain in her jaw and keening sounds clawing at her consciousness were a single, disruptive entity that pulled her from sleep into a frozen world of shaking limbs and chattering teeth.

She convulsed into a sitting position, skin blue in the dim morning light. Her jaw muscles flexed with agonizing tension and she was afraid she'd crack a tooth.

Movement was hard, a world beyond stiff. She nearly tumbled face first over the side of the clawfoot tub but managed to gain her feet during the awkward exit.

She forced the waiting hoodie over her head and slick torso, but wet legs defeated her attempt to pull on jeans. She left her clothes, desperate for the warm fire below. A hissing slug of whiskey finished last night's bottle and sent tendrils of heat into her blood stream.

She stumbled pantsless down the hallway, shells sharp beneath her numb feet. With her arms wrapped in a vice grip around her heaving ribs she couldn't hold the balustrade and nearly tumbled down the stairs into the foyer.

Her feet remembered the path to the fireplace in her camp and she used a beer bottle to poke at the grey ash until she uncovered the glorious orange of an ember. Cardboard from her case of water served as kindling and she coaxed it into flame before adding small pieces of wood.

Through it all, that keening sound jabbed at her ears.

A metal thermos with fresh water was set in the fire to warm for coffee and she used dirty clothes to dry off her legs before pulling on sweatpants and socks.

The shrill sound stopped and in the silence she heard the screech of seagulls before the aggravating noise resumed.

It was real, the sound. Not in her head.

She snatched a cigarette from a pack on the coffee table and inhaled against the rising tide of vomit in her esophagus. A brief, acidic battle ensued and she almost painted her feet with bile, but the mess settled back into her gut and she was able to stuff her feet into her boots.

* * *

The woman waiting across the channel was spindly and tall, thin as a rail post and dressed all in black, a tightly belted trench coat and long out of date cloche hat that framed her dark face. She hid her eyes behind oversized sunglasses.

The woman stood beside a shiny rented sedan. A Sebring or Altima, one of those bland cars that no one actually owned.

French grinned around her cigarette as the wind tossed her bird's nest mess of hair. She thought she recognized the woman from brief acquaintance. Remembered the spindly old bitch opening the door to Abbott's emaciated home.

So Abbott has dispatched his crow.

French was content to be patient despite the chill. She had food and water waiting inside. A warm fire and a toilet. If the cormorant across the channel needed to pee she'd have to squat on the grass and French very much doubted the old prude could engage in such bestial behavior. It amused French that to reach this place at this early hour, the old woman must have been dispatched almost immediately after the phone call. Flew into Bangor, probably, had to rent a car. Drive to this forsaken place. Had she slept? Was she tired?

The crow ruffled her feathers and that cold voice was made reedy as she called across the water.

"We need to talk!"

French grinned again, the ancient shriek blending with the call of seabirds. She shrugged and the breeze tugged her hair.

A minute passed and French thought she was winning the game.

"Mr. Abbott would like to talk!" The scarecrow stepped towards the edge and small stones tumbled towards the water. "I need to come across!"

Not on your life, French thought, but said, "Five minutes!"

She ambled back inside, flicking her cigarette onto the stony ground.

* * *

"Please don't smoke inside the car," the crone said, eyes inscrutable behind her absurd sunglasses. She had reminded French that her name was Hill, which struck French as both ambitious and suitably bleak.

French exhaled smoke, smothering the new car smell inside Hill's rental vehicle.

"I need to go into the house," Hill said, repeating her request.

French nodded and ash flaked free from the Salem's tip to flutter on the pristine dashboard. She'd taken a good half hour before rowing across to the mainland. Thirty minutes in which to pee, scrub her face and neaten her hair, eat an energy bar and have a cup of instant coffee. She brought the thermos with her, hot metal wrapped in a t-shirt. She unscrewed the lid and poured herself another cup without offering any to Hill.

"You're not allowed in the house," French said after a sip of the warm, bitter brew.

"Don't be absurd."

French shrugged and her windbreaker slithered against the seat back. She doubted the scrawny woman had enough meat on those long arms to handle the rowing.

"Have you slept at all?" French smirked.

"I remind you of your arrangement with Mr. Abbott." Up close Hill's skin was as grey as it was brown, her face powdery as if was flaking away in the daylight. French was tired of ugly things, the crabs, the skeleton, the crone.

"I'm revising the arrangement." French's voice was tight.

"You signed a contract."

"We can make a new contract."

"I need to see the cellar."

"Kick rocks."

French tapped ash onto the seat between them and Hill grimaced, pressing the button to lower her window.

"We're familiar with the history of the house before its acquisition by the Laurent family. Anything you discovered is the problem of the Catholic Church. Are you sure you want to take them—"

"What I found was wearing a digital watch." French interrupted, her smirk gaining in cruelty as the skin of Hill's face tightened across her sharp cheekbones. "A Swatch, to be specific."

"And you've shared this with…?"

French shook her head. "My counterpart doesn't know."

Hill raised one painted eyebrow, but released her unspoken question as a long exhalation. She placed her bony hands on the steering wheel as if she planned to drive them both into the channel.

"What do you want?" Hill asked.

"Five million dollars wired to my Schwab account by the start of banking tomorrow." The words came out so easily, like a movie line, something spoken by anyone other than Megan French.

"Impossible." Hill laughed.

"Abbott is worth between seventy-five and one hundred and ten million dollars." French felt like a kid riding a bike downhill at the terrifying moment when gravity takes over and survival is in the hands of unseen forces. "Five million by the start of banking tomorrow and what I found is his."

Hill's grin turned predatory and she lowered her sunglasses to fix icy blue eyes on French.

"And what if Mr. Abbott decides to simply take it?"

French grinned back, ignoring the butterflies in her stomach.

"Are you so ancient that you think I haven't concealed video, audio and written evidence in the cloud? Do you think I've left the physical evidence where it can be stolen from me? You have heard of the Internet, yes?"

Hill's bloodless lips thinned. "Everything in Hate House belongs to Mr. Abbott."

"And he'll have it when I look at my account tomorrow and see five million bucks."

French waved her cigarette out towards the property in question. "Shall I make up a room for you tonight?"

Hill slid the dark lenses over her eyes as if to ward against the sight of Hate House.

"I have lodgings."

French stubbed out the butt on the seat beside her hip.

Hill grimaced. "Disgusting habit."

French leaned towards her. "You smell old."

She shoved open the car door and climbed out, clambering down the slippery rocks to the boat bobbing in the channel. Hill's rental car thrummed to life above her and was backing away before French's ass met the bench on the boat.

She rowed back, the pain in her back and arms muted by the cyclonic thoughts racing through her. She knew she was behaving oddly, like a different Megan French from a different timeline who had never become a hermit. This French was bold and decisive.

Concealing a murder scene? Extortion?

Who was *this* Megan French?

Her mind's eye flashed to the great portrait of Simone over the doorway, towering over all below. As she had the night before, she imagined her own face in place of the old heiress.

Chapter Seventeen

Stomping around the island in her heavy boots, offshore gusts playing against her windbreaker *fwip-fwip-fwip* like toneless harp strings. "Look upon me ye mighty and despair," French proclaimed to the crab legions as they fled in scuttling waves.

Looking inland she saw no sign of Hill after the crone's hasty retreat, though her gaze lingered on the unkempt fence around the tiny graveyard. She wondered…

Around the island then to the seaward side. She waved to the lobster boat drifting a hundred yards off shore with no idea if she was even noticed.

Back inside through the front door like the Lady of the Manor, she collected the fishing line and hooks from the pile near her camp and peeled the lid off a can of Vienna Sausages. The hooks pierced them nicely and she carried the lot outside where she looped and knotted the ends around rocks and island jags before tossing the baited hooks out into the water.

She sat then, plucking the remaining sausages from the slimy goop inside the can and chewing them slowly, relishing the salt and chemicals.

I'm going to get fat out here, she thought before eating another slick sausage.

Tossing the can and the last bit of sausage onto the rocks attracted a pair of thick bodied gulls who dove for the feast, screaming and fighting as she rose to her feet.

Diagrams from Abbott's cookbook crossed her mind and her imagination conjured traps she might build.

Not that she would be in Hate House long enough to eat the local wildlife.

* * *

The cellar made her eyes water and she hurried to take several pictures of bones pulled from the makeshift grave. She needed to make good on her threat to place evidence online as insurance.

Coughing eventually overcame her and she fled up the spiral stairs, taking the pickaxe.

* * *

The front door was left open to bring in daylight and fresh air before French once again ascended the wide staircase.

Once more unto the breach!

More Advil had dulled the pain in her palms and she was glad she had bought gloves on her trip for provisions.

Pickaxe in one hand and the camp lantern in the other, she traveled east in the second story hall until she came to the first locked door, where she placed the lantern on the floor and took up a batter's stance.

The sharp end of the pickaxe slammed into the door and wood chips flew as the shock traveled up her arms. Cursing, she took aim and swung again, this time striking the lock plate below the knob and leaving a dent.

She coughed and spat, panting already from the exertion. Bracing her feet she reared back and swung again. The lock plate rang like a bell and the door flew inward to crash against the wall.

She dropped the tool and buried her nose and mouth in the crook of her elbow as the mausoleum air drifted into the hall. It was a dark room, stale from decades of disuse. Rays of light stabbed in between the boards over the windows and the atmosphere was thick with floating dust motes.

It was a bedroom, spartan in the extreme. A single bed and dresser. A small wooden desk with a tipped over chair. One window. One tall door that opened on an empty closet.

A cross was nailed to the wall over the bed.

A pedophile slept here.

She felt dirty being in the space and wondered if that was why Abbott kept it locked before remembering the small skeleton in the cellar.

Did you have kinship with these predators before you came to Hate House, or did the place infect you?

She used the pickaxe to pry several boards from the window to help air out the stifling second floor. Finished, she crossed the hall to a similar, locked door on the landward side of Hate House and set to work with her tool. More accurate this time, it only took two swings before the door gave way and she discovered another cell like room similar in every way to the first. Bed. Empty closet. Boarded window.

She pried off a board to let in more air and returned to the hall until she came to the bathroom and the glorious porcelain tub.

Back west, then, passing the staircase until she met another barred portal.

The room inside was similar and she didn't bother checking the closet. Rusty nails clattered on the floorboards as she yanked a board from the window and she crossed the hall to attack another door.

Sloppy work demanded six hard swings before she opened

the freshly mangled door before her. Fresh pains stabbed through the muscles in her shoulders as she leaned the pickaxe against the doorway before crossing to the window to pull a board free.

She had already turned away before realizing someone was out there.

* * *

She slipped on the steps leading down to the boat and landed on her hip hard enough to leave a bruise. Every pull of the oars summoned a foul word from her mouth and she climbed the mainland slope with a thunderhead forming on her brow.

From her vantage atop the slope the intruder was a stick figure two football fields away, inside the graveyard. Something about the figure's scale beside the tombstones suggested height, suggested a man and she immediately thought, *Grady?*

A tide of relief washed over her at the idea of Grady's return, of his being alive. It collided with the fiery anger at his abrupt departure and the two emotions erupted into steam that clouded her ability to think.

She climbed into the SUV and cranked up the engine, backing up in a half circle until she was facing away from Hate House and she hit the gas to bump and rumble down the dirt road.

The figure had gone still and she thought it was watching her.

If it was Grady she had no idea what she would say to him and was afraid for them both.

She feathered the brakes and threw the gearshift into Park, shutting down the big rental machine before climbing out to walk across the uneven yellow grass separating the road from the graveyard.

It wasn't Grady, but she thought she recognized the man in the black fedora with sunglasses in the style of John Lennon.

His black suit was the same one he wore to Fishercat. The same or identical.

What she hadn't noticed at the bar because she wasn't paying attention or because he'd removed it to go undercover, was the white flash of a priest's collar at his throat.

Curious, that.

She stopped at the open gate, close enough that she didn't have to raise her voice, but he spoke first.

"Megan French?" He removed his hat and she saw stubble atop his skull as blue black as the whiskers on his jaw.

"This is private property," she responded.

"I know. You are Megan French, representative of Marcus Abbott?"

"Who wants to know?" She winced internally at the juvenile belligerence in her question, but the weight of his regard unnerved her.

"I'm Flavio Ricci, here on behalf of the Diocese in Portland."

"You don't sound like Portland."

A smile ghosted across his lips. "I'm on loan from Boston, so to speak."

He reached inside his jacket and produced a white business card between two fingers. She stepped inside the graveyard without thinking and took it from him.

"Why are you on loan from Boston?"

He nodded as if it were an excellent question. "My role within the Church is similar to yours, investigations."

Her resting smirk deepened. "What are you investigating?"

He sighed and turned to look at Hate House, hunched in the distance.

"This is a dark place, the site of selfish and terrible behavior on the part of men."

"And the Church."

He nodded. "And the Church."

"Which still doesn't explain why you're here on private property."

He turned back towards her. "To meet you."

She snorted but took a step back. "You came all the way from Boston to meet me? Bullshit."

"It's not bullshit, Miss French." He replaced the hat atop his head and stepped around her, careful to stay out of her personal space. Up close she realized he was taller than Grady by several inches.

He left the graveyard and hesitated as if about to say something, but settled for, "Enjoy your day."

His long strides ate the distance and he had traveled far down the road before her mental gears caught and she made for the Suburban, closing the graveyard gate behind her.

Chapter Eighteen

French felt light headed from the swing between psychological highs and lows, from Ozymandius astride the world to a confused piece of flotsam tossed about on the waves.

Her thoughts resisted coalescing. Formless and darting, they remained beyond her ability to analyze. She found herself wandering to the seaward side of the island, tilting her face back to let the noonday sun caress her cheeks.

She wandered to the edge and saw one of her three fishing lines had come loose and was lost at sea. Squatting, she grabbed the next one and pulled it towards shore, hand over hand until its wet length was at her feet, the hook denuded of its Vienna Sausage.

"Well, crap."

She was unprepared for the last line to leap in her hand, raising a red welt across her palm.

"Holy shit!" All thoughts of priests and Abbott and Simone Laurent were banished as if by a strong wind as she struggled to pull the slippery line towards shore, but it kept sliding back through her palms.

Operating on instinct, she stood, twisted her hands into the line until it was wrapped about both wrists, whereupon she began backing up the rocks towards Hate House.

How long is this line?

She was near enough to fear backing into the house when a fish flopped out of the ocean and began snapping and flipping on land. French ran forward with a shout and shoved the fish further away from the ocean, unable to grab hold because of its slimy, violent motion.

She had no idea what it was, save that its scales were silver and it was over a foot long. After several failed tries, she gave up on carrying the thing and jogged back into Hate House, thundering towards the kitchen until she found a dusty pot.

Pot in hand she returned to the water and gave it a hasty scrub before laying the pot on its side, open end towards the fish, and shoving the flipping sea creature into its metal depths.

Angry birds circled overhead and a dollop of shit splattered like tartar sauce on the rock beside her, prompting her to hurry inside.

Cleaning it and cooking it would give her time to think.

* * *

The house's general foulness was leavened by the smell of fish charring in the living room fireplace.

Outside the open front door, birds fought over fish guts. A brazen black bird with a deadly beak screeched as it secured a pink length of intestine.

Saliva released itself in a mouth-filling flood when French snatched the fish from the fire, carrying it in yesterday's t-shirt to sit cross legged in front of the open door.

She flung slippery bones outside and her chin glistened with grease as she fed herself white chunks of meat with her fingers. The black seabird stood boldly in the doorway, its eyes implacable and doll like.

"Wait your turn," she said to the bird.

French lifted her gaze to Simone towering over both her and the bird alike. She dragged oily fingers through the knotted length of her own hair and considered herself alongside the dead heiress, the dead woman's short hair the height of style in decades long past. She grinned at the idea that it was she who had invaded *Simone's* mind by inhabiting Hate House, not the other way around.

Simone was on trial, not Megan French.

She preferred these thoughts to wondering about Flavio Ricci's cryptic appearance. Father Ricci, she presumed, though his energy was more secret police than priest. Despite his accent he carried himself with a European air of mystery. It wasn't hard to imagine him as an agent of the East German Stasi rather than of Rome.

When she could scrape no more tender flesh from the bones, French tossed the skin and spine out the door and the blackbird bounded after the delicacies with nary a squawk in thanks.

Standing involved much creaking and cracking of joints. She patted her pockets before returning to her camp to pick up the Spyderco, thinking that with so many visitors it might be wise to carry it at all times from this point forward.

But first...

* * *

Stripped to the waist, French knelt before a metal basin filled with fresh water, scrubbing her hair with the newly purchased shampoo.

Her skin was bluish with cold but it was a state to which she had become accustomed and she ignored it as she headed for the bathroom.

The lighting cast shadows in the wrong places and the mirror was so filthy as to be almost more hindrance than help, but the Spyderco knife was sharp and she set about cutting her hair over the sink. She brought bangs into being over her eyes and cut a ragged swath across the hair that touched her shoulder blades, so that it ended pertly below her ears at the hinge of her jaw.

Back in the foyer she showed Simone the haircut, her usual smirk nearing a grin.

The Latin carved into the petrified wood framing the doorway brought to mind a name from the files, Alice Molland, who was a witch. She wondered which of the words spelled out the woman's name and looked a question up at the Lady of Hate House.

It occurred to her that with shorter hair, her own neck was emphasized and that she would look good in a choker similar to the one Simone sported in the portrait. She thought she might take a bit of cloth from one of her shirts and try to fashion one.

* * *

Chapter Nineteen

French made a sullen picture as she rowed across the channel once again, the current trying to drag her south with the rising tide.

How many hours had it been since Hill left Hate House? Would Abbott have responded?

She shook out her tired arms before climbing behind the wheel of the Suburban and held a cigarette in her teeth as she bounced along the road to the gate, trying time and time again to bring her lighter's flame to the tip.

* * *

The mundane practicalities of extortion were proving tedious, including a twenty-mile drive to pay for a safety deposit box in which to hide Abbott's diary and recipe book.

Next she discovered that her photos wouldn't load until she managed to get three bars on her phone, and drove until she had a strong enough signal. She sent them to her email and buried them on a largely unused social media site.

Of voicemail messages from Abbott, she had none. Her email was nothing but spam she didn't bother to delete.

There was one message from a number she didn't recognize and she checked it, surprised to find it was from Doctor Booth, asking her to return the call at her convenience.

She hit redial and waited as it rang.

"Dr. Booth."

"Hi, it's Megan French returning your call?"

"Ah, yes, right." The Doctor paused. "I'm calling with the results from your tox screen."

"Oh good," French said. "What's the news?"

"Well, there were no traces of Rohypnol in your system," he said.

"I sense a *but* coming…"

"Yes." He paused. "There were strong traces of psilocybin and THC in your blood, Miss French."

"Psilocybin?"

"Hallucinogenic mushrooms."

She felt the blood rush from her face and quashed a reactive wave of guilt. She hadn't done anything wrong.

"He fucking drugged me," she whispered. "He sent me on a trip to the fucking moon."

"What's that?"

"I—nothing, nothing. How long do the effects last?"

"Depending on the dose, I'm referring to psilocybin, depending on the dose you're looking at four to six hours on average."

"Okay, okay. That's good." French ignored his obvious concern and curiosity. "Thank you."

The Doctor paused before saying, "Very well, Miss French. Good day."

French disconnected, staring at her phone.

Grady, that sonofabitch.

On the way back she took an exit and followed signs to a McDonald's located in a strip mall that had seen better days, half of its storefronts empty.

Chapter Twenty

After refilling the generator with kerosene from a fresh can lugged inside, French cranked on the lights in the foyer and headed upstairs. The Ochre Men were silent as she passed.

She brought her Spyderco and her pepper spray. She wore gloves and carried the pickaxe in one hand, the camp lantern in the other.

Up the stairs, careful not to trip. Boots clanging off the risers as she felt the burn in her tired calves and thighs.

DANGER INSIDE

That's what Grady had carved in the door sealed with his padlock.

As if he had a right.

French set the light down beside the door and plucked the lit Salem from her mouth, setting it carefully atop the lantern.

The smell came to her without the cigarette smoke clogging her nose. Marijuana. *Fucking Hell.* This was the Electric Kool Aid Acid Test, not Hate House.

Her body settled into the familiar batter's stance, pickaxe cocked over her right shoulder.

She swung and the sharp pick struck sparks from the hasp, tearing it from the wood.

The lock clattered to the floor at her feet.

Resting the handle of the pickaxe on her shoulder, she turned the knob, bumping open the stiff door with her shoulder.

As the cigarette found its way back to her mouth, she stepped into the Waldorf Astoria.

"Not expected."

It wasn't really the Waldorf, but that's what the corridor reminded her of at first glance. The dark blue, sound absorbing carpet. Pale blue and white paint on the walls, clean and unchipped with nary a patch of mold or water stain. It felt like she had left Hate House and arrived in a different building colored like the arctic.

The Waldorf Astoria in an old Sinbad movie, was more accurate. The air was hazy with smoke from an exotic brass brazier with gently glowing coals that cast a dim orange light into an opening behind it, as if the brazier were placed to guard something.

Whether to keep that mysterious something trapped or protected was anyone's guess.

Who lit this thing?

She reached back through the door for the electric lantern. Lifting it overhead, she tried to decipher the rhythmic sound tickling her eardrums. The electric glow struck sparks from the wainscoting. The polished doorknobs.

DANGER INSIDE

The faint crinkle of burning paper caught her attention and she plucked the cigarette from her mouth in shock. The tip was glowing, eating its way with bright tendrils of heat towards the filter. A huge length of ash broke free and scattered to the floor and she flicked the butt away before it could burn down to her fingers.

What the Hell is going on?

Doors lined the hallway, but fewer than on the second story, suggesting bigger rooms beyond.

Directly across from the brazier were double doors like those of a hotel suite. French felt reality growing slippery and almost believed she had stepped across some unimaginable distance to arrive—

She spun at a muffled thud.

Nothing moved in the hallway but she thought she heard whispers and maybe, very faintly…

Music?

Struck by the urge to flee, she backed towards the spiral stairs. She felt funny. Twilight Zone odd. We control the vertical, we control the horizontal odd.

A sudden rush of blood filled her ears and heat prickled the skin of her face. Her balance shifted and her stomach lurched. She staggered back towards the stair chamber and banged her shoulder painfully against the doorframe before yellow bile splashed from her mouth and struck the wooden floor.

She coughed and nearly fell to her knees, fingers scrabbling at the strangling blue choker she'd made. Dropping the long strip of cloth into the mess.

Had anyone heard?

Confused, she hurried to close the door and fled down the spiral stairs, emerging into the dark second floor hall. She trampled a path through the crab shells until she reached the wide stairs and it wasn't until she was halfway down that she realized the room was clouded in gloom, the big lights unlit.

After a nervous glance back up the stairs, she continued down and checked the lights.

Each had been switched off.

The generator, not running, was also shut down, the small silver key in the off position.

It took a hand to do that—

—*Don't picture the cookbook*—

A human hand.

She cranked the generator up and then the lights, driving back the gloom with a bright electric blaze.

"What the hell is going on in this house?"

No one answered and she walked outside on unsteady legs to suck in greedy breaths of salt tinged air.

Chapter Twenty-One

From her vantage point at the bottom of the giant steps leading down to the sea, French studied the third floor windows as the Atlantic foamed behind her. She saw nothing but the expected boards, as ragged as those on the stories below. There was no indication that those boards concealed elegance.

Though for all French knew, the rooms themselves were disintegrating like their cousins in the lower stories and it was only the hall that had been maintained in a state of elegant repair.

Recently maintained.

But she doubted it.

The carpet was vacuumed.

She was also certain, or fairly certain, that whatever she had experienced was real. There was nothing hallucinatory about it. The psilocybin Grady had slipped her was long past its ability to warp her mind.

Which explained nothing about what she had just experienced, including the nauseating vertigo.

Looking away at last, she made out two boats rocking on distant waves. She wondered if they were watching her and if they were really from Paper Bay.

Too many powers were interested in Hate House. Rich man Abbott. The Laurent estate, even richer. The paranoid lobstermen of Paper Bay. The Catholic Church.

French crouched like a small animal amidst circling predators, her only protection their competition with each other.

She imagined running. Setting the house on fire with her reserve of kerosene to destroy any evidence of potential crimes committed by her or anyone else. She imagined driving straight through the night back to Philadelphia where even the sight of The Righteous on Locust Street would be a welcome return to normalcy.

Five million dollars.

It would change her life. Leaving Locust Street behind and traveling to somewhere The Righteous couldn't follow. An island that had never heard of Dateline.

That was her goal.

Five million dollars and a new life. Screw investigating the house. Screw the third floor and especially screw the damned tower.

Control the secret in the cellar until she could take the money and run.

She trudged back inside to light a cigarette, have a drink and make a fire, in that order.

* * *

One drink became two and the warm fire unknotted muscles she didn't realize were clenched tight. She opened the diary, flipping pages in the hope of finding some mention of the cellar, but paused at an entry titled AS ABOVE, SO BELOW. Thinking it might address the mystery of the third floor, near as important as the mystery of the cellar, she discovered her eyelids drooping as she consumed entire sentences without memory of what she had read.

She closed the book and set it down.

I'll just rest my eyes for a minute.

Soon enough her snoring rose above the crackle from the fireplace.

* * *

The weight on her chest was soft and comforting, gently vibrating like a tiny motor. It was soothing. Pleasant. There was no rush to open her eyes, though eventually she did.

Bright yellow eyes with a vertical black slit stared back at her from a distance of eight inches.

Later, she thought it odd that she hadn't been startled into a shout, but vague memories of comforting dreams lingered as she awoke and so she stared into those yellow eyes and whispered, "Hello, damned cat."

It made a burbling sound as if to say, "I'm no damned cat," though indeed it was, black with a notched ear from a long ago battle.

"How did you get here?" She kept her voice quiet so as not to startle the tiny beast and it replied with another burble and sealed its fate. French named it Burble Cat, with the option of calling it the Cat Burbler when it suited the moment.

It tensed when her fingertips touched its side, but when she gently stroked the fur, it resumed that languorous purring.

A chuckle escaped her and it stood when her belly bounced, stretching before it stepped off her chest to the floor. She sat up, leaning back against the love seat and regarded it even as it regarded her.

"Would you like some water and a snack?"

It stared silently as if such courtesies were assumed, and she rolled gently away from it before crawling to her duffle. Her seeking hand located the plastic wrapping of a Snackables packet and she peeled it open so Burble Cat could help itself to the lunchmeat and chemical cheese inside. When it didn't immediately approach, she stretched out to place the food closer to the warm fire, further away from her.

Burble Cat made its graceful way to the repast, sniffed it, and settled down into a loaf position to begin nibbling.

An empty Bumblebee Tuna can became a water bowl, filled with Evian and slid over beside the food.

She watched for a while and listened to the moist sound of its eating, but eventually picked up the diary and returned to the section entitled AS ABOVE, SO BELOW.

It wasn't what she expected at all.

* * *

What could she do to me eight years into my confinement inside that wretched house? My witch? My tormentor?

She made my world smaller.

Like an animal conditioned to ignore a threat, I had ceased fearing Simone's terrible driver and his hearse-like limousine. Indeed, on his visits I chattered like an ape in a zoo, asking him for news of the world, reading aloud my delivery requests for his next visit, blithely ignoring how he failed to respond with anything other than grunts.

Conditioned to madness. Conditioned to my cage.

When he arrived on that rainy Tuesday, I remembered to wear pants and a shirt as I rushed out to the bridge, a child at Christmas eager to see what Santa has brought.

I sensed nothing amiss until he struck me with his fist and I found myself stretched out to my full length upon the stony span.

The casual lack of hurry he displayed would have terrified me had my senses not been scrambled, but he knelt astride me while pulling a folded cloth from his pocket in one gloved hand.

I bucked and tried to fight when he smothered my nose and

mouth with the cloth, hastening the speed with which the chloroform incapacitated me.

I awoke in a dark prison.

Terrified, I tried to sit up and immediately banged off a metal surface only a foot above me. I tried to stretch from my fetal curl and my bare feet struck a metal wall while my hands found another barrier just above my head.

I panicked then, overcome by unthinking fear like the animal I'd become. Screaming and crying, my nose dripped, I kicked and begged and banged until the pain in my hands forced me to stop. I sucked bleeding knuckles while my chest hitched and I wept.

Yes, Simone. To this I am reduced.

How long was I trapped in that tiny prison? Long enough that I released my bladder so that I lay in a wet, acidic stink.

At some point, incredibly, I slept.

I awoke to light and sound, metal screeching. Simone's driver stared down at me from behind his implacable sunglasses, lipless mouth twisted with disgust.

And yes, Simone, I was disgusting. Unwashed and stinking of piss, hair uncut and uncombed, cheeks unshaven.

Before I could sit up under my own power he grabbed my arm in a painful grip and dragged me roughly from the limousine's trunk to drop me on my belly like a worm.

Did you give him instructions to mount humiliation atop humiliation?

He kicked my thigh and then my rear. I cried out at the sharp pain and he kicked me again until I began crawling. He herded me then with more kicks until I was scrambling on hands and knees towards the bridge, mindlessly seeking the sanctuary of my prison.

The kicking stopped as abruptly as it started. He ceased his assault midway across the bridge and walked casually back towards the waiting limousine, climbing inside without a glance.

A moment later the vehicle backed away in an arc until he shifted gears and drove away, splattering mud in his wake.

I crept inside and wept until my tear ducts ran dry, then peeled off my soiled clothes, planning on a long soak in the tub upstairs.

Nakedly I ascended the grand staircase, but paused on the second floor landing when I saw that the door to the spiral stairs was open.

I did not think I had left it ajar and so I approached.

Your driver had indeed been inside, Simone. I found the velvet rope strung across the stairs where they rose towards the third story. A sign, perhaps stolen from a theatre, hung from the velvet expanse.

PRIVATE – NO ADMITTANCE

Private? Private? In my house??? What the Hell is beyond the rope? Back stage? You treat me like a member of the audience when I AM the show! I AM the entire ensemble!

What did he do, your driver? What changes did he wreak upstairs? Or was this simply another tactic to unbalance me, to measure my obedience, my castration.

How I hate you, Simone, but I will not cross your rope for the moment. I have no intention of doing so in the immediate future.

I wonder if your man will attack me again?

Scrawled beneath the entry in a rougher hand were the words: I KNOW HE WROUGHT CHANGES ON THE THIRD FLOOR BUT DON'T DARE INVESTIGATE. I WILL NOT GO UP THOSE STAIRS.

Chapter Twenty-Two

"You'll like Philadelphia," French said to the Cat Burbler, as the latter snored quietly in front of the fireplace. "I think Buster will welcome you. My apartment is very comfortable."

That she was taking the cat with her when she left was already decided, at least on French's end. She suspected Burble Cat would agree.

"When I have my money I'll make sure wherever we go, cats are welcome."

The black cat snored her assent and French set down the diary, tired of being inside Abbott's mind.

Aside from the attempted theft and infidelity and aside from the ugly lich Abbott had become, she found young Abbott entirely unsympathetic. She wondered why a woman as formidable as Simone Laurent had bothered with such a worthless trifle of a man, a boy really, worthy only of a quick screw before he was tossed aside and forgotten.

But Simone did not forget, it seemed. Especially if she had been wronged.

French was impressed. The will to psychologically torture someone over the course of a decade was no little thing. Hell, she'd been on the receiving end of Lucille Hargrave's worst intent for three years and that was nothing compared to what Simone had wrought.

She rose with a groan, briefly considered how little she enjoyed aging, and padded in her socks to stare up at Simone's portrait again.

"You could have bought yourself a dozen boytoys like Abbott. Better than Abbott. What was so special about him?"

Simone didn't deign to answer.

French leaned her elbows on the windowsill to stare at clouds skidding across the sky, unsure of whether they even noticed the tumbling ocean below. Like Abbott, she was cut off from immediate news, including weather reports, but it looked to her untrained eye like a storm was brewing.

* * *

The cat followed her up the stairs but became distracted in the hallway, batting around crab shells with its paws.

She dragged an old desk chair from a bedroom towards the room concealing the spiral stairs. When the cat wound around her ankle and made to enter, French made a sound and bent to gently shove the little animal back.

"Bad juju in here."

That something very real had occurred upstairs was a fact. That the temperature on the third floor was inexplicably below freezing was a fact. That vertigo had overwhelmed her was a fact.

Facts, none of which she understood.

Burble Cat looked up at her with seeming understanding as French closed the door and slid the desk chair beneath the knob.

"C'mon, let's go catch some crabs for your dinner."

Chapter Twenty-Three

French was on the landward side of the island catching crabs in her gloved hands when the slate grey clouds roared their displeasure. It was like a sluice gate opening and she was startled by the ferocity of the rainfall.

She dropped the bucket of crabs without thinking and snatched up the cat who had been burbling in her footsteps. This earned her terrible scratches on her wrist, but she was skidding into the kitchen within seconds and set Burble Cat down on the counter, glaring at the bloody lines carved into her skin.

"Dammit." She shifted her glare to the Cat Burbler but the little beast was so downtrodden and bedraggled with its sopping fur plastered against its ribs that her expression softened.

She looked through the door before closing it and saw that the bucket had landed upright.

"The things I do for you," she said to the cat before dashing outside to snatch up the bucket. "Shit-shit-shit."

She burst back inside as a titanic flashbulb lit the island behind her and thunder crashed hard enough to rattle her teeth.

"Holy—" She slammed the door shut against the wind driven rain and leaned against it, panting.

Burble Cat had vanished, no doubt frightened by the storm, and French carried the bucket of crabs to her camp in the living room.

Four of the nearly translucent crustaceans scraped against the inside of the bucket and she grimaced as she picked up a piece of firewood.

She smacked it down and ground it against the crabs like a mortar and pestle and soon enough they were reduced to slimy mush. She dumped the mush on the floor beside the water bowl and waited for the cat to smell its supper.

As she waited, night fell.

* * *

It was too damned dark in the house and whatever ease she'd gained from familiarity had been shattered by her attempted exploration of the third floor.

Water whipped in through the open window in the foyer and French was forced to drag the generator deeper inside, towards the stairs, rearranging two of the five lamps as well.

The blaze of light was most welcome.

In the living room she set out a number of candles on the coffee table and located spare batteries, reloading the electric camp lantern.

Thunder crashed and the house let loose a gurgling groan in response, reminding her that she needed to use the bathroom.

Abbott's diary exhausted her and though she pressed forward in search of details, she began to doubt that he ever wrote about the body in the basement.

Still, she wondered…how did he manage to get hold of a child? From his writing he never left the island except brief swimming excursions and a few midnight clamming expeditions.

Was he lying? Did he go out hunting in the dark? Paper Bay was a long journey on foot and that seemed unlikely.

Was the child brought to him?

She lit a fresh cigarette and cracked open a beer, somehow both anxious and bored. The inability to get online and continue digging gnawed at her. She flipped through the diary again and read about Abbott's masturbation habits. Tossed the big book aside.

"Buuuurble Caaaat."

Of course the cat didn't know her name. Didn't show her face.

(French wasn't sure when the cat became a *her*, but she was a her).

She watched the grey finger of smoke rise towards the gathering clouds obscuring the ceiling overhead. The storm was pushing the wind and rain inside, not allowing the smoke out. She coughed and rubbed at itchy eyes. Downed the rest of her beer and belched.

PRIVATE – NO ADMITTANCE

If she had seen the sign. The velvet rope. She'd have tossed both on the fire.

DANGER INSIDE

Was there really? So she had a weird reaction, what if it was because she was drinking too much? An after effect of the mushrooms? Or exhaustion? Her diet had been terrible since she arrived at Hate House, who knew what her blood sugar was doing?

Floorboards creaked beneath her tread as she paced. Wandered into the foyer and risked a glance up the great staircase. Of course she was uneasy. The cellar was murder central and the third floor held a mystery that defied exploration.

She shuffled down the dark hallway, glancing into the bathroom at the running toilet. Taking a quick look into the dining room where Grady was most definitely not lurking at the head of the table.

The kitchen still smelled like charred wood mingled with the ever present stink of Hate House. Lightning flashed and with her eyes on the window, she thought she saw a tall figure outlined on the far shore.

"What?"

She hurried to the door and yanked it open, shielding her face against the blowing rain until electricity flashed in the storm clouds and she saw…

Nothing but the humped shape of the SUV waiting where she had parked it.

No one was watching Hate House.

Hill was too old to stand in a torrential downpour and Flavio Ricci…okay, he might lurk outside in the rain but he wasn't there now and whatever she thought she saw wasn't him.

She flicked the cigarette outside and closed the door, wiping water from her face and plucking the damp front of her sweatshirt from her chest.

Tired. She was so tired.

The smell of smoke was thicker in the living room and she coughed when her throat tickled. Still, she added more wood against the wet chill and settled down atop her sleeping bag. What she had found so far with her intermittent online hunting wasn't enough. She needed a strong internet connection so she could begin searching beyond Google's reach. To use a Tor browser and dig into the dark web.

She wished she could turn on the TV or listen to a podcast. Anything to occupy her unsettled mind. She fumbled in the gloom and found her jeans by feel. Pulled out the business card left by the priest, Ricci.

What did he know?

She imagined Hate House as it must have been before Abbott, when it was in the grip of the Church. Eventually the storm and the moans of Hate House to soothed her to sleep.

Chapter Twenty-Four

A warm weight pressed against her chest and French stirred, grimacing against cotton mouth and the taste of sour beer.

Her thoughts were soupy and failing to congeal, but she recognized the purring for what it was and raised one gummy eyelid to behold Burble Cat's inscrutable yellow eyes.

Her dry lips cracked in a smile, but instead of saying, "Good morning, kitty," as intended, she blurted, "Oh shit."

Her stomach lurched again and her intestines writhed with pain. "Uh oh."

She sat up and the cat made an irritated noise before bounding to the floor.

"I'm sorry!"

She stumbled down the hall with the flashlight jammed in the waistband of her jeans, one hand pressed to her abdomen and the other clutching a roll of toilet paper.

The bathroom doorway beckoned her inside and she set the flashlight and toilet paper on the back of the sink before unzipping her fly and turning to sit—

Movement in the toilet startled her and she jerked out of her squat, fumbling for the flashlight and bringing its beam to bear.

The toilet bowl was boiling with crabs, iridescent in the bright beam.

French couldn't hold back a cry of disgust and her intestines answered with a convulsion that sent her stumbling for the nearest exit. The kitchen door.

A lucky grab snatched the toilet paper as she fled and then she was outside, stumbling down the unforgiving rock towards the whitecapped channel.

Her body said, *that's it!* She stopped, dropped her jeans and squatted to relieve herself in a hot, painful rush.

"Oh my god." Muttered curses followed.

A sharp stink enveloped her and she was embarrassed, despite her isolation. Said isolation confirmed with a hasty look all around. No narrow crone stood beside the rented Suburban on shore. No eerie Church inquisitor.

She cleaned herself up when she was certain her intestines had nothing more to share and stood, tugging her pants into place.

Be an investigator! Solve crimes! Live a life of romance and adventure.

She gave her waste paper to the channel and said, "Fuck mother nature."

* * *

A tuna fish can rolled ahead of her into the living room after she accidentally kicked it. Distracted by her angry gut, she thought nothing of it until she lifted her face and took in the disarray.

The contents of her duffle bag were scattered around the camp. Underwear, shirts, soap, tossed about will nilly. The food was tossed around as well, cans unopened but their wrappers shredded as if by feline claws. But no cat had stepped on the plastic wrapped Lunchables or crushed full beer cans until they spewed sticky lager across the floor.

She approached, careful not to step on anything as if she

were entering a crime scene. A white spill of cigarettes was gathered and stuffed back into the open package.

She noticed blackened paper in the fireplace and thought they might have been papers from the file drawer.

When had it happened?

She looked around, cocking her head to listen for movement but detected nothing. Surely it hadn't happened while she was outside relieving herself.

Which meant someone had stalked through her camp at night while she slept and in her haste to reach the bathroom she'd simply failed to notice the disarray in her camp.

Hairs on the back of her neck rose like quills.

She remembered passages from Abbott's diary:

They've been in the house again, I'm certain of it now.

Are they yours, Simone? Or envious fishermen from the village?

Is that what happened? The watchers from the boats come to harass her? Or something more diabolical, agents of the Laurent estate trying to…

Trying to what?

Scare her away?

Drive her mad?

Or was it Abbott himself trying to unnerve her? Despite what she thought she'd seen last night, she couldn't imagine Hill creeping through her camp while French snored mere feet away. But the woman had suggested Abbott might try to simply take the house and secure the evidence in the cellar, which suggested the ability to hire people to do so on his behalf.

She mindlessly gathered her belongings together. Her thinking was still too muddy for analysis and she walked on her knees to the fireplace to stir the embers into anger before adding wood. Soon she would fill her coffee pot and stick it in the fireplace to warm.

Caffeine would help.

She glanced at the time on her phone.

Banks would open soon.

She continued cleaning.

* * *

Warmed by coffee, she made the now familiar channel crossing, mildly impressed with how well the muscles in her back and arms were adapting to the exercise.

Bad habits to the contrary, she was getting a hell of a workout.

She clambered up the rocks with a Salem clenched in her teeth and paused at the sight of her car.

There were damp rectangles of white cardboard stuck to the windshield. Two of them side by side, reminding her of the signs carried by The Righteous on Locust Street.

The first said 2 KINGS 9:30-37, a passage she knew well from the signs carried outside her apartment. The Biblical text describing the death of Jezebel, the Old Testament's All Time Bitch of Bitches.

The sign next to it was easy to understand even without researching the Latin. HOMICIDA, meaning *murderer*.

She slid her fingers under this sign and peeled it off her windshield, accidentally tearing it in half before dropping both pieces to the ground. Exhibiting more care with the second, she removed it in one piece before letting it fall.

Perhaps she had seen someone last night after all? Examining the muddy grass around the SUV proved futile, the storm eliminating any traces of whoever left the signs.

She immediately ruled out a visitation by The Righteous. They were a deeply uncurious lot and there was no way for them to have found her so far north.

No, this was the work of someone who knew enough about her to exploit the reality of her life at home. Someone who might know enough about Abbott's diary to understand the significance of scattering her belongings, particularly her food.

Her world and Abbott's world colliding.

They may have even smuggled a cat onto the island as part of their mind game.

To what end, she didn't understand, but there were only so many people who might reasonably know about the signs as well as the contents of the diary.

Grady knew, but he was dead.

Abbott knew, but he was wheelchair bound.

Hill would know anything Abbott cared to tell her.

Hill, then.

French's lips curled into a cruel expression as she wondered how talkative the old woman might be with pepper spray in her eyes.

Chapter Twenty-Five

It was a miserable day, the kind of late autumn weather where dampness digs deep into bones.

French piloted the Suburban on a now familiar route, tires hissing over the rain drenched pavement, splashing through puddles as she accelerated past the speed limit in her haste.

When she saw the signal bars on her phone, she slowed and pulled off on the shoulder, right front tire sinking into the mud.

So eager was she to get online that she left the engine idling, the gear shift in Park. She pulled up the web site for her Schwab account. Entered her password too quickly and had to retype it.

There was no deposit from Abbott.

"FUCK!"

She screamed and banged her fist painfully against the steering wheel, breath fogging the windshield.

French dialed without thinking. The phone on the other end was answered immediately, as if they were waiting on her call.

"This is Hill."

"Where's my money?" French fought to calm herself but the breathing exercises were beyond her reach and she was panting like a runner after a hard sprint.

"It takes time—"

"It won't take time to email pictures to the NBC News affiliate in Bangor," French interjected.

"Wait, please." Hill spoke slowly, as if to calm an animal. "If you act with haste then this becomes a matter for both the courts and the media and neither you nor Mr. Abbott want that."

"You think I'm bluffing?" Saliva struck the inside of her windshield.

"No one thinks you're bluffing," Hill continued in her unruffled way. "Mister Abbott will pay what you asked but it couldn't be done as quickly as you asked. He needs until tomorrow to liquefy assets and transfer them to you."

"Bullshit," French snarled. "Abbott can snap his fingers—"

This time it was Hill who interrupted. "You made your ultimatum on a Saturday and today is Sunday. Mr. Abbott asks that you wait for regular banking hours to open tomorrow, which is Monday."

"What?"

French glanced at her phone and saw that it was, indeed, Sunday.

"If you're fucking with me, you and Abbott will spend the rest of your lives behind bars."

"No one will spend any time behind bars," Hill said. "We'll speak again tomorrow."

Words spilled through French's clenched teeth. "You listen close. Tomorrow morning that money is in my account or the first person I let in on the big news is the estate's agent."

There was a long pause. "Who?" Hill asked.

French disconnected before she registered the question. What did Hill mean, "who?"

She squirmed until she could get a hand into her pocket and pulled out a crumpled business card, deciding on instinct to place the call.

"How soon can you get to the Fishercat?"

* * *

Flavio Ricci sat across from French in a wooden booth against the rough brick wall. The lights were as dim as she remembered and Neil Young sang from the jukebox.

She slipped off her windbreaker and let it pool behind her on the bench. When she leaned her elbows on the table she immediately jerked back, peeling them free from the sticky surface.

Marie wasn't behind the bar. A barrel chested man with huge forearms and a shiny, bald skull had taken her place. He nodded when he saw her looking.

She half wished Mike and Percy were up at the bar bullshitting each other. It would be good to have friends nearby when talking to the man across the table.

"Do you believe in evil?" Ricci asked.

"I believe you're still wearing your sunglasses because you think it makes you mysterious."

A smile touched the corner of his mouth and he slid them down his nose before plucking them free. His thick black eyebrows emphasized the icy blue of his eyes. They were striking and memorable and she had trouble meeting their penetrating stare.

"You guys wanna see a menu or are we just drinking?" The bartender loomed over the booth, his belly threatening to rest on the table.

"Just drinking," French said.

The bartender smiled. "Professionals. I like it." A gold tooth twinkled in his smile. "What can I get you?"

When Ricci nodded she said, "Jamesons neat."

Ricci held up two fingers and said, "I'll have the same."

The bartender winked and rolled back towards the bar like a ship on the waves.

"Where were we?" Ricci asked.

"Evil."

"Yes."

"I believe in the evil that men do," French said.

He nodded, stroking his whiskered chin. "Do you believe a place can be evil?"

"Metaphysics are your department. I believe in this." She knocked on the table.

He nodded at the touch.

"Despite this," his index finger rested on the white clerical collar. "My function within the church is this." He knocked on the table. "But this house is something…unusual."

She tilted her head curiously.

He opened the leather attaché case resting on the bench beside him and pulled out a folder, handing it to her. She opened it on the table and saw printouts of old newspaper articles, decades out of date. Some from the early part of the twentieth century.

They all dealt with kidnappings. Missing children.

"That house represents a great failure for the Church," Ricci said. "A corruption built on top of a corruption."

"It's hardly the only one, is it?" She picked up the folder but it stuck to the table, tearing slightly. "Sorry."

He took it back.

"No, it's not the only one," Ricci slid the folder back into his attaché case. "But when the Church closed it down, we had hoped to be done with it."

The bartender returned with two tumblers half filled with brown liquor. He set them down carefully on the table and said, "Just wave when you want another round."

French smiled at him with a nod and he left.

Ricci lowered his head, considering his words. "We have an interest in allowing the evil of the past to remain buried."

He pulled out a thinner folder, also with printouts of newspaper articles. These were more recent, from the 1970's and 80's. She saw that the articles were from newspapers throughout New England.

"More children went missing when a new occupant took up residence in the house," Ricci said. "Mr. Abbott."

He pulled a newspaper wrapped in plastic from the attaché case. The Bangor Daily News. "This one is from last week, days before you entered Hate House."

French's eyes flashed. "You don't think—"

He held up a hand to stop her. "No! I don't think you have anything to do with kidnapping children." He rubbed the bridge of his nose. "But there is something deeply wrong with that house. When it's occupied, people, children, go missing."

French sipped her whiskey to buy time, rolling the liquor around in her mouth.

"When did you first hear of it?"

"A few weeks ago when Mr. Abbott sent me a letter and offered me a job."

"And the job is?"

"To prove he owns Hate House," French answered. "The Laurent estate sent their own representative and we entered the house together."

"Where is their representative?"

French took another sip. "He left about two days ago."

"Why?"

She shrugged. "He didn't tell me. I was out of the house when he left."

"And there's been no word from him or the Laurent estate since?"

"No word."

"Very curious."

"Very curious," she agreed.

He lifted his glass and drained half in a large swallow. Air escaped between his teeth and he dabbed at his eye with a finger.

"Let me ask...do you feel safe in the house?"

"Not entirely."

"Why?"

"It's big and old and drafty and strange people like you show up unannounced."

"Who else has shown up?"

She smiled and said nothing.

"The Church no longer owns the property but is not without means," he said. "It is our interest to have the house empty again. Would you consider accepting a fee to cease your investigation and leave the house?"

She finished her drink and set down the glass, turning it in her fingers. "What kind of fee?"

"Double what Abbott is paying you?"

She looked away, eyes finding the colored lights of the jukebox. "I'll think about it."

Ricci nodded and picked up the Bangor Daily News from the table, cursing quietly when it stuck to the table and tore. He pried it free and stuffed it back in his attaché case.

"Please do. I don't think it's safe for you inside that house." When he saw her expression he shook his head. "That's a concern, not a threat."

She smiled. "If ever a house was going to be haunted, it would be Hate House," she said. "But I don't believe in ghosts, only in the evil that men do."

He rested a hand on the case full of articles. "There is a great deal of man's evil connected to that house."

* * *

French and Ricci walked to their respective vehicles, her SUV towering over his car, a two door Honda the color of sand.

"Miss French?"

She paused with her door open. "Yes?"

"How did Mr. Abbott come to hire you?"

"What do you mean?"

He rested an arm lazily on the sedan's roof and stared across it at her, deep in thought.

"I mean why you? Surely there are investigators for hire in Rhode Island. Or in Maine, for that matter."

French shrugged. "My name was referred to him."

"By whom?"

"He made a point of noting my discretion and it seemed unwise to dig for information he didn't volunteer."

Ricci nodded and climbed into his car without another word. She climbed up behind the wheel and yanked the door shut before keying the ignition.

On the road she turned on her headlights.

A fog was rolling in.

Chapter Twenty-Six

A crawling child would have outpaced her as she guided the Suburban through fog so dense it created a white-out.

Even at that speed she nearly ran into the tall iron gates barring entrance to the Laurent property. White knuckled hands shoved the gearshift into Park. She opened her door and the fog billowed inside the SUV, an ugly white the color of an old woman's hair.

Her boots squelched over the damp mud as she approached the gate and slid the key from her pocket. The metal of the Schlage lock was wet and cold and as she opened it she felt its inadequacy, despite knowing it was all she could do to keep intruders out. She'd had to leave to check her account and speak to Abbott's aged crow, Hill. The meeting with Flavio Ricci had raised important questions.

She engaged in the pantomime of security as she returned to her vehicle, drove it through the gate, then climbed out once more to close and lock the gate behind her.

The relief she felt when back inside the secure cab of the SUV was palpable.

Low beams disappearing into roiling grey mist mere car

lengths ahead, French drove slowly, shifting and rocking in her seat as the big vehicle found every dip and pothole in the road.

The mournful lowing of a foghorn rolled in from the ocean and rattled her nerves. The fog pressed in on every side, suffocating.

A glance at her rearview mirror showed no sign of lights behind her yet she had the sensation of being followed. Rational knowledge that the gate was locked did nothing to ease her worry.

She was struck by the powerful urge to turn the vehicle around and drive like hell.

But what Hill said did make sense.

French had made her demands on the weekend when producing five million dollars would be more difficult. Waiting until Monday made sense.

Alone in that house for another night. Already certain that someone had been inside while she was asleep, trying to unnerve her.

To frighten her away?

Why bother turning these questions over in her head? She was as trapped by the promise of the payout as she would be by a nail pinning her boot to the floor.

One more night in Hate House and then she was leaving.

Who had referred her to Abbott?

Chapter Twenty-Seven

Climbing the steps from the channel with only the light from her phone was foolish and dangerous. It was a slow and deliberate process using her free hand to probe ahead. The seaweed stink enveloped her as if she was in the embrace of a codfish.

Familiarity helped her ascent through the horrible fog, as thick as soup but shifting as if mysterious beings danced just beyond her sight. The ground undulated as the crabs fled and she only stumbled twice in her march up the island towards the house. Eventually the great stone and brick bulk loomed out of the murk and she made her way along the dripping wall by feel until she came to the wood of the kitchen door.

Her steps were muffled and the kitchen walls were lost in vapor. It was stupid, so stupid to have left the flashlight at her camp. With so many windows unboarded and open, the fog had invaded every crevice of the house and her phone was near useless.

The walls were slimy to her trailing fingers and when those digits came to the gap of an open doorway, she imagined someone snatching her wrist to pull her into the dining room or library.

She knew she had entered the foyer when the sound of her

steps changed and she waved a hand ahead of her as she angled blindly towards the living room.

Sliding her feet forward to detect anything she might trip over she managed to pass through the archway without collision, but eventually bumped into a loveseat. From there she dropped to her knees and found the coffee table where the electric lantern waited.

It snapped alight and she huddled in the glowing sphere of its radiance.

The dampness soaked right through her windbreaker and she crawled towards the fireplace, finding wood and kindling by feel.

She coaxed flame from her reluctant lighter and leaned in to light newspaper beneath the kindling.

The fireball whooshed up to smash against the ceiling of the fireplace and she flung herself backwards with a startled shout.

"What the fuck?"

Sprawled on her back she patted her face, feeling the jagged tips of burnt bangs and smelling the stink of charred hair. Her cheeks felt sunburned and she shook her head.

How did that happen?

She flashed back to Josh grilling steaks outside, trying to coax heat from the coals by spraying a stream of Kingsford Lighter fluid. The fire bloomed in a mushroom cloud and everyone had laughed, even Josh.

She glanced back at the glowing lamp on the table and the swirling fog beyond, hiding the foyer and the generator and…

The kerosene.

She sniffed. All she could smell was her burnt hair. She hadn't done it. Had no memory of putting kerosene in the fireplace.

I have no memory of killing Grady in the cellar.

I have no memory of how I wound up in a boat at sea.

No. That way lay madness.

She crawled back to the fire and crumpled fresh newspaper.

This time it caught slowly, flames licking the kindling.

Doctor Acosta had discussed aspects of her job several times. Places where private investigation could impede her ability to manage things.

French had agreed that having a gun in her home was a threat to her own health.

How she wished she had one now.

* * *

Hate House had a voice, as ugly and glottal as Simone must have sounded in her last days. It moaned of its age and unhappiness.

Murmuring through the walls.

It's nothing, she told herself. Wait until dawn. Smoke cigarettes. Drink whatever you have left.

She smoked and drank in obedience to her own commands. She listened for Burble Cat but the small beast was off on feline business and nowhere she could detect.

A siren's song drifted to her ears, its origin lost in the mist. French was frightened and pressed her back against the loveseat.

A glance towards the foyer revealed nothing but shifting grey and she felt the hot prickle of tears.

She drank from a bottle and burped, the alcoholic fumes burning her sinuses. Emboldened by Dutch courage, she decided to push back the darkness with the standing lights in the foyer.

Straightening her spine took an effort of will but she rose slowly.

The beam stabbed out from the flashlight in her left hand as she flicked her right. The glittering blade of the Spyderco snapped out like an angry tooth.

Fuck Abbott. Fuck Simone.

Hate House was hers until she left by choice. Its secrets were her treasures until she sold them.

* * *

French ascended into darkness, wound as tightly as a spring loaded trap. Only people with the fevered imaginations of The Righteous and ugly dreams of Josh's hate filled family would have recognized this Megan French, teeth bared in a snarl, eyes slitted against the unexpected as she probed the roiling mist with her light.

Hate House had tormented her to the breaking point. Reduced her to a feral state she had only descended into once before in all her years.

The cornered rat has teeth. French's tooth was made of steel.

Red and blue jewels glimmered in the fog atop the landing. The stained glass window. Her path forward was barred by that ancient hag of the Laurent line, Josephine in her life sized portrait leaning against the wall. French's fevered gaze saw moisture dripping like saliva from Josephine's jaws and a devilish twinkle in her eyes.

She nearly gutted the bitch.

Though strangled by distance and fog, the sound seemed to come from her right. She moved in a scuffling slide, brushing crab shells out of her path, her breath a quick, heated panting. Saliva was drawn from her tongue to join the moist air around her and the roof of her mouth was as dry as the desert.

A chemical switch in her brain flicked off.

The momentary ferocity was swept aside by a fresh current of terror, a white capped wave that stripped the sharp teeth from her gums and made a joke of her flashlight and knife. The big muscles in her thighs fought to stop her progress. Her knees urged collapse. To make herself smaller in the dark.

Oh god.

Her emotions surged like tides in a mad moon's gravity and

her guts boiled. Vertigo assaulted her and she stumbled to her left, saved from collapse by the wall.

She waited, breathing hard as her pulse pounded in her ears, drowning out all sound. She had forgotten her medications and her emotions were unleashed.

The atmosphere inside the house was toxic. She could feel it seeping into her marrow like burrowing worms. The fog was mustard gas. Worse than the grave beneath the cellar floor, there was a nuclear waste dump poisoning her body even as the sick minds of Simone Laurent and Marcus Abbott poisoned her thoughts.

She licked her dry lips with a sandpaper tongue. Wished she had brought a bottle of water to moisten her cotton mouth.

It took a count of three to muster the effort to stand straight without support.

An odd sound made her ears prick up. Out of place in the second story hall.

A splash.

She panned her flashlight around to little effect and resumed a cautious advance. All that coiled animal danger had leaked from leaden limbs and the knife had become an anvil she could barely hold.

Her right foot struck a puddle, flinging drops of water. She aimed her light and followed it towards the source.

It was leaking from beneath the bathroom door.

Did I close this door?

Placing the blade of the Spyderco between her teeth, she rested the fingers of her right hand against the old wooden door, feeling the faint vibration accompanying the sound from inside.

It was hard to breath around the knife in her teeth but she needed her right hand for the doorknob. It turned beneath her fingers before she was ready.

The door swung inward and a cyclone of mist rushed at her. French grunted and backpedaled, gashing her own lip as she plucked the knife from her mouth and swung wildly. Her shoulder blades slammed into the wall and her breath exploded. She nearly dropped the knife.

But nothing followed. Nothing emerged from the foggy bathroom atmosphere stirred into movement only by the opening door.

"Fuckfuckfuck."

The gurgle and slap of running water was clearer now. She pushed off the wall and stepped into the flooded bathroom, splashing tentatively towards the noise from the overflowing tub.

Her breath caught in her throat as she looked inside…

Nothing lurked inside the overflowing tub. After gathering herself, she turned off the faucet.

The flow stopped to be replaced by the splash and slop of water tumbling over the sides.

She turned slowly, examining the misty room with her light. Seeing nothing to explain the running water.

She licked her bleeding lip. She wanted to retreat back downstairs to her camp. She wanted to go home.

She sloshed from the bathroom into the hall and heard it again. The siren song so low it was more like an earache than a sound.

It came from the other end of the hall. From the direction of the spiral staircase.

She was moving as if reeled in by an invisible fishing line. Her inner ear tumbled, her balance seesawed. Low moans of fear drooled from her wounded lip and when she reached Josephine's portrait she had to look away from the horrid caricature. The ghoulish line of Laurent!

She rushed it with a cry, jabbing her knife hand into the space where it leaned against the wall until she had the leverage to move its weight. The top of the frame tore free from the wall with a wet rasp and strands of ichor snapped before the hideous painting fell face first on the rotting carpet.

And still the siren sang a quiet song.

The waiting Ochre Men leered at her passing. Wolf whistling construction workers. Worse than teenage boys in high school halls.

She turned away from their rolling eyes and white grins. "You're not real." She repeated the mantra, "You're not real."

Warm breath tickled her ear.

"Hello Megan."

Chapter Twenty-Eight

The Ochre Man was so tall. His grip so strong.

Her knife so sharp.

The steel tip parted clay colored skin and his belly unzipped.

Hot human breath exploded in her face when she stabbed him. His eyes bulged white from a painted face.

It was all a single, crazed swirl of movement as a long arm caught her on the temple. A wild animal swat that sent her reeling into the wall face first. Forehead meeting wood and plaster.

Her world went dark.

* * *

She became aware of pain and touched her forehead with gentle fingers. Agony exploded from the swollen lump and she gasped, eyes opening in the foggy gloom.

She struggled to sit up against the wall, head swimming. Singing came to her as if from a distance, the tune familiar but the words unclear.

The flashlight threw light down the hallway from where it

lay on the floor and when she had enough strength, she stretched out her leg and hooked it with the heel of her boot, dragging it close enough to reach with her left hand.

Her right hand was red with blood, drying to a sticky mess. Playing the light about showed no sign of her knife.

She had stabbed someone. That had really happened.

Abbot's words came to her. *Are they yours, Simone?*

Hill's words followed. *What if he decides to take it?*

An Ochre Man had come to life and made an impossible step into three dimensions.

Lucidity chose that moment to wipe the scales from her eyes. *I'm tripping again. I've been drugged again.*

The clarity sloughed away when she stood. The singing was from somewhere behind her...

Focus.

Her light didn't show a body in the hall.

She moved the beam around until a flicker drew her attention.

A smear of blood on a doorframe.

She moved closer, holding her free hand out for balance. The swollen lump on her forehead pulsed in time with her heart and pain sent black lightning bolts across her vision.

It was one of the monk's cells she'd investigated yesterday. Moldering and spartan. She followed a blood trail to the closet door.

The door swung open with a creak of hinges. She noticed a shiny new deadbolt at eye level, left unlocked.

Light scoured the cramped interior of the empty closet and she thought she saw a seam on the back wall. Stepped inside to press against it.

A small door swung open

"Holy shit."

There was a tunnel.

* * *

French had to turn her shoulders to pass through the narrow space. Her light shined down the dusty length but was soon consumed by the darkness. She glanced over her shoulder.

The secret door was already twenty feet behind her. That earlier sense of dislocation returned, that Hate house contained distances and spaces that defied natural laws.

The print of a bare foot snapped her from her reverie. It was dark and fresh.

The ceiling opened up above her and the floor dropped away below her and she caught herself before tumbling head-long. Rungs had been set along the wall.

Up or down?

She let blood be her guide.

Stuffing the flashlight in the front of her jeans, she carefully reached out a hand, followed by a foot.

She descended

There were pipes running alongside the ladder and though she wasn't sure exactly where she was in the geography of Hate House, she believed she was in the wet wall containing the building's plumbing.

"You."

It was a simple statement of recognition directed at the house as she crawled through its secrets.

At the bottom she found another tunnel and slide stepped along a creaky wooden floor. She kept moving deeper into the guts of Hate House until she found a heap on the floor.

Grady's backpack.

You've been hiding in the walls, you sonofabitch.

It made sense now. Her scattered belongings. Lights turned off when she'd left them on. Kerosene in the fireplace.

The goddamned bathtub.

All that panic over his death. Over her responsibility. He'd caused that panic. Manipulated her. Drugged her to unbalance her mind.

The gaslighting sonofabitch.

"HOW DOES IT FEEL, GRADY?"

The words were huge in the cramped space, hanging in the air. Pain spiked from her bruised forehead and for a moment her vision split and she wobbled on her feet.

She closed her eyes, concentrating on her breathing, worrying about a concussion.

She opened her eyes and slowed her breathing, forcing herself to stay in the moment because a wounded and hostile man was roaming Hate House.

But where?

The tunnel hit a perpendicular cross passage and there was no blood to guide her.

Stop chasing him. Anticipate him.

If he was seriously wounded he might try to get off the island to find medical attention.

She stumbled back along her trail as quickly as the cramped space allowed.

* * *

French moved through the thinning mist over slippery rocks towards the stone stairs leading into the channel. Her vision was worsening, bifurcating and splitting. The rocks around her seemed to shift of their own accord.

At the top of the stairs she paused to brace her hands on her knees, breathing hard from the exertion, head throbbing, weary to the bone.

Nausea twisted her guts but all she could produce was a dry retching. When it ceased she could feel it biding its time, preparing to come back stronger.

The boat.

Closing one eye, she stared through the murk towards the sloshing sound of a boat on the water.

It waited loyally where she had tied it off. Grady hadn't stolen it.

She dragged her wrist across her nose and turned back to Hate House, its black windows like a cluster of spider eyes.

* * *

Chapter Twenty-Nine

Holding the railing for balance, French carefully ascended the spiral stairs as music drifted down from above. Sinatra or Tony Bennett. One of the crooners.

In the small room French found herself on her knees, retching again. Drool trailed from her mouth to the floor. Her hands pressed against her temples but the throbbing increased. A circle of black was closing around her peripheral vision. Tunneling. Narrowing.

No.

She played her flashlight across the door to the third floor hall, half expecting the hasp to be locked.

It wasn't.

Sticky brown liquid smeared the doorknob and whispered about Grady.

The brazier in the hall was lit and smoke spiraled lazily towards the ceiling.

Grady must have filled it with fresh coals before painting himself ochre. She could see where he had braced his hand on the clean wallpaper much as she was doing. The pristine hall seemed eager to lead her on, as if offended by the mess of Grady's passage.

The music was a little clearer, coming from behind the double doors. *Rosemary Clooney*, she thought. Her headache faded as a sense of giddiness took over.

A lure or a signal?

And what did the brazier guard?

The velvet rope made the choice easy. She remembered Abbott's diary.

I found the velvet rope strung across the stairs where they rose towards the third story. A sign, perhaps stolen from a theatre, hung from the velvet expanse.

PRIVATE – NO ADMITTANCE

What did he do, your driver? What changes did he wreak upstairs?

The rope had not barred the spiral stairs. Instead, it hung across the width of the double doors painted eggshell blue.

PRIVATE – NO ADMITTANCE

"What don't you want me to see?"

French was curious to learn what changes the driver had wrought and she unfastened the thick velvet rope, letting it fall silently to the carpet. When her hand found the doorknob she expected resistance, but it turned quietly as if recently oiled.

The sight of Grady jolted her to attention.

He was naked and dead, curled around his wounded belly like an animal.

SIMONE IS HERE

Written on the gleaming wooden floor in blood already drying to brown, letters running towards the cracks between boards.

SIMONE IS HERE

"Only you and me, Grady, and you're dead."

Crackling music spilled from a speaker as the needle lowered onto a spinning record. Piano. Something classical she didn't recognize.

Despite the initial shock, she was too tired and confused to feel much at the sight of his body. She anticipated that would come later and she would decide between doubling her Lexapro prescription or calling her therapist.

When she was gone. When she was home.

At present...

The room in which Grady had released his final breath was large and well lit despite the boarded windows. It was clean and expensively appointed, with all furnishings centered around the large, king sized bed. There were couches and settees, the old stereo system, expensive lamps of a bygone era and paintings under glass as pristine as the day they were created. Two doors led off to either side but her gaze returned to the bed.

The recently slept in bed.

The rich blue comforter was thrown back and the pillows were askew. Closer inspection revealed a few light colored hairs on the pillow case, pale against its midnight, and she suspected they were hers though she had no memory of this place.

On the floor at her feet was a crumpled sock and she plucked it up, stretching it out to see it was also hers. She recognized the annoying hole in the big toe.

She dropped the sock and walked across the polished boards without a glance at dead Grady, noting the edge of another clawfoot tub beyond one open door.

Hand on the doorway, she leaned inside to confirm it was indeed a bathroom and a single glance at the underwear on the floor beside the tub confirmed they were hers.

Grady the Panty Raider.

She sat on the bed to see if her body remembered the experience better than her mind, but her ass had nothing to say. She absently noted the lack of squeaking springs and wondered if that was by design. How often had Grady been sleeping up here instead of lurking in the walls?

How many times had he sprinkled powdered psilocybin

into her fireplace or injected THC into her Salems? Into her goddamned Lunchables?

Fingers brushed the short hair over her ear. *How stoned was I when he cut my hair to sprinkle on the pillow?* Because that's what had happened. She had not slept here.

Violation filled her bones with sour cold.

Dead Grady. A confusion of feelings. He deserved it, of course, but that did little to make it sit well.

Killing was not something she enjoyed.

She closed her eyes.

* * *

French was staggering through the apartment with both hands clutching her face. She was a shrieking teakettle spraying horrible amounts of blood.

Stunned by the blow from the fireplace poker she was calling out to Josh for help, forgetting who hurt her.

"Josh?"

Only his sobs, his muttered curses.

She sagged in the bedroom doorway and saw him silhouetted in the open window with his feet on the sill as if to jump.

"Josh?"

He glanced back and his eyes were cruel. "Thought I fucking killed you." He looked back outside while she reeled from the cold certainty in his voice.

In three long strides she crossed the room and slammed her hands into his back.

He was hurled into space and then he was dead.

* * *

The killer opened her eyes and began to plan.

Chapter Thirty

The steel pickaxe made short work of the boards over the bedroom window and soon she was covered in splinters sticking to her sweaty face and dampened t-shirt.

Billows of white fog ushered in the cool sea air and she breathed hungrily as her chest rose and fell, muscles warm but aching after the days of unexpected exercise.

There are actions one ponders and actions one must undertake immediately.

Defenestration was the latter.

French crouched and gripped Grady's shoulder, avoiding the congealing blood. His skin was rubbery and strange, sensations to be filed away and retrieved for examination at a later, safer date.

She rolled him on his back and quickly straightened his legs by the simple expedient of grabbing his ankles and backing up until the knees loosened their grip.

Rigor mortis had started to harden his pose, but had not yet finished the job.

His skin stuck to the floor, squeaking grotesquely as she dragged the dead weight around the bed. Hands on her knees, she paused to slow her heart rate before she sat him up beneath the open window and straddled his legs.

You creeping-around-in-the-dark motherfucker.

Violation was a fuel that burned hot.

Leaning in so close was horribly intimate, his face inches from her own, but she pummeled her fists under his arms until she had his armpits cradled in her elbows.

She stood.

He rose with her, dead meat sliding against her with horrid friction, his penis dragging a trail up her thigh, his face dropping to rest against hers until she could get him seated on the sill.

She shoved him away so hard she almost tumbled after and even in death Grady managed to kick her as he flew free.

The smack of one hundred and eighty pounds of meat hitting rock would echo in her nightmares.

"Fuck you, Grady."

Grabbing the lantern, she paused in the hall long enough to kick over the smoking brazier, glancing over the scatter of graying coals to the shape of stairs inside the alcove leading up to the tower. So steep as to be a ladder.

Of course there were more stairs.

* * *

The mist was so thick she could see little more than a few boat lengths beyond her bow. She dared only row so far, careful she could still see the camp lantern that marked the island, a bare glimmer in the fog.

The corpse resisted leaving the boat by the simple action of refusing to stand, so she had to shove him sideways on the bench until he was leaning out, the boat tipping as she crawled in the wet bottom to get beneath him and lift with an explosive grunt of effort.

His torso flopped over the side and the boat tipped precariously, but she scrambled and shoved until he his legs followed and sank into the water with a *plunk* rather than a splash.

She looked after the pale smear of his diminishing form as Grady vanished beneath the waves.

Her palms were bleeding when she grabbed the oars once more and the sinews in her back and arms were white hot with agony, but she made haste for the beacon.

Chapter Thirty-One

The sun was lowering towards the distant trees and the fog had thinned to a flimsy veil by the time French trudged up the wide staircase towards the second floor with the lights blazing in the foyer behind her.

Down the hall once so terrifying. Past the Ochre Men she no longer feared.

The struggle to reach the spiral staircase against all that had worked to impede her seemed like the work of years instead of days, but she ascended once again, bootheels clanging on iron.

She was terribly thirsty and craved a cigarette, but she had thrown everything Grady might have drugged out the window. The fire in the living room fireplace no longer burned, was no longer able to seduce her with its narcotic smoke.

The trusty camp lantern was set beside her on the floor of the room below the tower and she could see the trap door overhead. The shiny new lock easily spotted.

The mechanics of the matter were a struggle for her tired brain but soon enough she stood on a chair liberated from the bedroom, balancing precariously on the striped cushion.

The lock's hasp was loose enough to jam the tip of her trusty pickaxe between it and the wood it secured, even as her shoulders sizzled with lactic acid and her body screamed *enough*!

It was a moment made for remembering if she had a future, as French set herself against the lock and it surrendered with a snap.

The padlock hung impotently over her head as she climbed down from the chair, careful not to break an ankle at this stage of the game.

Whatever mad game this was.

Up the ladder then, shoving the trapdoor with her right hand.

She had no idea what to expect as it pushed up easily before bouncing closed. She shoved it harder and it swung past apogee, crashing over.

The final door was open.

The fresh smell of shit oozed down as she climbed, eyes wide and wary as her head rose periscope-like into the gloom above.

Someone was weeping.

Something rustled in the dark and she swiveled as her eyes adjusted to the gloom. Empty juice boxes and fast food wrappers made a path towards a child cowering in the corner.

His crying grew in strength as she climbed up into the room and knelt to make herself small. It was an unimpressive space after all the effort to reach it. Square with covered windows. The roof barely six feet overhead.

"Hey kid." A boy in thin pajamas, shivering in the un-insulated place. Whatever grief she felt over what she had done to Grady was buried by a feeling that had no name.

He twitched and flicked a glance. Startled to hear a woman's voice.

"My name is Megan French and I killed the man who put you here. I'm gonna take you home."

She stretched out her hand, though the muscles holding her arm up trembled from overuse.

It took time but she was patient.

Eventually small fingers touched hers.

* * *

It was a saltwater bath in her camp downstairs, but she wiped the child down and held back tears at the feel of his xylophone ribs.

He was pliable to the point of catatonic, but she got him into one of her hoodies. The garment hung down to his knees.

Seven? Eight? Too old to still suck his thumb, but she wasn't the one to tell him.

"Want to stop at McDonalds on the way home?"

He said nothing. Questions about where he lived went unanswered and she soon stopped asking.

To take him into Paper Bay meant exposing herself to investigation, despite the disposal of Grady's corpse. His blood was still scattered about the house and his camp still waited inside the walls. Bones remained in their eternal crouch in the dark cellar.

Burn it.

Would that exonerate her? Did it matter any more in the face of what she found in that tower. How much time she had wasted getting there?

Gimme five million dollars.

Nothing could ever justify her delay in finding the boy.

"Okay," she told him, crouching at eye level, but he turned so that she saw only a freckled cheek. "I'm going to row you across the channel and put you in my truck, which is huge and will keep you safe. Then we drive to town, right?"

She stood with her duffle bag over a shoulder and asked, "Would you rather walk or be carried?"

He didn't speak so she gently took his hand. She led him down the hall that had once seemed so long to the kitchen, which felt like the basecamp at the foot of Mount Kilimanjaro.

Molten sunset colored the western sky as they emerged from the house.

"Megan."

People were waiting on shore.

Chapter Thirty-Two

It pleased French to see mud on Abbott's shiny, expensive shoes and spattered on the undercarriage of his idling limousine. The wheels of Abbott's wheelchair were sunk into the wet turf, but though he was shrunken beneath an oversized grey suit and the blanket across his lap, his rheumy eyes danced with glee.

She thumbed a button on her cell phone and pocketed it. "Stay here, honey," she said to the boy, stepping forward as if to shield him with her body.

Hill was inscrutable behind her oversized sunglasses but Abbott's wet, wormy lips curled in a grin. "Hello, Megan."

"Why?" French asked.

He looked past her and an expression of naked longing swarmed across his face. It was an ugly thing. A junkie's hunger for the needle.

With the pressure of his gaze lifted she blinked, noticing movement in the distant graveyard. *Who?*

"I learned so much here," he mused before his gaze settled on hers. "Did you know Simone planned to frame me at the end of my sentence? I was to have one taste of free air before the authorities were notified about a body in the basement." He shook his head in admiration. "Her cruelty was poetic, but in the end she changed her mind and allowed me to go free. My Hell was only a game to her and she changed the rules on a whim."

"Why are you doing this?"

"My work is a crass limerick compared to Simone's, but I intend to put a period at the end of your sentence. The boy will be found inside Hate House and the police will have no one to suspect but you."

"*The boy* is right fucking here." French took a step forward and froze. A small, black automatic had appeared in Hill's right hand. "Wait—there are records of our business."

"Are there?" Abbott asked. "A handwritten letter? Do you still have it? A file that could have been assembled by anyone."

"Grady and I—"

"*Grady*. You emailed a fiction." Abbott squirmed in his chair, the motion unnatural and nauseating. "Did you get the best of him? Tell me how."

"Why are you doing this?"

"And you an investigator." His head swiveled atop the bird-like neck. "What is my mother's maiden name?"

"What?"

"Did you research me at all?" Abbott pressed.

"Of course," French shot back. "You're a cipher online. Almost non-existent."

"So much for the great gumshoe." Abbott flicked a glance at Hill.

"The name was Hargrave," Hill said.

"Lucille and I are cousins twice removed," Abbott added.

French's furious expression went slack and the rush of blood filled her ears.

"What was it she said after the grand jury acquitted you?"

French shivered at the memory as Abbott supplied the words.

"You will never know peace," he said. "Imagine my surprise at hearing from Lucille after so many years. I'd been waiting for an opportunity to put Simone's lessons to good use." He waved at hand at French. "And there you were. *You will never know peace.*"

"I haven't."

The impish grin returned to his wizened face. "It will get worse."

The distant movement had gathered itself into the familiar form of a man in black, his approaching steps concealed by the low rumble of the idling limousine.

French pulled the phone from her pocket.

"I just recorded you and posted it," she said.

"You have no signal," Hill said.

"Are you sure?" French tapped the screen and held it out for them to read.

It almost worked.

"I represent the dio—" A gunshot cut Flavio Ricci off mid-word and he staggered. The small pistol bucked as Hill fired a second time and Ricci's head snapped back. He fell hard and did not move.

Where normally French might have hesitated, exhaustion and the stress of recent events had stripped away a layer of civilization and she was moving without conscious thought.

Hill noticed her too late and French slammed into the older woman hard enough to knock her off her feet. French sprawled hard on her face, sliding across the muddy grass.

The gun had fallen between them.

"Stop!" Hill shouted as if hoping to freeze her, but French wriggled forward on her belly and slapped a palm down on the weapon just as Hill's ugly, old woman's shoe connected with her forehead.

French rolled away, clutching her skull with her free hand while waving the gun at Hill. She pulled the trigger and murdered a bit of earth as Hill yanked open the driver's door of the limousine and swung inside.

A second shot slapped the door like a giant hand against

metal and then the big limo was slewing backwards, engine roaring.

French took aim at the retreating vehicle, but lowered the pistol without firing. She brushed mud off her chest and turned.

Abbott waited in his wheelchair, wrinkled skin gone pale beneath the liver spots.

His mouth opened and closed like a fish out of water, a line of spit connecting his upper lip to his lower. He lifted a shaking hand as if to halt her.

"I have your money," he wheezed, abruptly short of breath. "Five million dollars."

French glanced at Ricci's body and down at the gun in her hand.

"No you don't," she said at last. She engaged the safety and stuck the compact gun in the pocket of her jacket.

"Wait!"

"No."

* * *

Waves slapped against the hull as French rowed out to sea towards the firefly lights. Evening surrendered to night and the purple sky deepened into black. The wind was cruel, whipping the nylon windbreaker against her arms as she rowed, hands cramping, breath whistling from her tired lungs.

Abbott shivered at the bow, leaking tears from his eyes and blood from a gash on his cheek. The boy sat on a bench at the rear, wrapped in Abbott's blanket.

French in the middle rowing. Breathing. Hoping. The electric lantern bright at her side. A beacon.

Motors caught her attention, their muted growls slithering over the water to her ears. She saw the lights drawing close from three directions and stopped rowing, setting the oars inside the boat.

The stars glimmered overhead, and she found Orion and the Big Dipper, the only two constellations she knew.

Three boats. Six men. Twelve angry eyes.

French felt like a toy poodle surrounded by junkyard dogs. The first boat nudged hers and the rowboat jolted. She grabbed the gunwale for balance and Abbott cried out. The child at the stern hunched lower in his blanket.

French held up both hands to show she was unarmed as long handled boathooks were extended by fishermen to secure her boat in the middle of the pack. All she could see of their faces were hard lines and bristling beards and she was afraid.

"I found something of yours," she said, pitching her voice to carry. She scrambled carefully to the stern, staying low to avoid rocking the boat. She knelt in the inch of icy water in the bottom of the boat and gently eased the blanket down off the boy's face. A flashlight beam stabbed out and crawled over her to him.

She looked around the gathered boats, shielding her eyes with her hand. Light flashed off metal and she thought one of the angry men held a gun.

"That asshole kidnapped this boy and kept him in Hate House!" She was shouting as much from fear as conviction. "I stopped him! He's the monster who lived there before when another one of your children went missing!"

"She's lying—" Abbott's words were cut off when a boathook *thunked* down against the bow beside him.

"I'm not lying," French continued. "He's a rich, sick monster who kidnapped a kid! Your kid!"

"That's Charlie Beaumont's boy," a voice called out and a moment later she lost track of the babble as the men shouted between the boats.

"You give him here," a big voice commanded and she gestured.

"Pull me closer."

The boat jerked beneath her and she fell back, soaking the seat of her jeans before she could scramble to her knees and gently take hold of the boy's shoulders. She stared into his vacant eyes.

"You're going to be okay. These men are from town and will get you home."

"Hand him up."

French looked up into a familiar face.

"Here he is, Mike." She helped the child to stand. "Abbott kept him drugged so he's still out of it."

Another man braced Mike as the old man reached down into the rowboat and snatched up the boy. It wasn't gentle but it was quick and a moment later the boy was aboard the lobster boat.

French glanced around at the surrounding men and definitely saw a shotgun aimed in her direction.

"What are you gonna do with him?" The gun jabbed at Abbott. Before French could answer another man shouted.

"You're gonna give him to us."

"You let us take him now," Mike said, holding a long boat hook at port arms.

"How—" French stopped when a boathook stabbed out from behind Abbott and dug into his shoulder. The old man shrieked with surprising volume and a second hook slashed out from a different boat to catch the fabric at his arm.

Abbott was dragged unceremoniously over the side. He splashed and screamed in the water.

Another boat hook snagged him and then a fourth. He was held up by the pull from different boats as if he was to be drawn and quartered.

A metal hook banged the gunwale beside French and she flinched, but it was Mike leaning down and cupping a hand to his mouth.

"You go back and burn that goddamned house down, you hear?"

French nodded wildly and he continued. "You set that fuckin' place on fire and then you leave. Don't ever come back."

"What will you do with Abbott?"

Mike glanced at the thrashing old man. "Gonna take him out and chum the water." White teeth flashed in his beard. "Now go!"

She was caught up in a surge of emotion when the boats sounded their horns. A gap opened up and boat hooks shoved her small craft through.

She grabbed the oars without hesitation and began pulling for shore.

* * *

The stench struck with awful vigor, the sickly sweet perfume of Simone Laurent's decaying self. If ever a place deserved to burn, it was Hate House.

Passing through the doorway into Hate House caused French to shiver with unease, but she pushed back the darkness by cranking up the generator and flooding the foyer with light.

She carried a half empty can of kerosene up the grand stairs to the second floor and unscrewed the cap, splashing it liberally over the baseboards as she traversed the hall, the crunch of crab shells beneath her boots a sound she would never forget.

She left the empty can in the room with the spiral staircase and glanced up, then down. All of it a game. A murderous game played by a wealthy sadist.

The fumes burned her nostrils as she trudged back downstairs and carried the remaining, full can of kerosene to the kitchen where she splashed it about. She left a wet trail in her wake as she traveled the hall, dousing the library and dining room until she eventually reached the living room where she had camped.

Kerosene soaked the yin and yang love seats and she dribbled a trail back to the foyer, splashing more flammable liquid around the doorframe. She only wished she could stay and watch the portrait of Simone Laurent burn.

"Fuck your house," she said to the portrait before stepping

outside for a last time. She paused to smoke a cigarette, looking at the firefly lights of the fishing boats out at sea.

She had been waiting for some kind of signal to tell her it was time, but when none came she shrugged and tossed the cigarette through the door into the house.

* * *

"Oh my God!"

French found Flavio Ricci sitting against the front wheel of her SUV, the side of his face sheeted with blood from a glancing wound to the temple, his free hand pressed against the leaking wound in his shoulder. Guilt swamped her and she knelt by his side, peering at his wounds as if she had the skill to heal him.

"I'm so sorry."

He shook his head. "Is it done?" His voice was weak but clear.

"It's done."

She opened the door and helped him stand before seating him in the passenger seat. He groaned with pain and his face paled beneath the dark blood.

"I need a hospital."

"I—" She hesitated. "They have to report gunshot wounds."

His thin lips stretched in a smile. "The Church will take care of that."

A moment later she was driving them slowly down the dirt road, briefly sketching out what had happened after he was shot. She apologized as the Suburban rocked on its springs and he waved it away.

"Tell me," he asked. "The child?"

"With his people."

"And Abbott?"

"With Old Man Atlantic."

Ricci digested the statement.

"What happened to Grady?"

"There was no Grady."

A glance in the rearview mirror showed the eastern sky orange with a false dawn. The air tasted of smoke.

"It's finished."

Hate House burned in their wake.

Chapter Thirty-Three

French dry swallowed a Lexapro and pondered the banality of evil on the long drive from Maine to Philadelphia. At a rest stop she pulled out her phone to scour the internet for news from Paper Bay. News of a shooting. A missing kid found. The burning of Hate House.

Google turned up nothing except a notice about the PANCAKE JUMBLE, a three town pancake fundraiser to benefit the consolidated high school.

A light flurry of snow began to drift from the iron sky as she stood beside the SUV. She ground out her cigarette beneath a boot and climbed back inside the Suburban.

Ricci was right. The Church had swept it all under the rug. It was odd to feel gratitude towards the Catholic Church, but life was funny that way.

Still, rusty gears turned in her tired brain and she wondered if a two time killer deserved to walk free.

She stopped for a restroom. To get coffee. To buy gas.

Light in the east tickled the dark but she knew it was only the false dawn and was not cheered.

Banality. The rental company charged her extra for returning the Suburban to the rental office without a full gas tank. For the cigarette ash scattered in the interior despite a contract that prohibited smoking. Expenses that wouldn't be paid by the client.

Gonna take him out and chum the water.

Was she a three time killer? Did Abbott count as hers?

She fell asleep in the cab ride to her apartment and only woke because her bladder sounded the alarm. Would there be Maine police officers waiting for her? Local Philly cops?

She didn't care as long as they let her use the bathroom before breaking out the cuffs.

A school bus belched exhaust as it rumbled past and she wondered how such things continued to exist. As if the world had continued turning during the nightmare at Hate House.

Her key worked in the lock and she kicked snow off her boots. Her legs worked well enough to carry her up the stairs to her apartment.

She unfastened two locks on the heavy wooden door and stepped into her stuffy home. The police were not there.

Instead she found a letter.

* * *

Hate House was finished. She knew this.

But the sight of the letter made her knees buckle.

The letter waiting on her kitchen table could have been left at any time she was in Maine. An examination of the locks on her door proved nothing. That there were no telltale scratches meant only that the intruder had used a key instead of picks.

Was the handwriting on the envelope Abbott's? She wasn't sure. She thought to compare it to his earlier letter but a quick look in her file cabinet revealed that Abbott's letter wasn't there. In fact, the file itself was missing.

Her mind was buzzing with white noise that drowned out her fear and the sense of violation.

Hate House was finished. Of this she was certain.

She carried the mysterious letter to her kitchen stove and turned on a front burner. Blue flame danced eagerly and she held the unopened envelope over the burner until the edge blackened and curled.

The burning letter landed in the sink and as it became ash she opened the nearest window to avoid angering the smoke alarm.

When the letter was reduced to grey flakes she ran the faucet and drowned the mess. The garbage disposal chortled as it ate what was left.

Golden light filled the kitchen window, but she couldn't feel its beauty. She was lost inside Hate House. The stink of the burning letter taking her back to that final act of arson. The madness and cruelty of the house turned into inhalable particulates. A smell that clung to her clothes. Oozed into her pores.

"Buster?" She was hoping for the safety of his company but the cat, mercurial at best, was probably pissed off by her absence and hiding under the bed.

She stripped right there in the kitchen, stuffing her clothes into a plastic trash bag before padding naked to the bathroom and climbing into the shower.

She sat carefully in the tub as the cold bullets of water grew hot and steam filled the room. Tension seeped from her muscles as she soaped her skin and worked shampoo into her hair.

Eventually she lay back and let the spray massage her into an uneasy sleep.

* * *

French awoke to the cooling spray of water and sat up, reaching forward to turn it off.

The dripping showerhead was loud in the sudden quiet and it was some time before she roused herself to stand, careful not to slip.

Her plans included Ambien and bed in that order, but she froze with one hand outstretched towards the medicine cabinet.

A word was written on the fogged mirror.

A name.

SIMONE.

* * *

Chapter Thirty-Four

Someone was following her.

French was trudging along Market Street trying to fit her entire being beneath the curve of a black umbrella, but the sleet was of devious nature and snuck around to spatter her shoulders and arms no matter what she did.

It was while huddling from a fierce gust that she looked away and happened to see her pursuer.

A long black coat and shoes unsuited for slush was all she could make out below the person's own umbrella. Something about his walk told her it was a man and something she couldn't define told her it wasn't a cop.

It wasn't one of The Righteous. They were fair weather foes at best and had never tried to tail her. Late morning made it unlikely the man was a mugger. That and his ugly black shoes, which looked like the cheap business wear of a copier repairman or used car salesman.

That left the Hargraves. Perhaps confused by lack of word from Abbott. They had never attacked her directly before. Had always acted on oblique angles, pulling strings to harm her, but that didn't mean they wouldn't grow frustrated, especially after she escaped Hate House.

She splashed towards the curb and squinted against the storm to study the passing traffic for cabs, but she saw none with their ON DUTY lights lit. A quick look back showed the man trudging closer and she hurried away, kicking up slush.

Up ahead was a SEPTA stop and she reached it well ahead of her pursuer, who never once changed his gait. The resolute plodding of his approach unnerved her, like something from a horror movie. Uncaring and unstoppable.

"Oh c'mon."

A trolley was coming, banging and slashing down the street on its nearly concealed tracks. Sparks flew from the wires overhead and she fumbled through her pockets for cash.

The metal behemoth splashed to a halt beside the stop and she waited impatiently for two passengers to disembark before climbing aboard, nearly slipping in her haste.

A moment later the trolley lurched away from the stop and she pushed past another passenger to stare out the window.

Her pursuer stood at the SEPTA stop, still hidden behind the umbrella.

She never saw his face.

* * *

French departed the train after several stops and ducked into the doorway of an office building. She pulled out her phone to call an Uber, glancing up and behind her to learn the address.

FOUR MINUTES. DRIVER NAMED HABIB.

She pocketed the phone and shook her umbrella open, holding it out like a shield against the freezing rain.

Someone was following her. This was not paranoia.

* * *

"It's not paranoia."

French tried to read the expression of the man in the brown

leather chair but he was a stranger without tells. Instinct told her to stand up and storm out.

She should have left the minute she walked into the outer office and learned that Sally Acosta was not in, but Sally had left word that her new partner would see French and French complied like an obedient puppy. She should have left when *American Pie* started playing in the outer office, a fucking depressing song to aim at people seeking therapy.

Wait, no, she should have never put herself in a position to have to hear *American Pie*. Sally had never insisted on an in-person session before, they did their work together (Sally always told French they worked *together*) over Zoom on the internet.

But Sally had been firm and French acquiesced because she was the goddamned patient and didn't understand the mysteries of psychotherapy.

The man in the brown chair wore an earth toned sweater over a collared shirt, white against his dark skin. His features were chiseled with deep lines and his black hair was streaked with silver.

His name was Khoury and she had trouble meeting his eyes.

"Who was he?"

He sounded like money and his accent was laced with a foreign seasoning she couldn't identify.

"I don't know."

"Why would he be following you?"

"I don't know."

A single eyebrow arched. "Are you telling the truth?"

She was startled into meeting his unblinking gaze.

"I think he might be working for the Hargraves," she finally offered.

He nodded, steepling his hands. It felt strange seeing him in Sally Acosta's office. Like a cuckoo bird who had stolen another bird's nest.

"And you think the Hargraves were behind..." His pause

was weighted. "Unfortunate occurrences on your most recent case."

"Yes."

"They followed you up to Maine and back home to Philadelphia."

"Yes."

"But the man who hired you to go to Maine was named Abbott."

It was sounding crazy even to her. "But his mother's maiden name was Hargrave."

He scratched his head, lips pursed.

"I know it sounds nuts," she said, her hands clenching.

He shrugged. "Does it? How far would a reasonable family go if you killed their son?"

The roof of her mouth went dry and she felt the blood drain from her face.

"I didn't—"

"What would a mother do to make sure you never felt peace?"

She was on her feet without realizing it, quivering with rage.

"Who the fuck are you?" She snarled.

He leaned back in his chair, steepling his fingers again. "It's important that you take an honest look at what you've done—"

"Fuck you!" She lunged for the door, storming into the outer office to the coat rack. Her trench coat caught on the spindly rack and she yanked hard, sending the entire thing crashing to the floor. She dragged the garment with her, stalking down the hall and outside into the storm before bothering to sling it over her shoulders.

"You motherfucker."

She stomped down the sidewalk as the freezing rain plastered her hair to her face.

Chapter Thirty-Five

Perched on a stool at a diner's counter, French cupped the hot coffee mug in both hands to warm them. A steady trickle of cold water drained from her coat to puddle on the floor beneath, the floor gritty with salt tracked in by the few patrons hardy enough to venture out into the storm.

Therapy was a sanctuary that had been defiled with mind games that reeked of Abbott. But how? Would Sally Acosta really have abandoned French to the wolves for a few bucks?

And to what end? Simple torture? Even the exercise at Hate House had an endgame, though she'd thwarted it.

And...

Abbott was dead, wasn't he? She saw the boat hooks grabbing his clothes and flesh. Saw him thrashing in the water and heard him screaming in despair. There was nothing of the lie in the hatred of the fishermen for Abbott. She *believed* them when they said they would take him out to sea and chum the water.

But she didn't see it, did she?

Blowing ripples across the surface of the coffee sent steam swirling. It was important that she accept a simple fact.

She did not see Abbott die.

Coffee burned her tongue, the bitterness appropriate to her

mood. Somehow Abbott's games had followed her from Maine. The letter in her apartment and the name written on her bathroom mirror were not legacies of a conflict resolved.

It continued.

She didn't realize she moaned in pain until the waitress paused.

"You okay, honey?"

French forced a smile. "Threw out my back. I'm fine."

The waitress's broad face broke in a sisterly smile and she winked. "Aging is a bitch. I live on Tylenol." She reached into the pocket of her yellow polyester uniform and pulled out a small plastic bottle. "Take two of these."

French was about to refuse when it dawned on her that she was full of aches and pains. She nodded thanks and placed the pills on her tongue. The waitress had a glass of water on the counter before French could reach for her coffee and she smiled in gratitude before washing the pills down.

As the waitress moved away to help another customer, French picked up the interrupted line of thought.

She had to change the locks on her apartment. Change passwords on social media, online banking…anywhere Abbott might have reached in to disrupt her life.

She began planning out a return to seclusion, simultaneously drawn to the idea of retreat and frustrated that she was being driven into a cave.

She still had Hill's tiny pistol. Should she get some ammunition? It wasn't hard in Pennsylvania, especially outside of the city. French didn't know much about firearms but she could take a picture of the gun and copy down the specs to show somebody who would know what she needed. Sally Acosta had cautioned against owning a firearm considering her mental state, but Sally Acosta had betrayed her, right? Fuck Sally.

French sipped her coffee and licked a spill of liquid off her wrist.

"Fuck you Sally."

* * *

The bell over the door didn't so much ring as it offered a metallic thud when French stepped inside the Army Surplus store and she hurried to close the door against the storm.

It was a dark, windowless place smelling of mothballs and crowded with stuff. There was a mannequin wearing a vintage gas mask and green fatigues, racks of jackets and coats, and pants in olive drab, desert tan and multihued camouflage.

UNCLE SAM WANTS YOU a sign shouted at her. Another rusting metal plaque read LOOSE LIPS SINK SHIPS.

She scraped icy water from the hair plastered to her scalp as a fat man with a grey beard emerged from a beaded curtain in the back.

"I was thinking about closing up," he grinned through the beard, revealing tobacco stained teeth. "Not a lot of business on a day like today."

French nodded but had little interest in small talk. She glanced at a glass case beside the cash register. "Do you carry Spyderco knives?"

"One or two," he sucked on his bottom lip. "But we have a passel of others. What exactly are you looking for?"

"A folding Spyderco for self-defense."

"Huh." He nodded. "Come over here."

He pointed with a fat finger at shelves beneath the glass. "That there with the orange is a Spyderco but these..." He stepped to his right and gestured for her to follow. "These are Gerber folding knives and they're better."

French studied them, dark composite handles, the blades looking sharp but the steel was matte instead of shiny. They weren't made for show.

"I want a gravity knife."

He nodded. "Okay, but I gotta ask, tool like this requires some knowledge to use properly."

"I know how to use it."

He rapped knuckles on the glass. "Alright then." Circling behind the counter he opened a sliding panel in the back and took out two closed knives. The handles felt good in her hand and she practiced snapping open the blades. One was a shorter, fatter blade. The other had a triangular tip.

"That there is modeled after a Japanese tanto, designed to penetrate armor." He set down a small leather sheath with a metal clip. "This goes with it."

She set the tanto down on the glass. "I'll take both."

* * *

"How much did they pay you, Sally?"

French disconnected and slid the phone in her pocket before stepping from the shelter of the doorway into the wind and wet. She didn't expect Sally Acosta to return her call, but it felt important to leave the message.

She was so tired.

Chapter Thirty-Six

The sleet had changed to snow by the time French reached her block. She had seen no sign of her earlier pursuer but thought it likely he might try to locate her near home. Despite her concern, she faced the practical reality that she had no groceries at the apartment and stopped at the corner store for cans of soup, milk and a few apples.

When a courier dropped an armload of packages on the sidewalk in front of her building, French knelt to help the woman collect them, holding her groceries in one hand and using the action as cover to look into nearby doorways.

"Hey, thanks a bunch," the courier said.

"*De nada*," French replied, placing a slim box atop the stack of packages in the woman's arms. She produced her keys and opened the street door before leaving a dripping path across the small lobby and trudging up the stairs.

There was a palpable sense of relief on being inside her building, as real as a warm blanket on a cold day. Month upon month of isolation had made this new apartment a home, even if Philadelphia was still foreign to her. She planned to call a locksmith to replace her locks and order liquor from the package store. In that order.

She fumbled out her pack of Salems and discovered it was empty.

"Well, crap."

On the third floor landing she heard a sound and bent down to hold her hand out towards Miniver, Mrs. Pappas' tabby cat. But the cat was having none of it and backed away.

It wasn't until ascending the final flight of stairs that she registered the footsteps of someone climbing behind her. She stopped atop the stairs and waited until the courier appeared below and started up.

"Oh, hey." The courier stopped with a tired grin. "Are you M. French?" She held up a package.

"I am."

"Cool." The woman started up again. "Thanks for earlier, most people would just walk on by." She shook her head. "I could've just given it to you then."

"No problem." French took a step down but the ascending courier wave a hand.

"Lemme bring it to you, all part of the service."

There was something oddly familiar about the woman and French slipped a hand inside the coat pocket with one of the Gerber knives.

"I need you to sign for it," the woman said, holding out the package. What was it that tickled her memory? The badly permed blonde hair? Something about her face?

As French reached for the package she heard the apartment door open behind her and turned—

A woman was lunging at her with a sack in her hands. French instinctively stepped back and lost her balance as her foot found only empty air before dropping to the step below. She snatched at the railing to stop her fall and dropped her groceries.

Bright pain exploded against her spine accompanied an ozone *SNAP* and her muscles convulsed. The sack was dragged over her head.

* * *

French had spent eons inside the apartment, its rooms the extent of her world, the walls become barriers at the very edge of her existence. It was not a happy place, but it was safe. Perhaps safety was all she could expect. If a home reflected the person inside it, then of course her apartment could not be a place of happiness.

Refuge, that's what it had been. A healthy place to heal and hide.

Now it was diseased.

Infected by invasion.

Now it was a nightmare.

* * *

She awoke in her home and knew in an instant it was no longer her home. Despite the hood over her head, she recognized the sound of her glasses smashing against the floor, her plates cracking against the wall. Some kind of desperate echo-location was at work and she knew she was in her kitchen, felt the passage of a stranger crossing to the sink and heard the sound of a fly unzipping. A grunt and soft thud had to be someone heaving themselves up on the counter. The hissing sound of urination was accompanied by an acrid stink that clawed through the hood to ravage her nostrils.

Tears of impotent rage stung her eyes. Her hands were bound behind her to a chair and she was as naked as a jay.

Cold pebbled her skin. Fear tickled the tiny hairs on the back of her neck.

Thudding footsteps announced the arrival of another person who spoke with a thick, glottal voice as if she had a cold.

"Clogged up the bitch's toilet," the woman crowed. "Litter box was a mess so I emptied it for her." She laughed.

"You have no class." This from the woman who pissed in

her kitchen sink. The two women laughed like carrion birds over roadkill. Their voices were southern. Tennessee maybe.

Tears cut streaks down French's face.

"Y'all gotta know your station, right?" A new voice, also female. This one was in charge. "Any bitch who puts on airs and gets above herself winds up tied to a chair."

The hood was yanked roughly from French's head and she couldn't stop a cry of pain as several hairs went with it.

"Right bitch?" The face pressing towards her was clumsily made up with garish colors, almost clownishly so. Her hair curled in a cheap perm and fake pearls adorned her neck. "You an alley cat who thought she was a parlor cat and look at you now!"

The woman with the cold was emptying a jar of flour on the kitchen floor while the third woman, the sink pisser, had her head inside the open refrigerator.

She turned around with a plastic mustard bottle in her fist, bony and mean in a t-shirt that read NO PEACE.

"What kind of woman don't have more than mustard and ketchup in the fridge," the sink pisser said. "And you thought you deserved a man like Josh Hargrave?"

She jabbed out the yellow bottle and squeezed until her knuckles went white. A blat of mustard splattered against French's cheek as she jerked her face aside. She blinked against the pain of mustard in her eye.

"What do you want?" French asked, trying to keep the tremor from her voice.

"*What do you want?*" The sink pisser mimicked. The gal with the cold spat on the floor. "Want you to know you're nothin' but white trash who got above herself, you stuck up bitch."

The sick one was fat with a broad, pock marked face and eyes like black marbles. She stood next to a camera mounted on a tripod and looked through the viewer.

"We're gonna educate you as to what you are," the clown said.

"Make you drink from that toilet," the sick one interjected with a grin.

"Bet y'all sucked his cock on the first date, no waitin' for a second date for you, huh? Men fall for that whore behavior but we know what you are."

The sink pisser threw the mustard bottle and it struck French's breast. "When we think you done learnt your lesson, we're gonna film your confession and send it to Dateline. They gonna rerelease your episode with new footage and pin you to the wall."

French looked with new horror at the woman with the awful perm and red, red lipstick. Unlike the others she was wearing a suit. A polyester number meant to look like the wardrobe of a TV correspondent.

She looked away to hide the shock of recognition. Her gaze fell on the pile of her clothes and boots a few feet away.

The clown crossed to the single window and closed the venetian blind. "Don't want no horny fella lookin' in at our naked bird hopin' for a show."

The room darkened significantly and she flicked on the overhead light from a wall switch.

"That's good for the video," the sick woman said.

The sink pisser left the kitchen and French heard more destruction from her living room. Objects torn from her closet.

"What happens after the interview?" She forced herself to ask.

The sink pisser reappeared with a metal toolbox in her hands. "Gonna nail your feet to the kitchen floor so you stay put 'til the cops come for you."

French swallowed and changed the subject. "How'd you get in here?"

"Key," the clown said.

"Was it Abbott or Lucille?"

French had long suspected The Righteous were well on their

way to crazy, but her words triggered something that terrified her.

The big woman behind the camera went completely still. Her flabby features went slack and her eyes unfocused.

"Don't you—" the sink pisser started before the big woman charged.

"DON'T YOU SAY HER NAME!" It was an immediate shift from stillness to motion without a moment's warning. As sudden as a landslide. Her hands slammed into French's chest and bowled her over backwards as if she weighed nothing.

The impact knocked the wind from her lungs and French gasped like a dying fish. Before she could close her mouth a bar of soap was jammed between her teeth and she fought against choking.

"Your cock sucking mouth ain't clean enough to say that name."

As they hauled her back upright the chair squeaked and shimmied and French recognized the piece of furniture they'd chosen for her prison.

A wobbly chair she'd found abandoned on the sidewalk for trash pick up. *Shabby chic*, she'd said at the time.

The clown laughed and said, "Are we rolling?"

The big woman returned to look through the camera to adjust its aim and said, "We're rolling."

French decided to roll the dice and turned to the clown.

French said, "Lauren, why would you come up to Philly in winter when its so much nicer in Memphis?"

"What?" This from Lauren the clown.

"Sorry, I meant Collierville," French shook her head in apology. "443 Dogwood Drive. Nice house but you don't cut the lawn often enough."

"What's she saying?" This from the sink pisser.

The camerawoman glanced at Lauren.

"Why're you sayin' that?" Lauren said.

"Lauren," French paused. "Mrs. Greene, I'm an investigator

and I've known who you were from the first time you showed up outside my apartment."

Lauren's garish mask twisted with anger but French cut her off.

"And I set up a deadman switch linked to your name," French lied.

"A what?" The sick woman wiped her nose on her arm.

French turned her eyes to the big woman. "A deadman switch that will trigger if anything happens to me. It will doxx Lauren's—excuse, me, Mrs. Greene's online banking. It will send prepositioned dossiers to child protective services in Collierville to threaten custody of—"

"You bitch!" Lauren shrieked.

French pressed on. "—Billy and Julie and alert their father."

"I don't believe you," the sinker pisser said and French grinned.

"You should, Jamie, you're on probation for another two years and this kind of stunt will send you right back to TPW, right?" French shifted her gaze to Lauren and whispered in a *just us girls* voice. "That's the Tennessee Prison for Women."

"You're a liar," Jamie the sink pisser said.

"No, I'm not." French shook her head. "And your friend is recording everything." She shrugged at the sick woman. "I don't have a file on you, I'm sorry. But you don't want to be associated to these women when they go down."

Hesitation gripped The Righteous but it wasn't enough.

Lauren grabbed a fistful of French's hair and pressed her face in close enough to smell onions on her breath.

"You're a liar and a murderer—"

French interrupted. "I murdered him and got away clean and you don't think I can rig a deadman switch?"

The apartment door opened and the three women froze.

French craned her neck around to see a man filling the doorway.

Chapter Thirty-Seven

"It's amazing how fast things can go from terrifying to stupid."

French was hunched over the bar in a shithole called DEWEY'S, white Christmas lights strung around the mirror behind the bar providing a vague suggestion of illumination.

A water puddle had formed on the bar where she'd planted her elbows. A lake was forming beneath her stool. She still wore her soaked trench coat. Her trusty duffle bag and a suitcase were beside her on the floor.

She was the only customer.

The bartender took in her flicking eyes. The tension screaming from her posture. Poured brown liquid into a glass without asking.

"*Gracias,*" she said.

"*De nada,*" he said, a beefy white guy who'd never been closer to Mexico than Virginia.

"It was this guy who's been following me. Black coat and mean eyes. Not too big but tough as nails, you know? The Righteous had no idea what to do so I bullshitted and said, *Hey Rick, will you escort these ladies out?*" like I knew him. He doesn't miss a beat and says, "We're leaving now, ladies." Got one of those hard ass Boston accents. He steps inside and gestures to the door.

French grinned and knocked back the bourbon. Hissed and pounded a fist against her chest. "They didn't know whether to shit or go blind. I start laughing like the joke's on them, see? And this really freaks them out. Like somehow *I'd* trapped *them*."

She nodded at the glass and the bartender refilled it, spilling a little but not bothering to wipe it up. Outside the sleet was scratching icy claws against the single window and the wooden building shuddered under a battering wind.

"Jamie, that's the one who peed in my sink, she just about faints. So I told them about Rick's temper. About how seeing me like this, you know, tied up and naked, he'd lose control." She shook her head. "Total bullshit. I have no idea if this guy has a temper." A shrug. "They untied me and split. You believe that?"

"They don't sound like the A-team," the bartender said.

"They're not even the D-team, these assholes." French shuddered. "But they were in my apartment and had a fucking key."

"The guy come back?"

"Not before I packed a bag and got the hell out of there."

"You want another?"

It was written all over her face. She wanted another and another until she could pass out on the bar. Her face clenched like a fist and she pushed back off the stool, catching it before it could fall.

"I better roll."

Outside the storm hit her like a full body slap, blowing her trench coat out behind her before she could button it closed. Worse than earlier in the day. Storm grey deepened into night dark, the nearest streetlight getting its ass kicked.

She twisted around warily, squinting against the slashing ice and rain, everything reduced to dark, shifting shapes.

It's not paranoia if someone's really out to get you.

She shouldered her duffle and picked up her suitcase from the slush, splashing down the sidewalk into the night.

* * *

How is this not over? How did it not end at Hate House?

* * *

"Hi, I'm trying to locate a patient. Flavio Ricci?"

"One moment."

The hum of background voices was drowned out by the clacking of computer keys.

"I'm sorry, honey. We don't have anyone by that name here."

"Maybe it's under Father Flavio—"

"The search keys off last names. We have no one named Ricci."

"Okay, thank you."

French disconnected the call feeling a little bit more alone.

* * *

The desk was cheap and the legs were uneven, the hotel chosen by the simple expediency of being the first she stumbled across. It smelled like mildew and bedbugs but it was out of the storm.

With the TV murmuring in the background, French sat in dry Steeler's sweatpants and a t-shirt with the HOTEL FRANKLIN stationary and a pen, bare feet tingling as circulation returned. The carpet slightly greasy beneath her toes.

ABBOTT was written on one sheet of paper, torn from the pad and placed at the far left corner of the desk.

LUCILLE HARGRAVE was written on another liberated sheet, placed at the far right corner.

She set down her bottle of beer and listened to it foaming in anger. Her pen scribbled the word MAINE and she tore off the sheet of paper. Placed it directly below ABBOTT.

INDIANA was scrawled hard enough to tear the paper and that sheet went below LUCILLE HARGRAVE.

Two different places to look for answers, assuming she could find them anywhere.

FACT: SOMEONE WAS STILL GASLIGHTING HER

The Righteous were fools but they'd been in her home. Her sanctuary. Someone had given them a key.

FACT: MARCUS ABBOTT WAS DEAD

He had to be. She saw the hooks dragging him from the boat. The angry eyes of fishermen glowing like hot coals.

FACT: I DID NOT SEE HIM DIE

Well, shit.

She considered Lucille and a trip to Indiana to confront her and achieve...what? If Lucille was this invested in tormenting her, would an in-person confrontation stop it in its tracks? French had lied to The Righteous about doxing them, but she began to consider ways she might retaliate against Lucille? Go on offense.

What other choice was left—

Wait.

FACT: HILL LEFT HATE HOUSE AFTER SHOOTING RICCI

Hill was alive.

Could Hill be behind this invasion by The Righteous? Was she still pulling strings?

Something thudded into the wall from the next room and raised voices made the fillings in her teeth vibrate.

FACT: I AM BURNING THROUGH FUNDS AT AN ALARMING RATE

Even this shitty hotel would be beyond her means before long.

Her chair complained when she leaned back to stretch. Despite the continued lack of news about the events in Maine, she didn't dare go to the police, certain that their involvement would trigger digging that would disturb the fig leaf the Church had pulled over Hate House.

She wondered how Ricci was doing? Wondered if he was well enough to help her again. Wondered if he would give a shit now that Hate House was in the rearview.

"Fuck me."

Her throat worked as she polished off the remaining beer. Dropped the empty in the plastic trashcan so that its thud was perfectly timed with a belch.

She opened up Google Street View and typed in a street address from memory. Moments later she was staring at Lucille Hargrave's lavish home in Indiana.

Offense felt so much better than defense.

Chapter Thirty-Eight

French awoke with the smell of mildew clogging her nostrils and the red light of dawn washing the window glass. She thrashed up to a sitting position, terrified she was back in Hate House.

Hate House burned.

She rubbed her face and her consciousness gathered itself. As it did, the room took on its proper shape. The walls papered and not stone, the furniture of the current decade. A TV stood on a dresser and the tiny desk was littered with papers from her effort at planning.

And she knew she was out, but not *out*. Hate House still had hold of her life. Had infected the psychological refuge of her therapy. Had invaded the physical refuge of her apartment. The forces unleashed in Hate House were still at work unraveling the threads of her life.

She padded barefoot to the bathroom, turning on the shower to warm before sitting on the toilet to relieve herself of last night's beer.

A moment later she was reclining in the tub as the hot water splashed over her body, a trick she had learned early during her psychological recovery after Josh's death. The massage of water and steady thunder of the shower created a meditative space otherwise unavailable to her.

Oh, she had made her decision before falling asleep last night. She knew it then and knew it now. But she had needed rest to regain strength to face the draining knowledge that her struggle with Hate House was not over, and that to wait longer was to prolong suffering.

The decision before her was whether to travel West or North. To confront Lucille Hargrave in Indiana or Hill in Rhode Island, assuming the old harpy was even there.

Rhode Island was closer.

* * *

She stood beneath the buzzing fluorescents in the badly lit concrete tomb of the parking garage, head swiveling as she set down her bags.

Using the light on her phone, she illuminated the dark space between her car and the next, which didn't mean someone wasn't hiding out of sight between the bumper and the wall. Her knees popped when she knelt and the floor was oily when she braced a palm against it, lowering herself on three points to peer underneath in the hope of seeing the feet of anyone concealed behind the car.

Nothing.

Wiping her hand against her trench coat, she finally approached the vehicle and snatched the note stuck beneath a windshield wiper.

She looked around, desperately aware of being out of her depth. She was alone. She heard no footsteps. The only sound was an engine on another level of the garage.

The note was brief. DO NOT USE YOUR PHONE. USE A PAY PHONE. CALL ASAP followed by a 617 area code number.

Boston.

She crumpled the note and dropped it before stowing her baggage in the back seat. Settled in behind the wheel and keyed the ignition.

The chime alerting her to an open door joined the steady ding from an unfastened seatbelt as she climbed out of the idling vehicle to pick up the note.

She ghosted out of the garage, her engine quiet in the way of modern cars. She half expected to see a menacing figure step out of the shadows to watch her depart but none materialized. Honking horns demanded she return her attention to driving and she did, letting herself flow with the traffic, wondering where the hell to find a working payphone.

The towers ahead beckoned to her and she headed for downtown.

Ten minutes and several curses later, she eased into the valet parking loop outside the Downtown Marriot on Market Street. She lowered her window as a valet trotted up in a blue Marriott uniform.

"Hey, I just checked out but left something in my room. Can I just pull over to the side and run in to see if they found it?"

"Yeah, no problem," the valet said, a portly man pushing fifty who probably imagined greater things than parking cars for a living.

French pulled over where he pointed and parked, leaving the keys inside.

"I left the keys in it just in case." She handed him a ten and he made it disappear.

The entrance was around the corner on Filbert and she hurried like a woman who lost her laptop. The lobby was loud and echoing and she passed a flight crew gathered around their bags before sliding through a long line at the check-in desk, with a muttered, "Excuse me."

She scanned the perimeter for a sign indicating RESTROOMS and headed beneath it down a short hall. A payphone was mounted in an alcove in between two swinging doors marked WOMEN and MEN respectively.

"Oh, you're fucking kidding me."

She had no change and reversed direction back to the lobby. Holding up a dollar she approached a bellhop, "Do you have change for a dollar?"

When he shook his head she headed to a woman at the concierge desk and received, "I'm sorry," in answer.

"Lady, I got fifty cents."

It was a tall guy in a satin 76ers jacket, fumbling in his pocket.

"Good enough." French held out her dollar but the guy shook his head, bouncing the quarters on his wide palm. She half thought he might have once been a pro baller.

"Nah, keep it. Merry Christmas."

His grin triggered a grin of her own and she nodded thanks, trotting back to the payphone with her treasure. When the hell had she last used a payphone? At least it was clean.

She slid the coins into the waiting slot and pulled the note from her pocket, dialing the number after a few clicks and buzzes over the line.

"Blanco." The voice that answered was terse. Boston tough. She remembered the tone when he interrupted The Righteous.

"You left a note on my car," she said.

She could hear the sound of traffic in the background and a rustling before his voice returned.

"Flavio Ricci sends his regards."

The statement was so dramatic, so *Hollywood*, that French started laughing.

Chapter Thirty-Nine

He looked like a Billy Blanco.

French had chosen to meet him in the macabre confines of the Philadelphia's infamous Mutter Museum on 22nd Street in the Center City part of town. A grim place for her grim mood.

When Blanco walked in, she was concealed behind shelves lined with jars of floating fetuses in various states of development. She wanted a chance to get a good look at this mystery man before he saw her.

And yeah, he looked like a Billy Blanco. A welterweight in a black raincoat somehow more serious than her own. Light brown skin and a badly healed broken nose. He sported a black fedora decades out of style, but he managed to pull it off. There was no mistaking his wiry build for weakness and people instinctively cleared a path for him.

He seemed familiar as soon as French laid eyes on him.

Over the phone he'd said, "Let me know where you are and I'll pick you up. We need to talk."

To which she'd replied, "Fuck you. I'm not getting in your car, freak."

"Flave said you were tough," he had replied. "Tell me where you want to meet."

He was raking his eyes across a display of skeletal deformities when she approached from behind.

"You look a lot like Ricci."

He did but he didn't. Something about their shared intensity, though Blanco didn't have that flash of white at his throat.

Blanco let his eyes find hers and she felt him digging inside her head.

"Miss French." He didn't bother doffing his hat.

"Why were you following me?"

"Flave asked me to keep an eye on you."

Her resting sneer spread into a smirk. "Tell me you didn't just call him Flave."

"It gets worse," Blanco said, deadpan. "Back in seminary I called him Flavor Flave." His delivery was sandpaper dry but she was fairly certain he'd just made a joke.

"How do I know you're not working for the Hargraves?"

"Or Abbott?" He said. "When you met with Flave at Fishercat's Saloon he put the Bangor Daily News down on the sticky table and it tore when he picked it up."

French considered this for a moment. "You a priest?"

"Not any more."

"I tried to check on Ricci. He wasn't at the hospital."

"He was moved down to Boston," Blanco said. "He's in good hands."

They were moving as they spoke and she paused in front of black and white pictures depicting horror.

"Leprosy is terrifying," she said.

He nodded. "I saw it in Brazil."

She wasn't sure what to do with that and said, "Why does Ricci want you following me?"

"Because he thinks whatever is happening to you isn't over."

They stepped around a trio of gleefully horrified high school girls ogling slices of human brain tissue in formaldehyde.

"What does he care?"

Blanco stopped in his tracks. "He said what you did erased an echo of evil left by the Church."

French pulled out her pack of Salems to buy time. Realized she couldn't light up inside the museum.

"You work for the Church?"

"No."

"Then why get you involved?"

"Because he asked."

* * *

Blanco lit a paper match and cupped his hand around it to protect the flame. French leaned in and the tip of her cigarette smoldered.

"Thanks."

He nodded, lighting his own cigarette before flicking the match into the street.

"I've been looking at the Hargraves," she said. "Lucille in particular."

"And?"

"And she left town two days ago. Trinidad. She was on an American Airlines 737 three hours after buying her ticket. According to her credit card transaction, she didn't even book a hotel room until she was in the air. She left in a hurry."

"As soon as Hate House burned." Blanco blew out a stream of smoke. "She's running from you."

"I'm not even sure what I could do to her."

"Really?" One of his eyebrows rose, a skill she envied.

"I could burn down her house like I did Hate House."

He stared at her without blinking.

"Seriously, I'm not sure how to get her to stop."

He shrugged, just spitballing...

"Scare her so much the mention of your name makes her faint." He shrugged again, suddenly fascinated by the burning ember tipping his cigarette.

"She's got a house in Zionsville and Josh's sister isn't far away in Meridian Hills. Nice neighborhoods. Quick police response time. Private security on both homes. Luke's sister has two kids of her own in high school. Public school, which surprises me."

She was surprised at her own businesslike delivery.

"Have you done something like this before?" He asked.

"No." She changed the subject. "Do you know who Grady was? I mean, really was?"

He rolled the cigarette with his lips so it lodged in the corner of his mouth. It bobbed as he spoke.

"I've been digging. He had a P.I. license but was exclusive to a couple of fat cats like Abbott. A cat's paw."

"Just a nobody." Her face remained impassive as she remembered the feeling of her knife entering his belly. The sight of him naked and dead on the floor.

Little killer. That's what Abbott called her.

Blanco studied the oily sheen on a puddle. "Where'd you put his body?"

French shook her head and he nodded in understanding.

"You know, Hill is still alive," she changed the subject again.

"Hill." He flicked his cigarette into the street, head wreathed in smoke. "She's a ghost. I have no idea who she is."

"She shot Ricci."

He gave her a look. "I mean, I have no idea who she is beyond shooting Flave. She doesn't exist in any database."

"I know, but I thought I'd see if she was haunting Abbott's house in Rhode Island. Because Abbott…Abbott's dead."

"Did you see him die?"

She shook her head, blood rushing in her ears. "No."

"You're not sure he's dead, are you?"

"He has to be dead." She remembered the old man's scream as he was dragged into the frigid sea. "He *has* to be."

Blanco's tilt of the head was the only sign of doubt.

"You think it's Hill and not Lucille Hargrave still pulling strings?"

"I don't know."

He adjusted the fedora on his head.

"So…Rhode Island."

Chapter Forty

The iron gate barring entry to Abbott's driveway was open.

"I want you to investigate Hate House."

The dead man's words as clear in her memory as if Abbott was sitting beside her in the car.

"It's the Versailles of Hate houses. The Empire State Building."

Dead. He had to be dead. French was terrified of what he might do if he were alive. What diseased fury would motivate him to action.

It was evening by the time she reached Rhode Island. There were no lights marking Abbott's address but the GPS wasn't fooled by the dark.

"You have arrived at your destination."

Her headlights splashed across the stone pylons on other side of the open gate before she guided the Acura through.

She remembered the narrow driveway down into the narrow valley, the narrow house awaiting them at the bottom, and realized how much she hated these old, narrow houses. If she ever bought a house it would be a sprawling, single story ranch on acres of open land. Narrow valleys and rocky islands need not apply.

Her eyes flicked about to take everything in. The leafless topiary. Skeletal trees. Empty and dead. Everything dead.

Abbott had to be dead. She saw him go into the water.

She pulled up to the circular drive and parked beside the narrow staircase that led up to the front door.

The open front door.

She turned the key in the ignition and the engine died, ticking quietly as she sat, staring at the gaping maw of Abbott's house.

Waiting for her.

She emerged from her car into a world of deathly stillness, disturbed only by the sound of dripping. Everything was wet. The skeletal plants dripped. The eaves far overhead dripped. Fat drops dripped down before the open door above.

Had it felt so dead on her previous visit?

Her boots clomped up the steps, thick treads scattering water with each splatting impact. She felt hollow comfort in her knives as the damp drained her resolve.

The gentle glow of her phone's light was quickly consumed by the interior gloom and revealed nothing more than details of the faded carpet runner, but her muscles locked in sudden fear. The idea of entering another decaying old house made her feel trapped on a loop, as if she had never escaped Hate House. As if every doorway was the entry to another rotting, ancient dwelling with a cruel and horrible history.

The memory of being restrained in her own home leaked forth like a weak spring from which she drank, allowing the angry waters to flood her limbs. While it didn't banish the fear, it acted as a blade with which she could slice through terror and create passage.

French stepped across the threshold into Abbott's house.

"Hello?"

Her voice was flat in the stuffy interior and didn't travel far, but she didn't expect a response. Where Hate House had seemed alive in its regard for their intrusion, Abbott's house was dead, no more aware of her passage than a mummified insect or scattered animal bones would notice her presence.

She took another step to shore up her courage and panned the light around, noting the ugly wallpaper above the wainscoting. Beneath the stuffiness was a smell she recognized. Urine and cleaning chemicals. The stink of a retirement home.

"Hill!"

Her shout limped away and was ignored by the dead house.

She found a light switch near the front door.

But the lights were dead like everything in the house.

She pushed deeper inside, glancing through an arched opening on her right and stopping in her tracks. Though little more than vague shapes in the murky room, it was clear she saw sheets draped over furniture.

A few steps farther offered a door to her left and she turned the knob, wincing at the rusty wail of hinges.

More sheet covered furniture of mysterious function.

Was this confirmation that Abbott was dead?

She entered the room and fought back a sneeze at the dust. Navigating a path with the aid of her light she eventually reached long curtains of a heavy dark material and pulled them aside to allow the daylight.

Wetting the tip of a finger, she touched the nearest sheet draped over a chair. Saw maybe a hint of dust on the tip of her finger when she looked closely with the aid of her light.

"Huh."

She made her way back to the hall and found the library by memory. The door was closed and she half expected it would be locked out of sheer perversity, but the knob turned beneath her hand and she stepped inside.

The books remained but the furniture was draped in the expected funeral garb. She crossed to the desk and pulled off the covering sheet, dropping the cloth at her feet.

Her nominal plan of searching the drawers was superseded by the sight awaiting her on the wall.

A life-sized portrait hung high up. She hadn't seen it on her previous visit. Had indeed been sitting beneath it unawares.

A shiver raced up her spine and the muscles of her belly tightened.

Simone Laurent glared down with contemptuous authority.

"Oh god, you're everywhere."

She remembered the name written in the steam on her bathroom mirror. Remembered Grady's dying message written in blood.

SIMONE IS HERE

What if he was being literal?

She collapsed into the desk chair and reached inside her jacket for the pack of cigarettes, happy to see she had a few left. The petty rebellion of smoking in his sanctuary was meant to sooth her, but French didn't like the tremble in her own fingers as she brought the lighter to the cigarette's tip.

Simone was dead. Abbott was dead. Grady was dead.

A sound intruded on her racing thoughts and she cocked her head without thinking. It repeated. A metallic note that vibrated towards silence.

She tapped ash onto the polished wooden desk and rose to seek out the sound.

It chimed again and drew her to the hall like a moth to flame. Deeper into the house, her boots quiet on the carpet runner, following her ears more than her eyes.

It was another wide entryway, the arch several feet higher than her head.

The room was ringed in curtained windows and glass cases full of oddities and trinkets, but occupying the room like a battleship at dock was a long table of polished wood, dark and heavy, its thick legs covered in elaborate carvings.

Lit candles stood in tall metal holders spaced down the length of the table. Their flames danced and the acrid sting of sulfur in her nostrils told French they were only recently awakened.

"Come, sit."

The woman seated on the other side of the table wore a high necked dress of dark fabric, long out of fashion. A black veil descended from her pillbox hat to conceal her face.

French dimmed her phone's light and pulled out a chair to sit opposite the woman. Though instinctively uneasy about having her back to the arched opening, she still felt an absence of life in the place.

The woman across from her didn't ping her inner radar at all and French wasn't sure what to make of it.

"What was that sound?" French asked.

A dark hand with long fingers gestured and French looked at the grandfather clock in the corner.

"It rang the hour." The woman's voice was thick with Caribbean inflections.

The black hands on the broad white circle of the clock's face was still, showing midnight.

"But we're not on the hour," French said.

"The clock is very old," the veiled woman said. "Who are we to argue with such age?"

"Who are you?"

"I am as old as the grandfather in the corner."

"What is your name?"

"Colline." The island sound sliding effortlessly to French.

A mechanical ding drew French's attention to another shadowy corner and a glowing point of red light. The anachronism stood on long spider legs.

A video camera.

"Why are you recording this?" French asked.

The veiled woman remained still.

"Who are you recording this for?"

Not even breath disturbed the other woman's veil.

French steepled her hands and shifted tacks. "Why are you in Abbott's house?"

"Whose house?"

"Why are you here?"

"Why are *you* here?"

French paused, unwilling to be sucked into sparring but sensing…not hostility. The woman's intentions were as veiled as her features.

"I'm here…" French paused. "I want to know if Marcus Abbott is dead."

The veiled head nodded and a hand indicated the deck of cards on the table in front of her.

French shifted uneasily, certain the cards had not been present earlier.

"You may ask three questions."

"Is Marcus Abbott dead?"

"Cut the cards."

"For real?"

Silence met her question.

French stood and leaned over the table, stretching out her hand towards the cards. The veiled woman could have easily slid the deck towards her but remained still.

French cut the deck, letting her fingers have their own mind. She sat back down.

The woman's dexterous hands lifted three cards in succession and placed them face up on the table. She leaned forward as if to study them, though French couldn't see her eyes. Eventually the woman eased back in her seat.

"The Tower represents sudden destruction by events outside of your control. It suggests you have not made changes to your life that need to be made. A decisive incident occurred and forced your hand."

"I—"

A long fingered hand rose to still her questions.

"The Devil represents slavery to an unhealthy idea. Something toxic. Combined with the Tower it represents a life shattering change forced upon you because you have not made necessary changes in your life."

French reeled at the accuracy of the cards, fighting the tide of belief by reminding herself that Tarot was horseshit. A con game for carnival rubes. She had to be on the lookout for the play to separate her from her money.

"Death, in this case, is not literal. It represents the removal of debris, the barrier preventing changes you must make. Much as a forest fire produces ash to nourish future forest growth… though first it destroys."

Anxiety made breathing difficult and French wished she had her Lexapro. She pulled out her Salems instead, prepared to argue if the Tarot reader objected, but the veiled woman said nothing.

She placed a Salem in her mouth and the tip jiggled with nerves as she tried to light it. She drew hard, too hard, and coughed out smoke like a sophomore experimenting behind the high school gym.

"What the fuck does any of that have to do with Abbott?"

"It suggests that Abbott is debris to be cleared aside. The necessary destruction of your life before growth can occur."

"Is he dead?" French asked.

"Ask instead, is he here?"

Silence. French inhaled more carefully and pursed her lips to blow smoke up and away from the woman. Flame popped atop a candle. She could hear her own breathing.

The woman gathered the cards together and shuffled them expertly. The riffling sound cacophonous in the quiet.

"Tell me when to stop," she said.

"Stop." The instinct was immediate.

The long fingered hands stopped and placed the deck on the table. She slid the top card from the deck and placed it face up on the table.

"The Nine of Swords," she said. "Your card is one of anguish, despair and pain. Deserved pain. You have committed a great injustice and know it. The guilt eats at you. Eventually it will devour you if you do not change your course."

French was at a loss for a place to tap her ash free and found a used Kleenex in a pocket. She placed it on the table in lieu of an ash tray.

"None of this is helping," she said after a long, quiet moment. "I came here to see if it was Abbott or Lucille Hargrave messing with me in Philadelphia. To make it stop."

"Marcus Abbott is not here," the veiled woman said. "Marcus Abbott isn't real. He does not exist. And Lucille Hargrave has fled the mainland for Trinidad. She has already purchased passage to Abu Dhabi."

"If it's not Hargrave because she's running and it's not Abbott because he's dead," she caught herself. "Because he doesn't *exist*. Who is tormenting me?"

"Do you truly want to learn, even after all you have learned today? Are you not frightened by a power that can so easily upend your life?"

"I'm terrified."

The veiled woman slid her chair back and stood. As she did so, the grandfather clock in the corner chimed and French looked at it, startled. The hands still showed midnight.

When she looked back the veiled woman was gone and she whipped her head around to discover the woman was somehow standing in the archway behind her.

"You will learn nothing more here, Megan French."

The woman ghosted out of sight in a soundless glide and French sprang to her feet, nearly toppling her chair.

She was not surprised to find the hallway empty when she reached it.

"Goddamn."

She trudged to the front door, thoroughly done with weird old houses, more unsettled and confused than when she arrived.

Pulling the front door closed behind her out of habit, she clumped heavily down the steps to her waiting Acura, the car forlorn and seemingly lost in time next to the Depression Era surroundings.

A quizzical expression crossed her face and she stared intently through the windshield as she approached. She thumbed the security button on her car and the locks thudded open.

So the car *had* been locked. Yet an envelope of expensive, bone colored paper waited for her on the dashboard.

Chapter Forty-One

The Canadair CRJ 705 was a small commercial jet and French was one of eighteen passengers on board. She swirled melting ice in her plastic cup, having asked to keep it after the flight attendant circulated for clean up following the drink service.

She had flown before but still found the experience awe inspiring as the jet descended through the clouds while the western sky burned orange.

The ground below was largely in shadow and she could make out the glow of houses and flow of headlights on roads that reminded her of glowing blood molecules traveling through arteries.

She crunched ice between her molars as her ears popped from the pressure change and ran an internal systems check to measure her mental state, though the Lexapro before take off more or less ensured at least a diminution of her ever present anxiety.

But she honestly wasn't sure how she felt beyond tired and curious. That she was a leaf floating on rapids was undoubtable, great forces pushing her around for reasons she couldn't fully understand.

She had been invited to a banquet at The Avalon Terraine in

Cape Breton, Canada. Unsurprisingly, an internet search turned up nothing except geological information about the rocky make up of Newfoundland.

After landing, she would spend the night in a hotel and travel by rental car according to the directions included in the invitation left on the dashboard of her car.

The invitation requested formal attire and she had bought a long, close fitting dress in shimmering black with matching heels. The steady depletion of her savings seemed a distant threat...whatever happened at The Avalon Terraine, she believed there would be closure of some kind.

"We'll be on the ground in five minutes."

French twitched in surprise, only then noticing the flight attendant holding open a plastic waste bag. She let her cup fall into the bag.

"Thank you," she said.

Down below she could make out the distinctive lights of St. John's International Airport. Long, straight runways with strobing safety lights and clusters of illumination around the low buildings.

A muffled thud announced the deployment of the Canadair jet's landing gear.

She was glad that Blanco was following on a morning flight and would be only an hour behind her when she drove out to The Avalon Terraine.

* * *

Customs went smoothly and the rental car, a Nissan Altima, was waiting for her. The Holiday Inn Express was close and easy to find and while it offered all the charm of a food court, it was clean and relatively quiet.

French hung the garment bag with her dress in the closet and kicked off her boots, peeling off her socks to let her feet breathe.

She ran a bath to chase away the chill and made a call while it warmed.

"Blanco," the voice on the other end said.

"Just checking in," she said. "Got to the hotel without any creeps following me or finding messages on the mirror."

"Good," he said. "I'll call you in the morning when I land."

He hung up and she already knew him well enough to know it wasn't rudeness. Billy Blanco simply didn't waste his time with unnecessary niceties.

She was glad he was coming, though, and whispered silent thanks to Ricci for putting his friend on the case.

Chapter Forty-Two

The sun was a blurry disk in an overcast sky and the CBC weatherman said they were expecting snow.

There was a Tim Horton's not far from the hotel and French walked over to get coffee and a donut, forgetting how much more wintery winter was in Canada compared to Philadelphia. A hat would have been smart. And gloves, she definitely needed gloves.

Still, she needed to get out of her hotel room. Her first act on awakening was to run the shower and close the bathroom door to fill the room with steam. When she turned off the shower she waited expectantly for words or a name written on the fogged mirror.

Yes, she needed to be in Canada, answering the invitation. The sense of personal invasion had become a pathology and she needed a decisive resolution if she was ever going to feel safe again in her home. Indeed, she was already planning on moving from Philadelphia when the maelstrom of Hate House was laid to rest. She needed a fresh start and couldn't afford to drag these fears with her.

Despite the warm interior, the horrid fluorescent lighting

and harsh white surfaces inside Tim Horton's drove her back into the cold, still wiping crumbs from her lips.

Butterflies filled her stomach and the coffee was not playing well with them. She was worried she might be sick and hurried back to the hotel.

The drive would take several hours and with a storm coming in, she silently added another hour to her travel.

It gave her too much time to kill. Time during which her tension ratcheted tighter and tighter and when lunch time came, she was unable to eat.

She popped a pill and chain smoked inside her room, using a plastic NO SMOKING sign as an ashtray. She stretched out in the tub and let the shower rain down warmth while she practiced her breathing. But practicing the exercises reminded her of the betrayal by her therapist, Doctor Sally Acosta, who exposed her to the mind games of a stranger named Khoury.

Billy Blanco called to tell her he had landed at St. John's International and rented a room at the nearby Comfort Inn. They discussed her revised departure time and he assured her he would be only an hour behind her when she set off for the address in Cape Breton, to visit a place that didn't exist on any map.

He mentioned casually that he would be unavailable prior to her departure while he acquired tools and she knew from the off the cuff delivery he meant guns and that was good.

And then it was time to dress and depart.

* * *

It was one hell of a dress and after years spent going to seed, she felt good putting it on, applying make up, making a largely futile effort to do something with her self-cut hair.

Even though she was the only one who would ever know, she was embarrassed to admit that she considered a garter to hold one of her Gerber knives. She settled on wrapping a strip of black electrician's tape around her thigh to hold the weapon in place. The uncomfortable pulling of the tape on her skin served as an excellent reminder that she wasn't tarting herself up for an evening on the town.

She slipped her feet into her boots and carried her heels in a bag and made her way downstairs, pausing to take a cup of coffee from the service in the lobby.

Her Nissan was waiting where she left it with no mysterious messages on the dashboard. She washed down another Lexapro with coffee and lit a cigarette before texting Blanco.

She was pulling out of the parking lot when the first snowflakes landed on the windshield.

* * *

Salt trucks and snowplows were active and though the drive was as slow as expected, it went smoothly. She flipped the radio dial, finding a French language music station that made a mockery of her high school language lessons but kept her mind occupied.

Sooner than expected, she began seeing signs reading CANSO CAUSEWAY, her route to Cape Breton island. It was snowing hard enough by the time she reached the Causeway that her car felt enclosed in a white bubble and she was forced to concentrate on following the red taillights ahead of her.

She was aware of a certain dark poetry in leaving mainland Nova Scotia. Her nightmare had begun when she left the mainland for the island on which Hate House was built. The end of the nightmare, she hoped, would be found on the island of Cape Breton.

Soon she was on the Cabot Trail, a road circling the island. Her GPS was unable to locate the address she typed in so she was forced to follow the directions hand written on the invitation. Trees and hillocks loomed as she passed on a winding, inner road and she imagined the rugged beauty all around her.

She was fortunate that reflectors on the sign flashed in her headlights and she feathered the brakes. At first the sign seemed to be floating in thin air, rusted white metal reading PRIVATE PROPERTY – NO ENTRY.

A swirl of snow quickly revealed that it hung from a chain stretched across what could only be the driveway for The Avalon Terraine.

She pushed open her door and the wind immediately pushed it closed, so she pushed again, harder, and was rewarded by a barrage of snowflakes invading the car.

"Shit."

Glad she wasn't trying to do this in heels, French walked carefully on the slippery road to the sign and followed the chain to a thick wooden post at the edge of the driveway. The metal of the chain was painfully cold and wet to the touch but it was easy enough to unhook it and walk it towards the wooden post on the opposite side, where she dropped it with a clank audible over the storm.

The driveway ahead was dark and she looked longingly back at the warm lights of her car, snowflakes dancing merrily in the beams of her headlights. Even the illusion of security appealed in that moment, but she hurried back anyway and settled inside.

The snow had wreaked havoc on her hair and her eyeliner was starting to run, but it would have to do. A Newfoundland winter wasn't ideal for fancy dress and her host would have to understand.

She grabbed the gearshift in her right hand and slid it into position.

The Nissan crept forward into the dark on the unplowed driveway.

Chapter Forty-Three

The Avalon Terraine looked abandoned. A low, two story building with an empty, snow filled parking lot. Her headlights washed across the glass double doors and flickered off windows. Sitting in the Nissan with the engine humming and the heater blowing warm air on her ankles and windshield, French eventually made out the red glow of what she presumed to be EXIT signs inside the wide room she thought to be a lobby.

It was some kind of hotel, though its efforts at secrecy threw that into question.

She suspected that the bulk of the hotel sprawled in a tumble of guest floors down the cliff side beyond her vision.

Beyond the working EXIT signs inside, French noted that all of the windows were intact. If it were truly abandoned she expected weather or vandals would have broken at least a few.

A twist of the key turned off the engine. The sudden silence and lack of blowing air seemed so utterly final that she wanted to turn the key again in the ignition, but she resisted.

A clutch purse was stuffed in one big pocket of her trench coat, and she carried the bag with her shoes.

Her boots sank into six inches of snow and she shrunk back

when a gust blew frozen crystals into her face, whipping the coat around her bare legs.

But she stomped forward on impulse before she could second guess the bizarre invitation and decided that if the doors were locked, she would turn right around and get the hell off Cape Breton.

But the door, while heavy, shifted at her touch and she braced herself to pull its weight of glass open before stepping inside.

The door closed behind her and cut off the draft and sound of the weather. In the silence, she immediately noticed that it was warmer inside than it should be if the place were abandoned.

Green eyes flashed in the darkness and French bit back a sound. She heard a cat meowing before the eyes vanished.

Leaving a trail of slushy boot prints, she crossed to where she had seen the green eyes and came upon what appeared to be a check-in desk. There she shrugged out of her trench coat and draped its black length over the desk.

A glance around the dim interior revealed more windows, carpeting and clusters of plush chairs arranged to facilitate conversation.

She made her way to one chair and sat, aware of the musty smell that rose from the cushion under her weight.

Snowy laces resisted her fingers but soon enough she had the boots off, followed by her thick socks, and stuffed them all inside the bag after sliding her feet into the elegant heels and tightening the strap across her instep.

Her heels clicked in the distinctive language of expensive shoes as she crossed back to the check in desk to leave the bag with her coat. Unlike many women, French had never struggled to walk in shoes like these despite rarely wearing them. A generally useless skill she appreciated in the moment.

Goosebumps rose on the bare skin of her arms and upper chest, the interior heating not quite up to par.

She had graduated from creepy, empty houses to a creepy, empty hotel and didn't much like the trajectory, but she crossed the lobby regardless, heading deeper inside.

* * *

There was a standing ashtray beside the single elevator and several cigarette butts had met their end inside. It didn't take a detective to realize that though they weren't fresh, someone else had been in that very place not long ago.

The slightly dented brass door of the elevator slid open when she pressed the call button and she entered the small chamber, noting the word MEZZANINE over a descending series of numbers from one to four.

Her stomach gurgled and she realized that despite everything, she was hungry. If there was to be a banquet then the Mezzanine made the most sense. The button glowed to life beneath the pressure of her finger and the elevator made a slow, scraping descent.

It stopped with a slight jolt and French held her breath when the door slid slowly open. The Jazz Age music seemed both cliché and appropriate, flooding inside along with light.

The aroma of food enveloped her as she stepped into the banquet room.

Never had she hosted more than a dozen people at a party, so she had little experience in planning food and beverages for a large number of guests, but what she saw laid out on three tables set against the southernmost wall looked like enough to feed forty or fifty people. She saw a large roast beneath a heat lamp, with thick slices of juicy beef already cut. She saw trays of seafood, steam rising, and pasta beside it. There were crocks of what her nose told her must be chowder and bisque and several large glass bowls containing different salads. There were rolls and cheeses, condiments and small bowls of berries to serve as palate cleansers. There were two stacks of plates along with silverware and cloth napkins.

A cat leapt from a banquet table as she approached and disappeared in the way cats do.

A dozen round tables were scattered across a floor she thought could double as a ballroom. Each was draped in a clean white tablecloth and adorned with four place settings, including wine glasses.

Across the broad expanse the room, floor to ceiling windows overlooked the Atlantic, though all she could see was the opaque night sky and white fingers of ice clinging to the outside of the glass. It gave the entire scene a fairy tale feeling and she considered the cliché of living inside a snow globe.

French scooped up a glass from a table in passing and headed straight for the bar where bottles of wine and liquor were arrayed in neat, military formations.

She picked up the first bottle and studied the label, with no idea what *Domaine du Joncier, Lirac, Regard* meant. But holding the recently opened bottle to her nose tickled her senses pleasantly and she poured herself a glass. Then splashed in a bit more for luck.

"Are you the new one?"

French stifled a shriek and almost dropped her glass. Did, in fact slosh some over the side to splash on the floor, as she turned and saw that a woman sat alone at the table farthest from her.

"What?" French asked, frantically trying to figure out if the woman had been there all along.

"Are you the new one?" The woman stood, tall and thin in a slightly wrinkled cocktail dress, black like French's own. The knees visible below the hemline suggested an age past that where short cocktail numbers were worn, and the woman had a headband that matched the Jazz Age music.

"I received an invitation to the banquet," French said after a strained moment.

"Of course you did." The woman approached French on unsteady heels, an empty glass in hand. She brushed by with a vague smile and refilled her glass from the bottle French had just sampled. Eyeing the spilled wine, she carried the bottle to French and said, "Let's top you off."

The claret gurgled into the bell of her wine glass.

"You're younger than I expected." The woman lifted a hand as if to touch French's cheek and French pulled her head back, covering the movement with a sip of wine.

The woman used a long finger to wipe wine and lipstick from her own lips. "Have you found a room yet?"

"No."

Mind swirling with confusion, French drifted to the nearest table of food and plucked a cherry from a bowl. It was delicious but she wasn't sure what to do with the pit under the woman's watchful eye, so she washed it down with a mouthful of wine.

"Is it just us?" French asked.

The older woman shrugged, ambling towards the wall of windows. "Maybe. You can never be sure who will show up."

"How many people are there?"

The woman shrugged again and French was struck by the disturbing idea that this was an act.

"What's your name, dear?" The woman was facing out to sea and the question seemed to emanate from her reflection in the glass.

"Megan."

"A lovely name," the woman said, turning back and moving towards her with a hand outstretched. "I'm Margaret."

The music changed as they shook hands. Big band sounds filling the high ceilinged space.

"This looks like a good dance floor." French tapped her shoe in emphasis.

"Oh, it is," Margaret said. "They used to set up the band over there." She pointed.

French twitched when she noticed another woman standing

against the far wall, staring with blank eyes at their conversation. She was also quite thin and while dressed for an evening social, her hair was a wild tangle and her make up a mess, lipstick smeared onto one cheek.

"Ignore her," Margaret whispered, leaning close. "All she does is complain, complain, complain."

French had trouble imagining the woman forming words, let alone complaints.

"Margaret, did you send me the invitation?"

Margaret placed fingers against her own breastbone with a *Who Me?* expression on her face.

"Oh no," she said. "The guest list isn't up to me."

"Have you ever heard of Hate House?"

"Oh no." Repeating what was apparently a favorite expression. She tilted her head back and her throat worked as she finished the wine in several large swallows. "It sounds dreadful." She winked and guided French with a hand on her upper arm. "A refill?"

French polished off her remaining wine and set her glass down while Margaret poured for them both.

"I feel rude not thanking my host," French said after another sip. It was very good wine.

The elevator door hissed open and two women entered, already smashed. They carried on in loud voices until they fell upon the banquet tables like hyenas, talking and gesturing with shrimp and rolls as if no one else was in the room.

"Oh god." Margaret steered French to a table near the windows where they sat. "They're so crass and I have no idea why they're here."

"I have no idea why *I'm* here."

A dangerous twinkle danced in Margaret's eyes and the wine smearing her lips looked like blood. "Shall we find out?"

"Yes."

"Say please."

"Please."

"Say, pretty please."

"Go fuck yourself, Margaret." French rose and walked away with Margaret's laughter trailing after her. She aimed for the elevator on instinct and pressed the button. A moment later the brass door slid open and she stepped inside, refusing to look into the banquet room while she pressed the bottommost button for the fourth floor, what she expected to be the penthouse in this upside down place.

The elevator descended with a scraping of metal and rattle of cables.

* * *

The door opened onto the fourth floor and she stepped back through time to Hate House. The Waldorf. The dark blue, sound-absorbing carpet. Pale blue and white paint on the walls. Twentieth Century luxury that ignored the passage of years.

Wind whistled outside and she felt it leaning against the hotel, snapping her back into the present. She was at The Avalon Terraine and would do well to remember that.

She was faced with a short hall. There were two, closed doors on either side before the hall ended in a set of tall, double doors with shining brass handles.

Time kept looping back on her. Events repeating themselves. She pulled a pack of cigarettes from her clutch purse and stuck one between her lips. The lighter flame danced high and fierce and she could hear the crinkle of paper as the tip of the cigarette smoldered with unusual vigor.

Oxygen. The fourth floor of The Avalon Terraine was flooded with abnormal levels of oxygen.

Her shoes were soundless on the thick carpeting as she approached the double doors and lifted a hand to knock.

But before her knuckles could touch the wood, she heard the sound of tumblers turning and one of the doors was pulled open from inside.

The veiled woman from Abbott's house stood before her, wearing the same, high necked dress from another era. Her rich, island tones tumbled from beneath the veil.

"Welcome to The Avalon Terraine, Megan French."

A thin, long fingered hand reached up to pluck the hat and veil from her head and revealed the dark, sharp features French knew all too well.

"Hill?"

"Yes, Ms. French," Hill said, the accent gone. She stepped aside and gestured for French to enter.

"Would you like to meet your host?"

French nodded and passed through the doorway—

The sight that met her eyes sent the blood thundering in her ears and drew all moisture from the roof of her mouth. Her bladder gained the weight of a lead lined safe and her guts decided on that moment to churn into action.

It wasn't Abbott waiting inside.

French opened her mouth as if to speak, but had to pause and wet her lips. She steadied herself and tried again.

"Simone Laurent?"

Chapter Forty-Four

"Breathe shallowly," Hill advised, a hand on French's arm to steady her. "As you've observed, we're in a high oxygen environment."

Unlike the seedy grandeur elsewhere in the Avalon Terraine, this room, this enormous room, was opulent. It reminded her of the dwelling of a Bedouin prince or Indian Raja, with drapes and rugs and incense burners made of copper. A museum's worth of statuary ringed the room and a fountain gurgled near the great wall of windows, the water spraying from between Poseidon's lips.

As if playing with time, the room also entertained an array of high tech equipment. A small, stunningly embroidered tent within the room held a bank of computer screens and she could see though not understand the running calculations in glowing type.

The cats were here as well, two of them stirring to study the intruder. And on the bed? Throne? A black cat regarded her with dangerous eyes.

"Come in, Megan."

Hill applied gentle pressure and guided French forward before shutting the door behind her. French fought to steady herself on her feet but it felt as if the floor was tilting. She looked away from the—

She focused on the ornate chair beside the—

On it rested a book and she could make out English lettering below what she thought might be Greek. Theogony by Hesiod.

"Mademoiselle Colline has been reading to me of the Gods. It helps to put my own appetites into perspective."

The voice was strong and slightly accented, summoning French's attention like a magnet draws iron filings.

She did not have a word for the enormous piece of furniture dominating the room. It was as much ornate bed as it was a throne, carved wood and metal draped in silks. Beside it were robotic devices she couldn't understand, blending past and present. Some looked as if they were developed in the alchemical past, all copper tubes and glass bulbs. Others screamed of a technology more advanced than anything she understood. The kind of thing the military experimented with at top secret facilities like Skunkworks out in Nevada.

The thin line attached to the wrinkled skin of a wrist was something French could understand. It carried blood.

"Simone Laurent," French said with more assurance.

"I have been called that for many years," the wizened woman said from her elevated position, looking down on French as a queen to a supplicant.

"But you're…"

"Dead?" Simone smiled and revealed perfect teeth despite her wrinkled skin.

Yes, it was clear she was old, very old, but she also hummed with a vibrancy that French envied. Her wrists were thin but her hands looked strong. Her head was erect on an unbending neck. That wrinkled skin held no liver spots and though her hair was a shocking white, it was thick and pulled neatly back behind her head with a twist of silk.

The portrait at Hate House had not done her eyes justice. They burned with the heat of iron just drawn from the forge, glittering and direct with a stare so invasive French felt as if fingers were tickling her brain.

"Thank you for coming," Simone said.

"Why am I here?"

A lazy smile played across Simone's lips and French was reminded of cats and their playful cruelty.

"I was curious," Simone said. "You were so weak, so outmatched, and while Marcus has never been much of anything, he had you so thoroughly ensnared I was sure he would win."

"Win?"

"But you beat him." Simone leaned forward eagerly with childish enthusiasm. "You killed his puppet and dragged him out to sea where the fishermen fed him to sharks."

French felt the blood drain from her face and Simone nodded.

"Yes, we have satellite footage."

Hill responded to an unseen command and crossed to a computer, turning the screen to face French. After typing for a moment a video window popped up and French recognized the telltale distortion of night vision.

She forced her gaze back to Simone.

"You don't care that he's dead?"

Simone actually looked confused. "Of course not, Megan. He was never more than a toy, and not even a good toy at that. I thought nudging the Hargrave girl towards him would be interesting…but you surprised everyone."

"The Hargrave girl?"

"Yes, Lucille Hargrave." Simone pursed her lips and French decided the old woman hadn't even had plastic surgery. "She's hiding in Abu Dhabi. Hiding from *you*."

Hill said something in what French believed was Arabic and Simone answered in the same liquid tongue. Both women laughed and Simone said in English, "I own the hotel she's staying at."

"And the airline she flew from Cairo to Abu Dhabi," Hill added smugly.

French turned away and took a wandering step, then another. She felt Simone's eyes on her back like a physical pressure.

"Who are those women," she gestured up with her chin. "At the banquet?"

"Broken toys. Misfit toys. Boring toys."

"Why are they just…hanging around?"

"Hoping for what I have."

"Hoping you'll make them rich?"

Simone laughed and Hill pretended to hide a cough behind her fist.

"Years are what I have," Simone said. "Decades."

Again responding to an unseen command, Hill returned to the computer and cut off the nightmarish vision of Abbott's death. A few keystrokes brought up a photographed document.

French approached at Hill's gesture and studied the screen. It was an old document, curled and faded, the ink barely legible. A birth certificate for Avril J. Colline.

"Nineteen forty—" French looked at Hill in astonished disbelief. Remembered Hill's speed outside Hate House when she shot Ricci. Her quick escape when French disarmed her. "That's impossible."

"No child," Hill said with that thick Caribbean melody. "I was born in 1946 and have been in Madame Laurent's service since 1970."

"But you were born…" She turned her gaze on Simone, mind churning with impossible mathematics. She made a leap and spoke before she could hesitate.

"You're not Simone."

Silence fell over the room. A cat burbled and shifted in its sleep.

The woman who was not Simone smiled in genuine delight.

"And that's why she bested Marcus and the Hargrave girl."

Simone and Hill exchanged glances. "She finds the truth and embraces it no matter how impossible."

"*Pui-jes vous presenter* Josephine Laurent," Hill said.

"I don't—my language skills are terrible." French said.

Simone leaned back and folded her hands in her lap.

"My name is Josephine Laurent," she said. "My late daughter was Simone Laurent. I am 167 years old."

French felt the floor tilt and Hill hurried her to the chair beside Josephine's throne like bed. French sat gratefully, mumbling thanks.

The black cat stood and stretched, strolling to the edge of the plateau-like bed to stare. French was startled by a moment of recognition. The cat made its familiar sound and she knew.

"Burble Cat?"

Eventually French was able to look up at the seemingly ageless woman.

"How is this possible?"

Josephine gestured with the wrist affixed to a blood line. "Ever improving technology developed with the Laurent wealth. To understand more you'd need a degree and I saw your transcripts, you lack the math."

Hill stifled another laugh behind a cough and French felt her fear diminish for the first time, replaced by anger.

"So you just sit here getting older and more bored and play with people's lives? Set them against each other like it's a fucking videogame?"

Josephine nodded. "Of course. That's not all I do, but moving people around is like looking down from Olympus without all the rutting. Endlessly entertaining."

That tiny anger was all French had and she clung to it like a raft, pouring her energy into it to fan the tiny flames.

"You're not a god, Josephine. You're just old."

Josephine threw back her head and laughed. After a moment, Hill joined.

"And again, that is why she won, Colline!" Josephine

crowed. Her mirth subsided and something like pity descended over her features. "Immortality, gods, it's a lot to absorb. I'm still grappling with the ideas myself. What will I do when I'm three hundred years old? Will games appease me? Shall I start wars? Have them build temples to me? Become Xerxes of Persia leading armies as a god made flesh? For the moment, if it helps you to grasp what you are dealing with, think of me as a nation state manifest in a single person."

"A what?"

"A country, child."

Deadpan. "You're a country."

"In power and wealth, yes." Josephine's face was serious. "Oh, not one of the big ones, more like…"

"Liechtenstein," Hill supplied.

"At least Belgium, Colline!" Color rose in Josephine's cheeks and her eyes danced at the jab.

"Burkina Faso," Hill retorted.

"Nigeria!" Josephine exclaimed. She turned to French. "You really should visit Lagos when you have the chance. Thriving and exciting in a way that no city in the United States is today, and so much more vast."

The idea of visiting an African country…of surviving that long…was a curveball French couldn't hit.

"I've never even thought of visiting Africa," French said. "That I'd ever have the opportunity."

"What if you had more years to consider where you would most like to travel, child? And the resources to do so?" Josephine twitched her chin at Hill. "Do you think Megan would like Lagos?"

"I think she'd like Botswana for the food and Mauritius for…" Hill shrugged. "Everything else."

The hand attached to the bloodline fluttered in feigned disgust.

Was she feeling giddy from the elevated levels of oxygen or was Josephine wielding some kind of strange influence? French was surprised to find a bubbling excitement eclipsing her earlier anger.

"I've never even been to Paris," French said in a small voice.

"Paris *est magnifique*," Hill said.

"Imagine it," Josephine said kindly.

French let her eyes wander, taking in the treasures in the room gathered from around the world.

"Why are you," French gestured vaguely. "Here?"

"In this lonely place?" Josephine asked.

"Yes."

"A good question it took us some time to answer, though it seems our science is only chasing much older knowledge. Have you heard of ley lines?"

French shook her head. "No."

"The Avalon Terraine sits atop what we call a ley line, but you might think of as…a natural concentration of the earth's energy," Josephine explained patiently. "Our technology taps into this energy." She pointed at the machines surrounding her.

"And Hate House? Is it on a ley line?" French asked.

"An excellent question," Josephine said. "Of a sort. We originally purchased the property because we thought so. If you consider that both positive and negative charges exist—this isn't a perfect metaphor—but if The Avalon Terraine possesses a positive charge, Hate House possesses its opposite."

"Is that why so many bad things have happened there?"

Josephine spread her arms in a *who knows?* gesture.

"This is hard to wrap my head around," French said quietly.

"What if you had more years to learn about these things?"

French stood abruptly and felt her head spin. Shame flooded her at the ease with which Josephine was manipulating her with ideas of exotic travel. Travel? That's how easily she was bought? Time to ponder universal fucking mysteries?

"You have no more years for me," French forced out. "No travel, no Botswana or Paris." She pointed at the ceiling, picturing the empty women gorging themselves at the banquet, drunk as loons. "I know what happens when you get bored with someone."

Instead of anger, Josephine wore a faint smile. "Have you kept me talking long enough?"

"What?"

"For your reinforcements to arrive?"

Hill glided back to the computer pavilion and her fingers danced across the keyboard. Another night vision satellite image displayed a bright and shifting smear of green light that gathered focus to reveal the hotel and parking lot as seen from above.

"Mr. Blanco's vehicle has already arrived," Hill said.

French saw the image of Blanco's car parked alongside her own. She fought against the confusing wave of guilt and hope that threatened to drown her.

"Don't be upset child," Josephine leaned forward from her cushions. "It was well played, I've simply been playing longer."

A quiet click announced the unlatching of the door behind her and French turned to see Blanco enter the room. He closed the door gently before turning to nod at Josephine.

French felt her stomach fall.

"Mr. Blanco has kindly offered to return your rental car should you prove unable," Josephine said.

"You fucking asshole," French said to Blanco, who returned her stare without expression until it was she who looked away.

"I'm done with this bullshit." French pivoted with a parade ground snap for the door, desperate to leave. Before she could take a step Josephine's quiet voice stopped her.

"But am I done with you, Megan?"

French turned back at the jovial menace in Josephine's voice.

"Pieces remain on the board," Josephine said. "You right here and Lucille Hargrave in Abu Dhabi, and both of you remain sane." She produced a small leather coin purse. "Now that I have decided to play my hand directly, it comes down to a choice."

"What choice?" French hated herself for asking but fear had revisited her and she was unable to remain silent.

Josephine produced a large, gold coin from inside the purse and held it out to French, who took it in a reluctant hand.

"Megan, I have to decide on whom I will focus my attention."

French looked at the coin in her hand, worn and ancient.

"What if I decide to leave?"

Hill spoke from behind her. "I will kill you."

"I beat you before."

Hill laughed and Josephine joined her.

French felt her insides turn to ice and thought that although Hill carried no weapons, she was certain the older woman was more than capable of killing her. Of course, there was also Blanco.

"I just want this to be over," French said at last.

"Yes," Josephine said. "A toss of the coin may mean your part in this is over and I will turn my attention to the Hargrave girl."

"If you don't do that?"

Josephine smiled as if French were a particularly slow child.

"Flip the coin and call it in the air. Let it land on the carpet. Mademoiselle Colline will tell us the result."

"This can't be happening," French whispered.

"It's happening, Megan, flip the coin," Josephine said.

"Flip the coin," Hill said.

Megan French took a deep breath and flipped the coin into the air.

About the Author

John C. Foster was born in Sleepy Hollow, NY, and has been afraid of the dark for as long as he can remember. A writer of thrillers and dark fiction, Foster was raised in the wilds of southern New Hampshire before hauling stakes for the ersatz glow of Los Angeles. He has since relocated to the relative sanity of NYC. Foster is an enthusiastic amateur cook, partially to offset all the griping that results from pushing his increasingly decrepit body through the rigors of martial arts training.

John's novel *Dead Men* was published by Perpetual Motion Machine Publishing (PMMP) in 2015 and his second novel, *Mister White*, was published by Grey Matter Press in April of 2016. His debut collection of short stories, *Baby Powder and Other Terrifying Substances*, was published by PMMP in January 2017. His short stories have appeared in numerous magazines and anthologies including *Shock Totem*, *Dark Moon Digest* and *Dread – the Best of Grey Matter Press* among others. He lives in Brooklyn with the actress Linda Jones and their dog Coraline.

www.johnfosterfiction.com

Also by John C Foster

Leech

Rooster

The Isle

Night Roads

Baby Powder

Mister White

Dead Men